Praise f

THE GUAR

NATIONAL BESTSELLER

·

"A blisteringly readable, yet literary-quality take on one of the hoariest of topes, the haunted house novel. . . . *The Guardians* fires on all cylinders: it's a headlong, absorbing narrative enriched by an unflinching literary conscientiousness. They say you can never please everyone: *The Guardians* comes damn close." —*Vancouver Sun*

"Andrew Pyper's *The Guardians* is everything you could ask for in a thriller. It's psychologically unnerving, moves like a bullet, and is fraught with so much tension you might crack a tooth reading it. Outstanding in every way." —Dennis Lehane, author of *Mystic River*

"A beautifully crafted haunted-house thriller. The horror [Pyper] evokes has less in common with Stephen King and things that go bump in the night than with the fevered imagination of Joseph Conrad ferrying himself and the reader into a heart of darkness. . . . Compellingly readable and stylistically impressive." —*Calgary Herald*

"With its deft prose and pristine pacing, *The Guardians* is an intelligent and engrossing page-turner." —*Winnipeg Free Press*

"Pyper connects plot strands with vivid imagery [and] bold prose . . . [he] has set a high bar for thrillers . . . and other Canadian crime writers will be hard-pressed to top him." —*National Post*

"Pyper reveals his skill with pacing as the story takes on the speed of midnight dash through a graveyard. And please note: This is not schlock horror dripping with gore. Pyper expertly creates terror through mood and setting. We hear what keeps going bump in the night, but never quite see it." —*The Globe and Mail*

"[*The Guardians*] is a dark, brooding, compelling story about the loss of innocence and the ubiquity of evil, with a finalé as bittersweet as your 50th birthday party." —*The Times* (UK)

"A screenplay-ready meditation on the loss of youth, and the fact that the past is *terra incognita* in [Canada]. . . . It's no bad thing to have our literature now and then influenced by disciplined plotting, vivid characters, sharply drawn evocations of modern-day mayhem—the very specialties of crime fiction." —*The Walrus*

"An ambitious excursion into Stephen King territory. . . . With a well-executed narrative, both past . . . and present, strong characterization and some truly arresting images, *The Guardians* is a compelling and genuinely creepy read." —*The Guardian* (UK)

"Pyper delivers a fast-paced, gripping and truly spooky tale with panache." —*Irish Independent*

"Hauntingly good . . . *The Guardians* will chill you far more than winter ever could." —*Chatelaine*

"Pyper's plot hits a near-perfect pace." —*Maclean's*

"Dreadfully good . . . *The Guardians* is exemplary—disbelief gets suspended, the pages race by, the prose itself is seamless . . . and you'll stay up way too late reading it." —*Hamilton Spectator*

"The writing is so convincing, even the most skeptical readers may find themselves shaking with fear . . . A white-knuckle thriller balanced with a satisfying character study." —*Edmonton Journal*

"A very creepy story . . . Pyper has such a gift for character and setting." —*NOW Magazine* (starred review)

"So much more than a thriller. Truly great writing, haunting, intelligent, human, terrifying. Pyper is a genius." —Deon Meyer, author of *Thirteen Hours*

"Pyper's distinctive, highly visual writing style compliments his plot perfectly. The story's developments are all unexpected, but it works. Every twist and turn in *The Guardians* is shocking, yet still feels right . . . Though Pyper gets beyond the traditional tropes of the horror genre, he mines it for all it's worth and gives readers what they're really looking for: can't-tear-your-eyes-away fear. *The Guardians* gave me nightmares, but I didn't want to put it down." —*McGill Tribune*

"Like good chocolate, you find yourself finishing a chapter and wanting 'just one more.' [*The Guardians*] is a hard book to put down. . . . A haunting, menacing ghost story." —*Cadence Magazine*

"In *The Guardians*, Andrew Pyper draws on an impressive range of gifts: a fine command of all the devices of suspense narrative, nimble characterizations, and a knack for the felicitous phrase. The story is altogether scary, compelling, and full of delightful surprises, but be prepared—it just might get under your skin too."—Dennis McFarland, *New York Times* bestselling author of *The Music Room* and *A Face at the Window*

"Like any good haunting, *The Guardians* is at first just a whisper in your ear, a dark form in the window across the street. Then page by page, with the patience and skill of a true master, Andrew Pyper ratchets up the tension, the suspense, the fear until you find yourself white-knuckled and breathless. Andrew Pyper is the rare writer who has it all; he's a poet, a magician, and a seer into the frail human heart. In this moving, utterly gripping, and gorgeously written novel, he brings all his formidable talents to bear. Don't miss it." —Lisa Unger, bestselling author of *Die For You* and *Beautiful Lies*

"A splendidly eerie haunted house story, and a superb evocation of small town life. *The Guardians* gripped me from its opening line and never let go." —John Connolly, bestselling author of *Every Dead Thing* and *The Lovers*

ANDREW PYPER

THE

GUARDIANS

ANCHOR CANADA

Library and Archives Canada Cataloguing in Publication is available upon request.

ISBN 978-0-385-66372-4

The Guardians is a work of fiction. Names, characters, places and incidents are
products of the author's imagination or are used fictitiously. Any resemblance to
actual events or locales or persons, living or dead, is entirely coincidental.

Printed and bound in the USA

Published in Canada by Anchor Canada,
a division of Random House of Canada Limited

Visit Random House of Canada Limited's website: www.randomhouse.ca

10 9 8 7 6 5 4 3 2 1

For my Guardians then—
Jeff, Larry, Mike, Robin, Alan

And for my Guardians now—
Heidi, Maude and Ford

THE GUARDIANS

MEMORY DIARY

Entry No. 1

We watched them come.

A lone police cruiser at first. The officer's shirt strain-ing against the bulge around his waist. A look of prac-tised boredom on his face, a pantomime of seen-it-all masculinity performed without an audience. We were the only ones who saw him walk, pigeon-toed, into the house. The only ones who knew he wouldn't be bored for long.

When he came out he wasn't wearing his cap anymore. His thin hair, grey but darkened with sweat, was a greasy sculpture of indecision, pointing in several directions at once. (Later, we wondered about the cap. Had it fallen off in the first jolt of shock? Had he removed it himself in a reflex of some sort? A show of respect?)

He tumbled into the car and radioed in. We tried to read his lips, but couldn't really see his face through the willow boughs, swaying reflections over the windshield. Was there a numbered code for this? Or was he forced to describe what he'd seen? Did he recognize, even in the shadows that must have left him blind after entering from the bright outside, who they were? However he put it, it would have been hard for anyone to believe. We weren't wholly convinced ourselves. And we knew it was true.

Soon, two more cruisers pulled up. An ambulance. A fire truck, though there was no fire. Some of the men went inside, but most did not. A scene of grimly loitering uniforms, sipping coffee from the Styrofoam cups they brought with them. The last of history's union-protected, on-the-job smokers flicking their butts into the street in undeclared competition.

There was nothing for most of them to do, but they stayed anyway. An only partly hidden excitement in the way they scuffed their shoes over the cracked sidewalk and rested their hands on their belts, knuckling the handles of holstered guns. It was a small town. You didn't get this sort of thing too often. You didn't get it ever.

We stood together, watching. Unseen behind the curtains in the front room of the McAuliffe house across the way. Our noses grazing the diaphanous material that smelled of recently burned bacon and, deeper still, a succession of dinners scooped out of the deep fryer. When the paramedics and bearded man in a suit who must have been the coroner finally emerged from the house with the black bags laid out on gurneys—one, and then the smaller other—we held our breaths. A gulp of french fry, onion ring and chicken finger that, to this day, is the taste of loss.

We remember all this, though still not everything.

And some of the things we remember may not have happened at all.

[1]

THE CALL COMES in the middle of the night, as the worst sort do.

The phone so close I can read the numbers on its green-glowing face, see the swirled fingerprint I'd left on its message window. A simple matter of reaching and grabbing. Yet I lie still. It is my motor-facility impairment (as one of my fussily unhelpful physicians calls it) that pins me for eighteen rings before I manage to hook the receiver onto my chest.

"I don't even know what time it is. But it's *late*, isn't it?"

A familiar voice, faintly slurred, helium-pitched between laughter and sobs. Randy Toller. A friend since high school—a time that even Randy, on the phone, calls "a million years ago." And though it was only twenty-four years, his estimate feels more accurate.

As Randy apologizes for waking me, and blathers on about how strange he feels "doing this," I am trying to think of an understanding but firm way of saying no when he finally gets around to asking for money. He has done it before, following the unfairly lost auditions, the furniture-stealing girlfriends, the vodka-smoothed rough patches of his past tough-luck decade. But in the end Randy surprises me when he takes a rattling, effortful breath and says, "Ben's dead, Trev."

Trev?

This is my first, not-quite-awake thought. Nobody's called me that since high school, *including* Randy.

"How?"

"A rope," Randy says.

"Rope?"

"Hanging. I mean, he hung himself. In his mom's house."

"He never went outside. Where else could he have done it?"

"I'm saying he did it in his *room*. Up in the attic where he'd sit by the window, you know, watching."

"Did his mom find him?"

"It was a kid walking by on the street. Looked up to see if that weird McAuliffe guy was in the window as usual, and saw him swinging there."

I'm quiet for a while after this. We both are. But there is our breath being traded back and forth down the line. Reminders that we aren't alone in recalling the details of Ben's room, a place we'd spent a quarter of our youth wasting our time in. Of how it would have looked with the grown-up Ben in it, attached to the oak beam that ran the length of the ceiling.

"Maybe it's for the best," Randy says finally.

"Take that back."

"I didn't—it's just—"

"Take that stupid bullshit *back*."

"Fine. Sorry."

Randy has led the kind of life that has made him used to apologizing for saying the wrong thing, and the contrite tone he uses now is one I've heard after dozens of defaulted IOUs and nights spent sleeping on my sofa between stints in rented rooms. But then, in little more than a whisper, he says something else.

"You know it's sort of true, Trev."

He's right. It is sort of true that with the news of Ben McAuliffe's suicide there came, among a hundred other reactions, a shameful twinge of relief.

Ben was a friend of mine. Of ours. A best friend, though I hadn't seen him in years, and spoke to him only slightly more often. It's because he stayed behind, I suppose. In Grimshaw, our hometown, from which all of us but Ben had escaped the first chance we had. Or maybe it's because he was sick. Mentally ill, as even he called himself, though sarcastically, as if his mind was the *last* thing wrong with him. This would be over the phone, on the rare occasions I called. (Each time I did his mother would answer, and when I told her it was me calling her voice would rise an octave in the false hope that a good chat with an old friend might lift the dark spell that had been cast on her son.) When we spoke, neither Ben nor I pretended we would ever see each other again. We might as well have been separated by an ocean, or an even greater barrier, as impossible to cross as the chasm between planets, as death. I had made a promise to never go back to Grimshaw, and Ben could never leave it. A pair of traps we had set for ourselves.

Despite this, we were still close. There was a love between us too. A sexless, stillborn love, yet just as fierce as the other kinds. The common but largely undocumented love between men who forged their friendship in late childhood.

But this wasn't the thing that bridged the long absence that lay between our adult lives. What connected Ben and me was a secret. A whole inbred family of secrets. Some of them so wilfully forgotten they were unknown even to ourselves.

Only after I've hung up do I notice that, for the entire time I was on the phone with Randy, my hands were still. I didn't even have to concentrate on it, play the increasingly unwinnable game of Mind Over Muscles.

Don't move.

It's like hypnosis. And like hypnosis, it usually doesn't work.

Everything's okay. Just stay where you are. Relax. Be still.

Now, in the orange dust of city light that sneaks through the blinds, I watch as the tremor returns to my limbs. Delicate flutterings at first. Nervous and quick as a sparrow dunking its head in a puddle. An index finger that abruptly stiffens, points with alarm at the chair in the corner—and then collapses, asleep. A thumb standing in a Fonzie salute before turtling back inside a fist.

You know what I need? A week in Bermuda.

These were the sort of thoughts I had when the twitches showed up.

I need to eat more whole grains.

I need a drink.

The hand-jerks and finger-flicks were just the normal flaws, the software glitches the body has to work through when first booting up after a certain age. I had just turned *forty*, after all. There was a price to be paid—a small, concealable impediment to be endured for all the fun I'd had up until now. But it was nothing to worry about. It wasn't a real problem of the kind suffered by the wheelchaired souls you wish away from your line of sight in restaurants, your appetite spoiled.

But then, a few months ago, the acceptable irregularities of the body inched into something less acceptable. Something *wrong*.

I went to the doctor. Who sent me to another doctor. Who confirmed her diagnosis after a conversation with a third doctor. And then, once the doctors had that straightened out, all of them said there was next to nothing they could do, wished me well and buggered off.

What I have, after all, is one of those inoperable, medically unsexy conditions. It has all the worst qualities of the non-fatal disease: chronic, progressive, cruelly erosive of one's "quality of life." It can go fast or slow. What's certain is that it will get worse. I could name it now but I'm not in the mood. I hate its falsely personal surnamed quality, the possessive aspect of the capital *P*. And I hate the way it doesn't kill you. Until it does.

I spoke to a therapist about it. Once.

She was nice—*seemed* nice, though this may have been only performance, an obligation included in her lawyer-like hourly fee—and was ready to see me "all the way through what's coming." But I couldn't go back. I just sat in her pleasant, fern-filled room and caught a whiff of the coconut exfoliant she'd used that morning to scrub at the liver spots on her arms and knew I would never return. She was the sort of woman in the sort of office giving off the sort of scent designed to provoke confessions. I could have trusted her. And trusting a stranger is against the rules.

(There was something else I didn't like. I didn't like how, when she asked if I had entertained any suicidal thoughts since the diagnosis and I, after a blubbery moment, admitted that I had, she offered nothing more than a businesslike smile and a tidy check mark in her notepad.)

One useful suggestion came out of our meeting, nevertheless. For the purposes of recording my thoughts so that they might be figured out later, she recommended I keep a diary chronicling the progress of my disease. Not that she used that word. Instead, she referred to the unstoppable damage being done to me as an "experience," as if it were a trip to Paraguay or sex with twins. And it wasn't a journal of sickness I was to keep, but a "Life Diary," her affirmative nods meant to show that I wasn't dying. *Yet*. That was there too. Remember, Trevor: You're not quite dead *yet*.

"Your Life Diary is more than a document of events," she explained. "It can, for some of my clients, turn out to be your best friend."

But I already have best friends. And they don't live in my present life so much as in the past. So that's what I've ended up writing down. A recollection of the winter everything changed for us. A pocket-sized journal containing horrors that surprised even me as I returned to them. And then, after the pen refused to stand still in my hand, it has become a story I tell into a Dictaphone. My voice. Sounding weaker than it does in my own ears, someone else's voice altogether.

I call it my "Memory Diary."

Randy offered to call Carl, but we both knew I would do it. Informing a friend that someone they've known all their life has died was more naturally a Trevor kind of task. Randy would be the one to score dope for a bachelor party, or scratch his key along the side of a Porsche because he took it personally, and hard, that his own odds of ever owning one were fading fast. But I was definitely better suited to be the bearer of bad tidings.

I try Carl at the last number I have for him, but the cracked voice that answers tells me he hasn't lived there for a while. When I ask to have Carl call if he stops by, there is a pause of what might be silent acceptance before the line goes dead. Randy has a couple of earlier numbers, and I try those too, though Carl's former roommates don't seem to know where he is now either (and refuse to give me their own names when I ask).

"Not much more we can do," Randy says when I call him back. "The guy is *gone*, Trev."

There it is again: *Trev*. A name not addressed to me in over twenty years, and then I get it twice within the last half-hour.

I had an idea, as soon as Randy told me Ben had died, that the past was about to spend an unwelcome visit in my present. Going from Trevor to Trev is something I don't like, but a nostalgic name change is going to be the least of it. Because if I'm getting on a train for Grimshaw in the morning, it's all coming back.

Heather.

The coach.

The boy.

The house.

The last of these most of all because it alone is waiting for us. Ready to see us stand on the presumed safety of weed-cracked sidewalk as we had as schoolchildren, daring each other to see who could look longest through its windows without blinking or running away.

For twenty-four years this had been Ben's job. Now it would be ours.

MEMORY DIARY

Entry No. 2

There were four of us.

Ben, Carl, Randy and me. Grimshaw Guardians all. Hockey players on the high-school squad that travelled the county's gravel roads to do battle against the villain-ous Cougars of Milverton, cheating Rams of Listowel, cowardly Sugar Kings of Elmira. We were just sixteen years old the one and only season we played with the seniors, but we were decent enough—and the school small enough—to make the team. The only boys among just-turned men.

Randy:

A featherweight winger looping skilfully—if a little pointlessly—in front of the other team's net. It always seemed that he liked to skate more than score. Sometimes,

Randy would forget that there were others playing *against* him. Kids who wished to see him fail, to crumple to his knees and never get up again. It was usually a look of puzzled disappointment, not pain, that I would read on his face when he limped to the bench following these punishments.

Why? his eyes would ask as he took his place at the end of the bench, rubbing the charley horse out of his thigh.

Why would someone do that? I was just having fun.

Carl:

Short, but solid as an elm stump. Hair he left long so that it waved, black as a pirate flag, as he skated. Carl was the Guardians' unpredictable pugilist, a rarely played fourth-liner who would skate up to a kid who had nothing to do with the play at hand—and, often, against whom no grudge was held—and commence a windmilling of fists into the poor fellow's face.

Who knew if Carl would have been the fighter he was without the dark eyes and drooping smile that conveyed unintended menace? How less inclined to serve up knuckle sandwiches—and, later, less susceptible to needle and pill—if his dad had been another kind of man, one who didn't leave and never return?

Sometime late in the third period of the first game of the Guardians' season there was a bench-clearing brawl. It was an away game against the Exeter Bobcats, a team whose only real talent was for medieval hand-to-hand combat. We knew things were about to get nasty when their coach started tapping the shoulders of players on his bench and pointing at us. Then, with a collective whoop, they stormed over the boards and set upon us, their fans sending a volley of scalding coffee cups over our heads.

I mention this because, in my experience, who you first go to help in a riot is as sure a test of true allegiance as any I know.

So who did I rush to that night to prevent a Bobcat from pounding his face into the ice? I went to Randy, because he was my friend. And because he was squealing for help.

"Trev! Carl! Ben!"

And all of us came.

Once we'd thrown Randy's attacker off him we were able to form a circle and hold our own. In fact, we ended up faring better than many of our older teammates, who left Exeter that night with split cheeks and teeth in their pockets.

On the bus ride home we, the youngest Guardians, were permitted to sit at the back, an acknowledgment of our success on the battlefield. I recall us looking at each other as we rolled out of the parking lot, unable to hold the giddy smiles off our faces. Which started the laughing. We laughed three-quarters of an hour through a snowstorm, and though we expected someone to tell us to shut our mouths or they'd shut them for us at any second, they never did.

Ben:

Our Zen mascot of a backup goalie. Because Vince Sproule, our starter, was eighteen and the best stopper in the county, Ben almost never saw ice time, which was fine with him. His proper place was at the end of the bench anyway. Mask off, hands resting in his lap, offering contemplative nods as we came and went from our shifts, as though the blessings of a vow-of-silence monk.

Ben was the sort of gentle-featured, unpimpled kid (he made you think *pretty* before pushing the thought away) who would normally have invited the torment of bullies, especially on a team composed of boys old enough to coax actual beards from their chins. But they left Ben alone.

I think he was spared because he was so plainly *odd*. It was the authenticity of his strangeness that worked as a shield when, in another who was merely different, it would have attracted the worst kind of attention. They liked Ben for this. But they kept their distance from him because of it too.

Trevor (Me):

A junk-goal god. Something of a floater, admittedly. A dipsy-doodling centre known for his soft hands (hands that now have trouble pouring milk).

There was, at sixteen, the whisperings of scouts knowing who I was. Early in the season the coach had a talk with my parents, urging them to consider the benefits of a college scholarship in the States. Who knows? Maybe Trev had a chance of going straight to pro.

Of course, this sort of thing was said about more than it ever happened to. Me included. Not that I wasn't good enough—we'll never know if I was or wasn't. Because after the abrupt end of my one and only season as a Guardian, I never skated again.

I had known Randy since kindergarten, when I approached him and, offering to share my Play-Doh, asked, "Do you want to be in my gang?" I remember that: *gang*. And even though I was alone, Randy accepted.

Ben joined us in early grade school, Carl a year later. That was grade three.

My father, not known for his wisdom (though he took runs at it on the nights he hit the sauce harder than usual), once told me something that has proven consistent with my experience: while a man can accumulate any number of acquaintances over his life, his only true friends are the ones he makes in youth.

Yet why Randy, Ben and Carl and no others? I could say it was the way we saw ourselves in each other. The recognition of my own foolishness in Randy's clowning, my imagination in Ben's trippy dreams, my rage in Carl's fisticuffs. How we had a better chance of knowing who we were together than we ever would have on our own.

What we shared made us friends. But here's the truth of the thing: our loyalty had little to do with friendship. For that, you'd have to look elsewhere.

You'd have to look in the house.

We were in Ben's backyard, out behind his garden shed, the four of us passing around a set of *Charlie's Angels* bubble-gum cards. I remember the hushed intensity we brought to studying Farrah Fawcett. The wide Californian smile. The astonishing nipples piercing their bikini veils.

We were eight years old.

And then there's Mrs. McAuliffe's voice, calling Ben inside.

"I'm not hungry," he shouted back.

"This isn't about dinner, honey."

She was trying not to cry. We could hear that from the other end of the McAuliffes' lot. We could hear it through the garden shed's walls.

Ben crossed the yard and stood before his mother, listening to her as she wrung her hands on her Kiss Me, I'm Scottish! apron. He waited a moment after she finished. Then, as though at the pop of a starter's pistol, he ran.

And we followed. Even as he crossed Caledonia Street and onto the Thurman property, we stayed after him. Ben scooted around the side of the house and we came around the corner in time to see the back door swing closed. Our feet had never touched this ground before. It was the one place we never even dared each other to go. Yet now we were running into the house, each of us fighting to be first, all calling Ben's name.

We found him in the living room. He was leaning against the wall between the two side windows. His crumpled form looked smaller than it should have, as though the house had stolen part of him upon entry.

"My dad's dead," he said when we gathered to stand over him. "She said it was an accident. But it wasn't."

Randy frowned. It was the same face he made when asked to come to the blackboard to work through a long-division equation. "What do you mean?"

"It *wasn't* an *accident!*"

He was angry more than anything else. His father was gone and it was his weakness that had taken him. A coward. Ben had been shown to have come from shoddy stock, and it was the revelation of bad luck that held him, not grief.

So we grieved for him.

Without a look between us, we knelt and took Ben in our arms. Four booger-nosed yard apes with little in our heads but Wayne Gretzky and, now, Farrah daydreams. Yet we held our friend—and each other—in a spontaneous show of comradeship and love. We were experiencing a rare thing (rarer still for boys): we were feeling someone else's pain as acutely as if it were our own. Ben wasn't crying, but we were.

More than this, the moment stopped time. No, not stopped: it stole the meaning from time. For however long we crouched together against the cracked walls of the Thurman house's living room we weren't growing older, we weren't eight, we weren't attempting another of the million awkward steps toward adulthood and its presumed freedoms. We were who we were and nothing else. A kind of revelation, as well as a promise. Ben had been the first of us to take a punch from the grown-up world. And we would be there when the other blows came our way.

We were pulling Ben to his feet when we heard the girl.

A moan from upstairs. A gasp, and then an exhaled cry.

I remember the three versions of the same expression on the faces of my friends. The shame that comes not from something we'd done but from something we didn't yet understand.

We'd heard that older kids sometimes came to the Thurman house to do stuff, and that some of this stuff concerned boys and girls and the things they could do with each other with their clothes off. Though we didn't really know our way around the mechanics, we knew that this was what was going on up there in one of the empty bedrooms.

I'm uncertain of many details from that afternoon, but I know this: we all heard it. Not the moaning, but how it turned into something else.

What we heard as Carl pulled the back door of the Thurman house closed was not the voice of a living thing. Human in its origin but no longer. A voice that should not have been possible, because it belonged to the dead.

The moaning from the girl upstairs changed. A new sound that showed what we took at first to be her pleasure wasn't that at all but a whimper of fear. We knew this without comprehending it, just stupid children at least half a decade shy of tracing the perimeters of what *sex* or *consent* or *hurt* could mean between women and men. It was the sound the dead girl made upstairs that instantly taught us. For in the gasp of time before we stepped outside and the closed door left the backyard and the trees and the house in a vacuum of silence, we heard the beginnings of a scream.

[2]

THERE'S A TRAIN to Grimshaw leaving Union Station at noon, which gives me three hours to pack an overnight bag, hail a cab and buy a ticket. An everyday sequence of actions. Yet for me, such tasks—pack a bag, hail a cab—have become cuss-laced battles against my mutinous hands and legs, so that this morning, elbowing out of bed after a night of terrible news, I look to the hours ahead as a list of Herculean trials.

Shave Face without Lopping Off Nose.

Tie Shoelaces.

Zip Up Fly.

Among the fun facts shared by my doctors at the time I was diagnosed with Parkinson's was that I could end up living for the same number of years I would have had coming if I hadn't acquired the disease. So, I asked, over this potentially long stretch, what else could I look forward to? Some worse versions of stuff I was already experiencing—the involuntary kicks and punches—along with a slew of new symptoms that sounded like the doctor was making them up as he went along, a shaggy-dog story designed to scare the bejesus out of me before he clapped me on the shoulder with a "Hey! Just kidding, Trevor. Nothing's *that* bad"? But he never got around to the punchline, because there wasn't one.

Let's try to remember what I do my best to forget:

A face that loss of muscle control will render incapable of expression. Difficulties with problem solving, attention, memory. The sensation of feeling suffocatingly hot and clammily cold *at the same time*. (This one has already made a few appearances, leading to the performance of silent-movie routines worthy of Chaplin, where I desperately dial up the thermostat while opening windows to stick my head out into the twenty-below air.) Vision impairment. Depression. Mild to fierce hallucinations, often involving insects (the one before bed last night: a fresh loaf of bread seething with cockroaches). Violent REM sleep that jolts you out of bed onto the floor.

For now, though, I'm mostly just slow.

This morning, when my eyes opened after dreams of Ben calling for help from behind his locked bedroom door, the clock radio glowed 7:24. By the time my feet touched carpet it was 7:38. Every day now begins with me lying on my back, waiting for my brain to send out the commands that were once automatic.

Sit up.

Throw legs over side of bed.

Stand.

Another ten minutes and this is as far as I've got. On my feet, but no closer to Grimshaw than the bathroom, where I'm working a shaky blade over my skin. Little tongues of blood trickling through the lather.

And, over my shoulder, a woman.

A reflection as real as my own. More real, if anything, as her wounds lend her swollen skin the drama of a mask. There is the dirt too. Caked in her hair, darkening her lashes. The bits of earth that refused to shake off when she rose from it.

That I'm alone in my apartment is certain, as I haven't had a guest since the diagnosis. And because I recognize who stands behind me in the mirror's steam. A frozen portrait of violence that, until now, has visited me only as I slept. The face at once wide-eyed and lifeless, still in the mounting readiness of all dead things.

Except this time she moves.

Parts her lips with the sound of a tissue pulled from the box. Dried flakes falling from her chin like black icing.

To pull away would be to back into her touch. To go forward would be to join her in the mirror's depth. So I stay where I am.

A blue tongue that clacks to purpose within her mouth. To whisper, to lick. To tell me a name.

I throw my arm against the glass. Wipe her away. The mirror bending against my weight but not breaking. When she's gone I'm left in a new clarity, stunned and ancient, before the mist eases me back into vagueness so that I am as much a ghost as she.

Impotence. Did I fail to mention that this is coming down the pike too? Though I could still do the deed if called upon (as far as I know), I have gone untested since the Bad News. I think I realized that part of my life was over even as the doc worked his lips around the P-word. *No more ladies for this ladies' man.*

Is *that* what I was? If the shoe fits.

And let's face it, the shoe fit pretty well for a while: an unmarried, all-night-party-hosting nightclub owner. Trevor, of Retox. Girlfriends all beautiful insomniacs with plans to move to L.A. I don't know if any of them could be said to have gotten to know me, nor did they try. I was *Trevor, of Retox*. Always up for a good time, fuelled by some decent drugs up in the VIP lounge of the place with the longest lineups on Friday nights. I *fit*. Though never for long. I hold the dubious distinction of having been in no relationship since high school that made it past the four-month mark. (I was more often the dumped than the dumper, I should add. The women I saw over my Retox years occupied the same world I did, a world where people were expected to want something other than what they had, to be elsewhere than across the restaurant table or in the bed they were in at any given time. It was a world of motion, and romance requires at least the *idea* of permanence.)

Who else was there with me in Retox-land? My business partners, though they were something less than friends, all work-hard–play-hard demons, the kind of guys who were great to share a couple nights in Vegas with but who, in quieter moments, had little to say beyond tales of how they got the upper hand in a real estate flip or gleaned the "philosophies" from a billionaire's memoir. On the family side, there was only my brother left, and I spoke to him long-distance on a quarterly basis, asking after the wife and athletic brood he seemed to be constantly shuttling around to rinks and ballet classes out in Edmonton. My parents were gone. Both of major cardiac events (what heart attacks are now, apparently) and both within a year of moving out of Grimshaw and into a retirement bungalow with a partial view of Lake Huron. That's about it. I've been alone, but well entertained.

And then the doctors stepped in to poop on the party. Within three weeks of the Bad News I sold Retox and retreated into the corners of my underfurnished condo to manage the mutual funds that will, I hope, pay for the nurses when the time comes for them to wheel, wipe and spoon. Until then, I do my best to keep my condition a secret. With full concentration I am able to punch an elevator button, hold a menu, write my signature on the credit card slip—all without giving away my status as a Man with a Serious Disease. In a way, it's only a different take on the "normal act" I've been keeping up since high school. It's likely that only my best friends from that time, my fellow Guardians, know the effort it takes.

Then, in a small town a hundred miles away, one of them ties one end of a rope to a ceiling beam and the other around his neck and the normal act has fallen away. There is only room for the lost now. To let the dead back in.

That's it, Trev. Keep moving. Keep it simple.

Button Shirt.

Find Seat on Train.

And when the call for Grimshaw comes, do what every shaking, betraying part of you will fight doing and get off.

MEMORY DIARY

Entry No. 3

When I remember Grimshaw now, a collage of places
comes to mind. The Old Grove Cemetery. The rail line
that snaked through town, straightening only in front of
the station, polka-dotted with bird shat. The sky: low,
cottony and grey. The trail that followed the river right
out of town and could, it was said, lead a runaway all
the way to Lake Huron. The sort of things everyone who
has grown up in a small town has their own version of.

And like every small town, Grimshaw had a haunted
house.

321 Caledonia Street. Once the Thurman place,
though who the Thurmans were, and when it was theirs,
we didn't know. Although it was red-bricked and wide-
porched like most of Grimshaw's older homes, it was
distinct in our minds, broader and higher, set farther

back from the street. We saw foreboding significance in its broken weather vane, a decapitated rooster spinning around in the most mild breezes as though panicked, a literal chicken with its head cut off. Yet other than this, it was its sameness that left it open to stories we could dream taking place in our own kitchens and bedrooms. It was a dark fixture of our imaginations precisely because it appeared as normal as the houses we lived in.

The house was occupied only for brief stretches. Outsiders who'd been recruited to be the new bank manager or Crown attorney and thought a place of such character was worth an attempt at restoration. The money pit it inevitably turned out to be chased such dreamers away. Or, if you went with the versions we told each other, they were sent out screaming into the night by furious spirits and bleeding walls.

Ben McAuliffe lived across from the place. It allowed us to look out from his attic bedroom and through the maples that darkened its double lot, trying to catch a flash of movement—or, worse, a toothily grinning ghoul—in one of its windows. It spooked us. But no more than the werewolf and vampire comics we traded among ourselves that delivered brief, dismissible chills. Even then, we didn't think there was such a thing as a real haunted house.

Of all the things we ended up being wrong about, that was the first.

All of us had families. Parents, from the long-gone to the present-but-only-in-body to the few (all moms) who tried hard to make contact but didn't know, when it came to teenage boys, where to start. There were siblings too. My older brother had already left for college in Kitchener. Ben was an only child of the kind given miles of his own space by his mom, who rarely left the house after Ben's dad died. Randy, on the other hand, came from a big, red-haired Catholic brood, five kids who, viewed together throwing dinner rolls at each other or administering Indian sunburns in their rumpus room, seemed to number closer to a dozen. But with the possible exception of one, none of the other familial players in our lives figured in what was to turn out to be Our Story.

We were boys, so you're supposed to look first to our dads in having a hand in making us the way we were, but for the most part, they were as absent as our teachers and the other elders advanced to us as "role model" candidates. My own father was an accountant at the town's utilities office. Compromised, mildly alcoholic. An essentially decent man possessed of faults some children might have chosen to be wounded by, but for me were just the marks that living the better part of his life in Grimshaw had left on him, and therefore were forgivable.

But we had another father. One we shared between us. The coach. He had a name—David Evans—that struck us as too unutterably bland to belong to someone like him. For us he was always "the coach," a designation spoken in a tone that somehow combined affection, irony and awe.

The coach wore wire-frame glasses, Hush Puppies, hid a receding hairline under a wool cap on game days.

He looked more like an English teacher—which he in fact was between nine and three thirty, Monday to Friday—than a leader of anything more athletic than the chess club. But his rumpled-scholar appearance was both who he really was and a disguise. We all got him wrong at first, which was how he wanted it. We were always getting him wrong. And then, out of the blue, he would say or show something that struck us as so essential and unguarded and true we became his. We believed. We wanted more of *that*.

The league's other coaches considered our success a freakish series of flukes. It wasn't any tactics or motivation our coach brought to the dressing room that lifted us to the top of the standings. How could it be? He didn't *look* like a hockey man. He didn't even *swear*.

They got him wrong too.

But what was it to get him right?

We knew he was married. Childless. Moved to Grimshaw five years earlier from Toronto. There were questions we had about him. Not creepy suspicions (of the sort we had about Mr. Krueger, for instance, the knee-patting driver's ed. instructor), just a handful of missing links in what we could gather about his story. Information that might explain why, beneath the coach's calm surface, we could sense something being held down, a muffled second voice. It might have been anger. Or a sadness too unwieldy to be allowed free run within him. There was, we sensed, something he might be helped with.

But he was the one who helped us. Our guardian. It was hard to see how this could ever be the other way around.

———

Our school hired a new music teacher at the beginning of our grade eleven year. Mr. Asworth, the old music teacher, had left over the summer. (Yes, we had much obvious fun with his name, as in "Hey, what's his *Assworth*?" whispered between us as we filed out at the end of class, an insult he seemed to think he deserved, given the way he pretended not to hear.)

Naturally, we'd tormented him. Makeout sessions in the drum-kit storage room, blowing cigarette smoke out of the tuba, snapping Melissa Conroy's bra until a red line was blazing across her freckled back. And as for Asworth teaching us to *play music*? His attempts to coax a melody out of Carl's flatulent trombone or get Randy to stop ringing the triangle and hollering "Come 'n' get it!" in the middle of "The Maple Leaf Forever" met with nothing but cacophonous failure.

Asworth's replacement, Miss Langham, was a different story.

In her presence we called her only Miss, but between us (and in our dreams) she was always Heather. At twenty-three, the youngest teacher at Grimshaw Collegiate by a decade. Long, chestnut hair we imagined slipping a hand through to touch the solitary mole on her throat. Green eyes, at once mirthful and encouraging. Tall but unstooped, unlike some of the senior basketball girls when they walked the halls, ashamed of their commanding physicality. Until Miss Langham arrived to teach us a surprisingly moving brass-band version of Pachelbel's Canon, we had witnessed only prettiness, tomboys, the promise of farmer-daughter curves. But Miss Langham exceeded any previous entry in our schoolboys' catalogue of feminine assets. We had no name for it then, and I hardly know what to call it now. Grace, I suppose.

I believe I can say as well that we were all instantly in love with her. Desire was part of it, yes. But what we really wanted was to rescue her one day. Show her our as yet unappreciated worth. Grow into gentlemen before her very eyes.

Sometimes, after school, we would head up to Ben's bedroom, gather at his window and wait to watch her go by. She was renting a room at the nurses' residence up the hill on the hospital grounds ("No Male Visitors After 8 P.M.," a sign at the door declared). Most days she would take Caledonia Street, advancing with long strides up its slope, a leather satchel bumping against her hip. Alone.

When I think of the Thurman house now, what comes to mind isn't a horrific image or stab of guilt. Not at first. What I see before any of that is Miss Langham walking home along the sidewalk past its brooding facade. A juxtaposition of youth and poise against its clutching shadows. Her sure step, the hint of smile she wore even when no one was coming the other way to wish good day to. Heather Langham was all *future*. And the house possessed only the wet rot, the foul longing of the past.

This is how I try to hold her in place as long as I can, before the other pictures force their way through: Miss Langham clipping past Grimshaw's darkest place. It was, for all the moment's simplicity, an act of subtle defiance. We never saw her cross the street to pass it at a safer distance, as we ourselves did. In fact, she seemed oblivious to the house altogether. A refusal to acknowledge the rudeness of its stare.

But in this, of course, was the suggestion that she knew she was being watched. She was a woman already well used to being looked at. Usually, this looking inspired admiration and yearning in the observer. But we could sense that the Thurman house—or the idea of whatever inhuman thing lived in it—instead felt only bitterness. A reminder of its place in death and hers so vividly in life.

[3]

THERE ARE MOMENTS when the tremors disappear all on their own. Whole chunks of time when my body and I are reunited, warring soldiers clinking tin mugs over a Christmas ceasefire. I'll be looking out the window, and the hands that had been squeaking against the glass will be calmed. Or now. Sitting on the milk run to Grimshaw, the train starting away from the platform with a lurch, my heart giving enlarging shape to Randy's announcement of the end of things: *Ben's dead, Trev.* As we pick up speed, I can feel the closing distance between myself and the past, an oncoming collision my newspaper-reading and text-messaging fellow passengers are unaware of. And yet, I am still. Silently weeping into the sleeve of my jacket but physically in control, my limbs awaiting their orders.

You can't help anyone, a voice suggests within me. *You can't help yourself. Why not do what Ben did while you're still able?*

Not my voice, though it's instantly familiar. A voice I haven't heard in twenty-four years.

The train rolls out from under the covered platform and the city is there, the glass towers firing off shards of sunlight in a farewell salute. All at once, I'm certain I will never come back. I escaped something in Grimshaw once. But it won't let me go a second time.

Ticket, please, the voice says, laughing.

"Ticket, please," the conductor tries again.

It was thought, when they built the four lanes running west between Toronto and the border at Detroit a couple years before I was born, that the highway's proximity to Grimshaw would lend new purpose to what was before then not much other than a service town for the county's farmers. But there was no more reason to take the Grimshaw exit than there had previously been to limp in its direction on the old, rutted two-lane. Like many of the communities its size on the broad arrowhead of farmland stuck between the Great Lakes, it remained a forgotten place. Never industrial enough to be outright abandoned in the way of the ghost towns of Ohio, Pennsylvania and Upstate New York, but not alert enough to attempt re-invention. Grimshaw was content to merely hang on, to take a subdued pride in its century homes on tree-lined streets, the stained facades of its Victorian storefronts, its daughters or sons who met with success upon moving away. Now, entering it as a stranger, one might see a gothic charm in the wilful oldness of the place, its loyalty to the vine-covered, the paint-peeled. But for those who grew up here, it was only as it had always been.

There are times of the year when certain places seem to be themselves more than any other time. Springtime in Paris, Christmas in New York. Toronto frozen at Valentine's. Even before the bad things happened, I saw Grimshaw as a Halloween town. Sparsely streetlit, thickly treed. The houses never grand but large, built at a time that favoured rear staircases, widow's-peaked attics, so that they all had their own secret hiding places. Founded by Scots Presbyterians and consistently conservative in the backbenchers it sent to Parliament, Grimshaw had little sympathy for the mystical. Any mention of the supernatural was considered nothing more than foolishness, the side effects of too many matinees indulged at the Vogue. Ghosts? "Catholic voodoo," as my father put it.

Yet at the same time, it was its dour Protestant character that endeared its inhabitants to the everyday tragic, to the stories of broken lives and cruel, inexplicable fate. For our parents, the dead lived on, but only in dinner-table and church-tea tales of misfortune.

Grimshaw's adults could never see their home as haunted. Their children, on the other hand, had no choice.

The train slows as we approach the town limits. The hardened fields yield to weedy outskirts, the low-rent acres of half-hearted development: the trailer park, the go-kart track, the drive-in movie screen with "See U Next Summer!" on the marquee (a promise that, by the vandalized look of things, has not been kept for a dozen years or more). Then the more permanent claims. Shaggy backyards crisscrossed with laundry lines. A school with paper witches taped to the windows. Dumpsters left open-mouthed, choking on black plastic.

Within a minute, we are rolling into the old part of town at a walking pace. It gives us a chance to study the Inventory Blowout! offerings at what used to be Krazy Kevin's car lot, where Randy's dad worked, to catch a whiff of the fumes rising from the Erie Burger's exhaust. There is even a welcome party of sorts. Three kids smoking against the wall of the station, giving us the finger.

When the train stops I am alone in getting to my feet, hauling my bag off the rack and stepping down onto the platform. The cars already moving again, easing into the west end of town, where they will pass the high school, the courthouse before speeding out onto the tobacco flats. All places I'd rather view through double-paned glass. But now I'm here. The Grimshaw air. The midday moon staring down, bug-eyed and bored.

A gust blows a Big Gulp cup against my leg. Dust devils swirl over the platform, and within them, the laughing voice again.

Welcome home.

MEMORY DIARY

Entry No. 4

Randy was Howdy Doody–freckled, knob-elbowed and goofy-haired, but girls liked him. It was hard to know precisely what charms he possessed that got him into perfumed back seats and onto darkened basement futons more frequently than the rest of us. The easy answer would be his "sense of humour," which was how most of the girls who came and went, unblamingly, through Randy's teens would have explained it. But I'm not so sure. Yes, Randy was funny. But he was more of a joke than a comedian. Someone to be next to and feel that here was a fellow who needn't be taken seriously. I think this is what girls saw in Randy, and still do. He made the idea of two people being with each other for a time so much simpler than it was with anyone else.

Take Carl, for instance. Girls liked him too. In his case, it was a combination of good looks and a reluctance to speak that was often mistaken for an air of mystery. But Carl was restless. For him, female affection was something to gorge on, swiftly and roughly, then leave behind without clearing his plate. His habit was to break up with his girlfriends without telling them, refusing to return their calls or meet their eyes in the school hallways. Unlike Randy, Carl made girls cry.

Ben, on the other hand, mostly did without. Not that there weren't sideways opportunities offered to him. Quieter girls, too studious or artsy to attract more aggressive attention. Instead, they made themselves available to Ben (in camouflaged ways), and he went about his business. And what *was* Ben's business? Living in his head. Reading dragon and time-travel novels. He wrote poetry. Stranger still, he *read* poetry.

But what Ben did more than anything else was watch. Our backup goalie, following the play from the bench like a shoulder-padded Buddha. A silhouette in his attic bedroom, staring at the house across from his.

Of the four of us, I was the "married man." Funny to think how true this was at the time. And how, for the more than twenty years since I last saw Sarah Mulgrave, I've been about as far from married as a man can get.

The obvious explanation for this would be the Thurman house. It messed all of us up in different ways.

Addiction. Professional failure. Emotional amputations. For me, it was never being able to love—or be loved by—a woman again.

Personally, I favour an even more sentimental explanation: Sarah was meant to be mine. And the wound I am to bear is to have had her taken from me.

Even today, I whisper "Sarah Mulgrave" and she is with me. A wrinkled nose when she laughed. Hair the colour of a new penny. A mouth that articulated as much when listening as when speaking: sharply etched, blushed lips, amused creases at the corners. And green eyes. Lovely in their colour but lovelier in what they promised.

Sarah came to all the Guardians games, and though this earned her inclusion among the "puck bunnies" who fawned over Carl and the older guys on the team, the fact is she had little interest in sports. She would never have shown up to sit at the top of the stands, clutching a hot chocolate beneath the maniacal, hockey-stick-munching beaver of the Akins Lumber billboard, were it not to shout for number 12. Me.

Afterward, if my dad wasn't using the car, I would drive her home. The last of the wood-panelled Buick wagons. Hideous but handy. Because on those evenings we would take a spin out of town. Spook ourselves by switching the headlights off and flying over the night roads. Knowing that no harm could come to us because we were *young*—not children anymore, but still immune to what grimly went by the name of the

Real World. The car hurtling into darkness. A foreplay of screams.

We would slow only once we passed the "Welcome to the Village of Harmony" sign. Park in an orchard of black walnut trees. The pulsing silence of a killed engine.

It was often cold out. But the shared heat of our skin fought off the chill until we lay side by side, our breath visible exclamations against the windows. My dad would take measurements of the gas he left in the tank, so in heating the car, we had to weigh the risk of discovery against the fear of frostbite. The result was sporadic, short hits of warmth from the front vents. To avoid getting up and baring my ass to those who might drive by, I learned to turn the keys in the ignition with my toes.

Sarah's dad was friendly but strict. He liked me, and was even prepared to look the other way when his daughter was returned home an hour past curfew, her cheeks flushed, smelling faintly of cherry brandy. But the unspoken deal between us was that he was permitting these liberties on the condition that, sooner rather than later, I would propose to Sarah. He married Sarah's mom when they were both only a couple of years older than we were then. Teen weddings in Grimshaw were far from uncommon. Many kids knew what their professional lives were going to be by that time, the house they would one day inherit. What was the point in waiting?

It was a plan I was happy to entertain myself. I had no sense, as Carl and Randy had (and maybe Ben too, though who could tell?), that we were too young to judge who was right for us, that more sophisticated, realized women awaited us in our post-Grimshaw lives. There was nothing I could imagine wanting beyond Sarah anyway. I would marry her, just as her father wished. Why not? Sarah and I would look out for each other and let our lives, long and benign, wash over us.

And I would give my right arm (for what it's shakily worth) to know how that life would have turned out. Sarah could have waitressed, I could have found work on a construction crew or factory floor. We would have had our own apartment, something on the second floor over a shoe store or laundromat, the bedroom in the back. Just the two of us (the three? the four?), getting along fine without a coach or Heather Langham or friends I felt I should be ready to die for. Without a Thurman house.

For *that*, go ahead. Take both arms.

[4]

My room smells of ammonia and wet dog.

I'm on the top floor—the third—of the Queen's Hotel. A brick cube whose one gesture toward grandeur, a tin cupola over the corner suite, had over the decades been painted with coats of blue and yellow and green that wouldn't stick, so that these days it appears psychedelically polka-dotted. Other than a couple of motels on the edge of town—the inexplicably international Swiss Cottage and Golden Gate—the Queen's is the only place to stay in Grimshaw. For this reason alone, it enjoyed a reputation for fanciness that was never deserved. Though there were sporadic efforts to renovate its rooms or hire a "French chef" to pour sherry and cream over the menu, eventually the Queen's always returned to its fatigued self.

I open the window that looks out over Ontario Street and breathe. Grimshaw is a farming town, and in the summer and fall there is always a breeze carrying the perfume of cow manure to remind you of the fact. Not to mention the afternoon traffic of eighteen-wheelers hauling livestock to slaughter. Pig snouts and cattle tails and chicken feathers poking through the slats of passing trailers. As a kid, I felt that only the pigs knew what was coming. Watching them now, the pink nostrils flaring, I feel the same thing.

I lie down on the bed for a time. I must have, because when there's a knock at the door, that's where I am.

"Who is it?"

"Wayne Gretzky. Team Canada needs you, son."

I open the door and Randy is standing there. And while I am almost light-headed with happiness to see him, I have, at first, an even more overwhelming thought.

Good God, you look old.

And then, after a glimpse of ourselves in the hall mirror: *We both do.* The indoor skin, the lines of shoulder and chin grown soft. Randy and I look as though some internal dimmer switch has been lowered, pulling us into partial shadow.

What the hell happened?

The worst part is we know the answer.

The project of Being a Man had shifted with overnight suddenness, so that we awakened one morning with the hungover certainty that something was wrong. All the things we had been working for, what we had managed to achieve, now required maintenance. For most it is a home, a family. For Randy, an acting career limited to bit parts and commercials. For me, it was Retox, the girlfriend with a bar code tattooed on her inner thigh. Whatever it was, it would prove to be too much. Some of it was bound to slip away. It *had* been slipping away.

But here Randy and I are together again. Overdressed and middle-aged, improbably standing in a bare room of the Queen's Hotel like actors in a Beckett play who've forgotten their lines.

You too.

That's what we see in each other's eyes, what we silently share in the pause between recognition and brotherly embrace.

I see it got you too.

"Well," Randy says, slapping both of my shoulders. "We're here."

"Yes, we goddamn are."

"Have you been around town yet? It's like a time capsule. The world's most *pointless* time capsule."

"Can't wait to see all the sights."

"I guess Ben's the only one who could have brought us back."

"Ben's the only one who could have got us to do a whole lot of things."

I was referring only to harmless stuff, of how Ben could talk us into goofing around with a Ouija board or playing Dungeons & Dragons, but as soon as it was out, I heard how it could seem that I was speaking of something else.

"You know what's funny?" Randy announces finally. "The last time I was in the Queen's, it was with Tina Uxbridge."

"Todd Flanagan's girlfriend?"

"It was her idea, swear to God. I liked Todd. But I liked Tina more."

"She had his kid, didn't she? In grade twelve or something?" And then: "Jesus, Randy. Maybe it was *yours*."

"*Not* mine. Trust me, I checked the calendar."

"Wait. I'm still a little dizzy here. You slept with *Tina Uxbridge*?"

"Just down the hall."

"You amaze me, Randy."

"And *she* amazed *me*."

I look around the room, checking the corners.

"I tried," Randy says. "Followed up again on every number Carl ever gave me. Nobody knows where he is."

"He ought to be here."

"Did you ever talk to him?"

"Not much the last few years."

"So you never saw him after things got bad."

The two of us still standing in the room's entryway. I should move aside, give us some space. But I need to hear what Randy is now obliged to tell me.

"He was using, Trev."

"Did you—I don't know—confront him?"

"Confront *Carl*?"

"No. I wouldn't have either."

"He called every once in a while. Then, maybe two years ago, even the calls stopped."

"He never called me."

"He was *ashamed*," Randy says. "He looked up to you more than any of us."

"He did?"

"The best hockey player. Successful businessman. You were steady."

I'd been standing with my arms crossed over my chest. Now I release them, hold them out in front of me and let them shake. "Who's steady now?"

It's meant as a joke, but it only makes Randy uncomfortable. I step aside to let him into the room. He goes and stands at the window. Speaking against the glass.

"I visited Mrs. McAuliffe this morning," he says. "Apparently Ben had a will. And he named you executor of his estate."

"What estate?"

"You mean aside from some hockey cards and a jar of dimes? Not much."

The room closes in on us, stifling even the idea of speech. It's not that we've so quickly run out of things to say, but that there's too much.

Randy turns to face me. "What are we going to do?"

"In Grimshaw? At three-thirty on a Thursday afternoon?" I shuffle over to Randy and deliver a smart smack to the side of his face. "Let's get a drink."

We were sitting in music class on a Tuesday morning in early February, waiting for Miss Langham to walk in and give us one of her let's-get-started smiles, when Ben turned around in his chair to face me and whispered, "I had the most fucked-up dream last night."

There was nothing unusual in this. Miss Langham was often a minute or two late for us, her first class of the day. She had a gift for comic entrances. We never laughed at Miss Langham, though. We were too busy fixing her quirks into our memory: the sound of her footsteps scuffing hurriedly down the hall and—*slap!*—a dropped textbook on the floor, followed by a Girl Scout cuss that we held our breath in order to hear.

Butternuts!

Frick!

Then her hand gripped on the doorframe, spinning her into the room. Her flushed apology. The wisp of hair that had come loose and she now curled her lower lip to blow out of her eyes. The later she was, the better we behaved.

As for Ben, he was always having dreams. Surreal, circular narratives he would begin relating to me as we waited for Miss Langham, laying his flute on his lap and leaning back, making sure we weren't being over-heard, as though the latest clip from his subconscious was something others were eager to monitor, to use.

Ben's dreams were a little strange. What was stranger was when he saw people who weren't there:

A man with goat horns, standing at the top of his attic stairs.

A boy with one arm freshly cut off and waving wildly with the other, as though to a departing ship, standing in Ben's backyard when he looked up while mowing the lawn.

An old woman who might have been his grand-mother if she hadn't died the year before, looking out from his bedroom closet, red scars in place of eyes.

On this Tuesday, waiting for Miss Langham's arrival, what was a little out of the ordinary wasn't Ben telling me he'd had another weird dream the night before, but how he looked when he did. His skin showing tiny blue veins, as it did after he'd sat, unplayed, for a couple of hours in a freezing-cold ice rink.

"I'm not even sure it *was* a dream," he said.

"What was it about?"

"Me, looking out my bedroom window. Everything

like the way it is when I'm awake. The one streetlight that works, the one that doesn't. The trees, the houses. Nothing happening. I'm almost falling asleep—like a kind of *double* sleep, because it's a dream, right? And then, there's . . . *something*."

"Something?"

"I don't even really see it. I just notice that something is different. Something that's *moving*."

"What was it?"

"I told you, I didn't really see it."

"The thing you didn't see. What'd it look like?"

"Like the shadow of a tree, maybe. But not."

"So it had *feet*? This tree?"

"It wasn't a tree."

"A person, then."

"I guess."

I looked to the door. I was more than ready for Miss Langham.

"I don't think it was alone," Ben said.

"There were two people?"

"I got the idea it was holding on to someone."

"And where'd it take them?"

"Round the side of the Thurman house. It was scary, Trev. Seriously."

"Good thing it was just a dream."

"I told you. I'm not sure it was."

"What's wrong with you? You okay?"

"I . . . I think . . . you . . ."

"You look like you're going to puke."

I remember pulling my feet out from under his chair, just in case.

Ben took a deep breath. Swallowed. "You need to hear the fucked-up part."

"Okay."

"Like I said, I couldn't really *see*. But I could *feel* who it was. The person it was carrying into the house."

"*Into* the house? I thought you said it just went round—"

"Good mor-*ning*!"

Not Heather. A buxom lady in support hose writing her name on the blackboard. We'd seen her before, doing the same thing at the front of our math, geography, history classes.

"Where's Miss Langham?" I asked without raising my hand. Then, after not getting an answer: "Where's Heather?"

The supply teacher kept writing her name. In fact, she slowed down to buy the extra second required to come up with an answer to the question she knew was coming next. A question that came from Randy.

"Is she okay?"

The supply teacher put down her chalk. Thumbed her glasses back up the slippery bridge of her nose.

"Miss Langham is unavailable at this time," she said.

And before we could ask anything else, she was tapping her baton and telling us to open our sheet music to "The Maple Leaf Forever."

Something else was worth noting from later that afternoon. A good deed.

We went to visit Paul Schantz in the Cedarfield Seniors

Home as part of a "community outreach" program the Guardians' board of directors thought up, the idea being that team players would go to visit kids with cancer or other fans who couldn't make the games, and someone from the *Beacon* would be there to take a picture for the next day's paper. It didn't turn out that way. In fact, Randy, Ben, Carl and I were the only ones to sign up.

According to the scrawled letter he sent the coach, Paul Schantz was a Guardian himself "during the war" (meaning the *First* World War, I figured out when I did the math). When we arrived, he'd been wheeled out to meet us wearing a team jersey so big he looked like a wrinkly dwarf inside of it. Then we pushed him to his room, too small for the five of us. We wanted to leave after two minutes.

"You have any kids?" Carl attempted at one point.

Paul pinched his chin. "I'd say we had eighteen over the years." He was recovering from a stroke, so it was hard to know exactly what he said. Then he explained that he and his wife had been foster parents.

"You ever miss them?" Ben asked.

His face clouded over. "All of them. Except one."

"A bad apple."

"There's bad. Then there's worth."

"Worth? Worth in what?"

"*Worse. Worse!*" He fought to get this out, leaving his chin white with spit. "There's always something worse than you think. Closer than you think."

That was about it. One by one my friends excused themselves to visit the men's room and didn't come back. Until only I was left.

"It's been good to meet you, Mr. Schantz," I said, backing toward the door. "And I hope we can bring the cup home this year, just like—"

"There's some places you should never go."

It was a strange thing to say, if in fact he said it. But I remember the moment not for the words I thought I heard him mumble, but for the look on the old man's face. A kind of insane clarity.

He was talking about the Thurman house. I couldn't say why I was so sure, other than the look of him. He'd been just this withered stranger, his legs painful-looking sticks on the footrests, yet now he was sitting forward, his eyes alive and searching.

Then he collapsed back into his wheelchair. I was wrong: he wasn't reading my mind. As I slipped out, I heard him mutter, "Sometimes I wet my back."

I bet, I thought as I made my way toward Ben, Randy and Carl, who stood waiting at the end of the hall. *Doesn't mean I have to be there the next time you do.*

But before I reached them, I heard the old man's words a different way.

Sometimes the dead come back.

I already mentioned that my father worked for the utilities commission. A union rep with his own office in the basement of Municipal Hall, back in the days when offices had ashtrays and a bottle of whisky in the bottom drawer and windowless doors that could lock shut. He didn't work too hard.

But he often brought stories home with him. Juicy stuff, as far as Grimshaw went. Battles between neighbours over the staking of property lines. The mayor owing five grand in parking tickets. Noise complaints against an apartment behind Roma Pizza, from which a woman's shrieking orgasms (or what my dad called "the sounds of a cat in heat") awakened dozens in the night.

Because they shared a filing system, police gossip would also flow through the basement of Municipal Hall. Usually, this side of my father's nightly news was sad more than thrilling. Domestic knockabouts, drunk-driving charges, old people discovered a few days dead on their linoleum floors.

Yet that night, I could tell my father had a scoop when he took his place at the head of the kitchen table. Hands placed on either side of his dinner plate, staring down at what my mother had spooned out of the casserole dish with the sombre look of a judge reading a jury's verdict to himself before announcing it to the court.

"Langham," he said finally. "She's a teacher of yours, right? The pretty one?"

"Music," I said.

"She wasn't at school today."

"No."

I watched him use his knife to bulldoze food onto the back of his fork. Slip it into his mouth. Chew.

"What about her?" I asked once he'd swallowed.

"They're looking for her."

"They?"

"It'll be in the paper in the morning."

"She's not just sick or something?"

"That's what I'm hearing. The cops. Asking if anyone's seen her."

"The police think she's a missing person after one day? Don't they usually wait seventy-two hours or something?"

"They've got information. Suspicions." My father raised his hands, palms out. A gesture to signal the limits of his insider's knowledge.

"Do they think she's all right?"

My father lowered his fork. *Pretty.* That's what his eyes said to me, man to man across the table. *I don't blame you.*

"My guess?" he said. "She found some fella and got the hell out of here. Struck me as a sensible sort of girl."

Then he told my mother this might be her best shepherd's pie ever.

After hockey practice that night, we gathered at Ben's house. Sitting on the mouldy pillows and atop the books that towered around his bed. And on it, cross-legged, was Ben himself. I remember he wasn't wearing shoes or socks. His feet oversized, patchy with hair. Nasty feet for such a slight, dream-prone boy.

I had told them earlier what my dad had said. We were lacing our skates in the dressing room, and I had to whisper to keep from being overheard by any of the other players. Once I finished, there wasn't a chance to hear their reactions, as the coach poked his head around the corner and told us to hustle out there, that holding on to the lead up our asses wasn't going to help us beat the Sugar Kings on the weekend. But even as he said this—in the same way he would have at any other evening practice—I thought his eyes lingered on us for a moment. An unreadable expression contained only in the look itself, as the rest of his face was kindly as usual. Yet in his eyes there was sadness, or distress, something he couldn't wholly contain. Or maybe something he *wanted* us to see. A feeling he shared. Was protecting us from.

Up in Ben's room, I learned that I wasn't the only one to have heard Heather Langham rumours. On the bus rides home from school, in our kitchens, whispered between our parents, we heard versions of a story—or pieces of a handful of stories—beginning to circulate around town.

First, there was Miss Langham running off with a student.

Nobody had seen Brad Wickenheiser today, had they? There was an absurd but persistent rumour that he'd done it with Mrs. Avery, the vice-principal, on a school trip to see *Othello* in Stratford. And he was in Heather's grade twelve music class. French horn. (*French horny*, as he called it, idiotically, to the girls on either side of him.) According to Randy's source, Brad Wickenheiser and Miss Langham were doing it right now out at the Swiss Cottage Motel on the edge of town. He was in love with her. But she was just in it for the sex with a young stud. I remember that phrase in particular: *young stud*. The way it made me uncomfortable, and a little jealous, like standing in the showers with the older boys after a game.

"Really?" I asked when Randy was done with his breathless telling. "*Really*?"

"Bullshit," Carl said.

"It's what I heard."

"Carl's right," I said. "Brad *Wickenheiser*? No way. He's a moron."

"She's not screwing his *brain*, Trev."

"Still. I'm not buying it."

"Neither am I. And I'll tell you why," Carl said, jabbing a finger into Randy's chest. "It's bullshit because it's *my* bullshit. Told Andy Pucinik in gym. Born-again Jesus Saves wanker. I *knew* he'd like it."

Then Carl told his own story, a more fanciful version of my father's dinner-table suggestion that Miss Langham had simply left town. But this time it wasn't her tiring of Grimshaw that prompted her to take off without warning—it was an identical twin sister. A Langham girl just as beautiful as Heather, but without the winning manners. The *bad* Heather.

"Aha!" Randy said. "Maybe it's the *twin* who's banging Brad Wickenheiser at the Swiss Cottage."

And then came the horror story. All the more horrific for being the most believable. And for me being the one to tell it.

An anonymous tip had been called in to the police. Male, gravel-voiced. Telling the cops he'd had "some kinda fun" the night before, taunting them to go see "where that bitch used to sleep." When they got to the nurses' residence the police found sticky boot prints on the carpet outside Heather's room. They kicked the door down. Inside, walls sprayed with blood. Obscene messages fingerpainted in gore over her Leonard Bernstein and Mozart posters. But no body. Only a necklace laid over her pillow, the heart-shaped locket we had seen her wear in class some days, and wondered whose image might be contained within, impossibly wishing it might be ours.

According to this version, her murderer was a mysterious lover-turned-stalker, an attractive sociopath who gave her the locket (he gave *all* his girlfriends lockets). She had come to Grimshaw after he started to show signs of being unstable. But he'd found her.

It was only when I finished that we noticed the snow. The first squall of the season dropping heavy flakes over town, whitening and silencing.

"That's not it."

Ben's voice surprised us. For the past while, it seemed like he wasn't even listening, and we had come to nearly forget he was here. But now we were all looking at him. Watching his head slowly shake from side to side.

"It didn't happen that way," he said. "Or not exactly that way."

"How would you know?"

"Because when I saw her, she was alive."

That's when we all went ape shit. Demanding to know why he hadn't told us this sooner, how he could know anything from a dream.

"You never said it was Heather when you told me in music class," I said.

"I didn't know then."

"When I know something, I know it."

"I'm happy for you, Trev."

"Okay. Back up. This monster—"

"I never called it that."

"Fine. This not-a-tree-but-looks-like-one has someone in its arms. Heather. And she's trying to get away."

"I just said I could tell she was alive."

"For fuck's sake," Carl said.

"I'll second that," Randy said.

"Ben? *Ben*?" I moved from where I was sitting to stick my face in his line of sight. "Just tell us what you saw."

Ben's nasty feet. The toes curled up, trying to hide.

"A man—what I suppose could *only* be a man—had Miss Langham in his arms last night," Ben said. "Her eyes were open. Like she couldn't believe whatever was happening was actually happening."

He took in a breath, and we thought he was readying for more. But he just exhaled it all wordlessly out again.

"That it?"

"Pretty much."

"Is it or isn't it?"

"None of this matters."

"Why not?"

"Because if she's still alive, I'm not sure how much longer she's going to be."

I came in even closer to him. "Where is she?"

Ben pointed out the window. Not up into the sky where the snow was illuminated by the orange street-light but down, at what stood across the street. We knew what was there without looking. We looked anyway.

For a long time, none of us said anything.

Not true. Ben was murmuring something, the same thing, the whole time.

"I don't know . . . I don't know . . . I don't know . . ."

"*What* don't you know, oh wise one? Oh great seer of visions?" I said, hoping it might come out funny. It didn't.

"I don't know," he said for the last time. "But I think it was the coach."

[5]

RANDY PUSHES OPEN the door to Jake's Pool 'n' Sports. Though I've never been in the place before, I immediately know I'm home. My grey overcoat and polished Oxfords might mark me as an outsider among the early-bird clientele, the hockey-jerseyed, puffy-faced men who line the bar, frowning up at the flatscreens showing highlights from last night's game, but that's who I would have been had I stayed. Who I am still, even after all the time away.

We remain marked, we small-towners dressed in what, as Randy and I walk into Jake's, feels instantly like borrowed city-slicker duds. Beneath the camouflage, all of us in this room are branded by shared experience and ritual as indelibly as members of a religion who are alone in understanding its rules and expectations. I've noticed over the years how we recognize each other among strangers: something draws me to those who have grown up in a Grimshaw, despite our efforts to hide every embarrassing hickdom, every clue that might give away our corn-fed, tranquilized youths.

Part of what we share is the knowledge that every small town has a second heart, smaller and darker than the one that pumps the blood of good intentions. We alone know that the picture of home cooking and oak trees and harmlessness is false.

This is the secret that binds us. Along with the friends who share its weight.

We take a table in the corner and order a pitcher from a pretty girl wearing the referee's stripes they make all the servers wear. She reminds me of someone. Or a composite of someones. There is a quality to her movements, the intelligent smile and playfully serious eyes, that I've seen before.

"She looks like Heather," Randy says.

"Oh yeah?"

"Not exactly *looks* like her. More like she *reminds* me of her. Don't you think?"

"Don't see it myself," I lie.

The truth is, the waitress doesn't look like Heather Langham all that much, though they share some general characteristics— height, age, style of hair. But the girl in the referee outfit who now comes our way with a tray balanced on the flat of her hand has the same rare brand of charm as Heather had. An aura, I suppose. A goodness that doesn't disqualify desire, as goodness alone can often do.

She returns with the frosted mugs, pours draft from the pitcher. It's Randy who chats with her. His goofy, going-nowhere banter that waitresses are happy to play along with. He's firing off queries regarding what's good on the menu ("All I can say is the kitchen passed inspection last time around," she says), what she's studying ("I took a year off backpacking in Europe last

year, so now I'm chained to this place to save up for tuition")
and if she grew up in town ("Grimshaw bored and raised!").
Then Randy notices the ring on her finger. A platinum band
with an emerald shard embedded in it.

"Now that's a lovely stone. Matches your eyes," he says,
taking her hand in his to inspect it more closely. "Don't tell me
it's an engagement ring? You'd *kill* me."

"I don't know. Pre-engagement, I guess."

"No worries, then," Randy says with a laugh. "*Everything* is
pre-engagement when you think about it, darlin'."

As Randy and she tease, he turns to give me a wink both the
waitress and I are meant to see, a shared pleasure in the moment.
It's the first bloom of alcohol, the comfort of being with a friend
you know well and who asks nothing of you. As for the waitress,
she doesn't seem in any particular rush to leave our side, though
she shows no special interest in us either. She is simply, gener-
ously, unselfconsciously making our day and nothing more.

As the afternoon turns to evening, the pitchers come and go
in steady succession. The sudden emotion that had gripped us
earlier is replaced with easy talk, catching up. He takes me on a
comic tour of the low points of his acting career ("I've got
nothing *but* low points!"), the cattle calls and megalomaniac
furniture-commercial directors and gigs as an extra on a handful
of Hollywood blockbusters, most notably as "a bartender who
slides a Manhattan over to George Clooney . . . which apparently I was doing wrong somehow, because they cut me out and
spliced in somebody else's hand." I tell him about my Parkinson's.
How I sold Retox and was doing little but waiting for things to
get worse. Somehow, though, I felt I related all this misfortune
in the same tone Randy related his: plainly and without self-
pity, each of us acknowledging that we had been visited by our

measure of failure and regret, as everyone has at our stage of the game.

And through it all, we remember Ben. How his life was wasted on a pointless obsession. And then his death, so preventable and yet unsurprising, even fated. But we quickly shift away from the outcome of Ben McAuliffe's narrative to a greatest hits of scenes from his youth, his dorky visions, his sleepy goaltending. Soon Randy and I are laughing and coughing and laughing again, which we're thankful for, seeing as it makes our anguished tears look to the rest of the room like beer-fuelled hilarity.

Some time later I make my way to the men's room and see how busy the place has gotten. The work crews kicking the mud off their boots, the girls-night-outers squeezed into their finest denim. Even a clutch of suits tossing back a couple of after-work quickies before heading home to the newer streets north of the river.

And then two faces I recognize. Stepping out of the crowd and offering hands to shake. A big fellow in a Canada Post parka first, followed by his stout, patchily bearded friend.

"Trev? Holy shit! I was right. It's you!" the first one says, and claps me in a bear hug.

"Todd?"

"Glad to know the grey hair didn't throw you off too much."

"Todd *Flanagan*?"

"Last name too. Nice work."

"How's Tina? You two still together?"

"*Long* gone," Todd reports. "Tina was not a stick-around sort of girl." Todd loops his arm around the bearded guy's neck. "Here's another test. Can you recall the name of this walking sieve right here?"

"Vince Sproule," I announce, catching in the toothy grin a glimpse of the eighteen-year-old he once was. "Grimshaw's greatest goalie ever."

"He *was* quick, wasn't he?"

"Not so much these days," Vince says, pretending to snatch an oncoming puck out of the air. "Three kids and too many Egg McMuffins can slow you down after a while."

Todd and Vince were Guardians too, teammates on the high-school team. And though they were only two years ahead of us at the time, they look a decade older than we do now, bloated and shambling. But content too, I'd say. The added pounds that come with snacks in front of the game-of-the-week and unrenewed gym memberships.

"A terrible thing," Todd says, his hand on my shoulder. "About Ben."

"It is."

"Guess you're here for the funeral."

"Randy too."

"No shit?"

"He's sitting over there. In the corner."

Todd and Vince squint over the heads of other patrons to find Randy waving back at us, like a long-lost cousin at airport arrivals.

"It's a goddamn team reunion," Vince says.

"Wish it could have been for better reasons," Todd adds, and I'm moved by how plainly he means it.

"We're going to miss him," I say.

"Us too," Todd says. "It's a funny thing. I probably saw him more than anyone the past while."

"You visited?"

"I'm a mailman," Todd says, pointing to the Canada Post patch on the chest of his jacket as though to offer proof. "Been delivering to Ben's neighbourhood pretty much since I took the job. I'd wave up at him in that window, Monday to Friday, before going up the steps to drop off the bills."

"Did he ever come down? To talk?"

"Not a once."

"Always was an oddball," Vince Sproule says, shaking his head. "But then there's a point when oddballs turn just sad. You know what I mean?"

"I do."

"Never much of a goalie, either," Todd says.

"It's a good thing we had you, Vince."

"You ever wonder how far we could have gone that year, Trev?" Todd asks.

"I don't really think about it."

"It was tragic. What happened. But maybe not just for, you know, those *involved*. You were a pretty good sniper yourself."

"It doesn't—"

"Who knows who would have noticed you. You could have—"

"I told you, I don't think about it. I do my best not to think about a lot of things."

"Sure. I can understand that," Todd says, nodding as though at an insight into his own condition he'd long been blind to.

Then something happens that delivers a sharp stab of jealousy: our waitress, the pretty referee, walks up and gives Todd a kiss on the cheek.

"Don't you just love this guy?" she says before slipping back into the crowd, and though it's just more waitress banter, it's obvious that she *does* love him. Lucky Todd Flanagan. Tina Uxbridge might have fooled around on him a few hundred times before dumping him. But if this referee is Todd's new girlfriend, he's bounced back quite nicely.

Todd is grinning like a monkey. "You remember Tracey."

"Tracey?"

"She was a lot smaller then."

Then I get it. The bundle of squawking joy Tina used to bring to the Guardians games.

"That's your daughter?"

"You fancy-suit, big-city guys. They all as sharp as you?"

"She was just a baby."

"Still is."

"Well, I have to thank you, Todd. You've just made me feel incredibly old."

"C'mon. You didn't need me for that, did you?"

I carry on to the men's room, and when I return Todd and Vince have joined Randy at our table, a fresh pitcher already between them. I suppose it's all the beer that helps in creating the sense that the four of us still have so much in common, when really all we talk about is how lousy the hockey got on TV after they started giving "these Russian pretty boys five million to fake a concussion every time the wind blows" (as Vince puts it), our women troubles, the body's first betrayals that attend the lapsing of its forty-year warranty.

Or maybe I'm wrong in that. Maybe we *are* still friends, and I've just forgotten what they are.

Eventually, Todd and Vince announce they have to go home and get some sleep. Todd has his mail rounds in the morning and Vince has to replace the brakes on a minivan at the garage he co-owns before they have to put on Sunday clothes for Ben's funeral in the afternoon. Yet even then we stay on for one more pitcher to add to the previous half-dozen or so, all served by Tracey Flanagan, Todd's baby girl.

When we finally head out into the night, the air has cooled several degrees. I stand with Randy on the sidewalk, deciding which way to go. Around us, the town has been sharpened by the cold, the old storefronts grey and looming.

The two of us shake off a chill. It's the shared notion that for all the time we were inside Jake's Pool 'n' Sports, in the deceptive warmth of light and company, Grimshaw was waiting for us.

I think we were hoping to find it gone. Torn down to make way for a triplex, or finally razed for safety reasons, leaving only an empty lot behind. We don't entertain these possibilities aloud, in any case. Once we'd paid our tab at Jake's, it was still only nine, and Randy wanted a cigarette, so I joined him on a tipsy wander through the streets, taking the long way back to the Queen's.

Neither of us acknowledged it when we turned the corner onto Caledonia Street. We started up the long slope toward the hospital, noting how remarkably little had changed about the houses, the modest gardens, even the mailboxes lashed to the streetlight poles to thwart kids from tipping them over. When the McAuliffe house comes into view we automatically cross the street to be on the same side it's on. We pause in front for a moment, gazing up at Ben's window.

And then, unstoppably, we turn to follow what was his line of sight for most of his waking adult life.

It's still unoccupied, judging from the black, uncurtained windows, the wood trim bristled with mildew, the knee-high seedlings dotting the yard. Nevertheless, given the little care paid to it over the last thirty or more years, the Thurman house looks reasonably solid, testimony to the stone foundation and brick work of its builders over a century ago. Even the headless rooster still tops the attic gable.

"Why don't they just tear it down?" I ask.

"Can't. It's privately owned."

"How do you know?"

"Mrs. McAuliffe told me. It's been handed down and handed down. The owners are out-of-towners. Never even visit."

"Why not sell?"

"Maybe they're waiting for an upturn in the market."

"In the *Grimshaw* market?"

"I wonder if it misses him," Randy says, stubbing his cigarette out under the heel of his shoe. "Ben must have been its only friend."

"He wasn't its friend," I say, sharper than I expected to.

We stay there a minute longer. Staring at the Thurman house from the far side of Caledonia Street, a perspective we had returned to countless times in sleep-spoiling dreams. Watching for what Ben had been watching for. A white flash of motion. Opened eyes. A glint of teeth.

I'm first to start back to the hotel. The moon leading us on, peeping through the branches.

Randy laughs. "Guess it knows we're here now."

I do my best to join him in it, if only to prevent the sound of his forced humour from drifting unconvincingly in the night air. And to push away the thought that we had already made mistakes. Coming back to Grimshaw. Pretending that we could avoid certain topics if we simply told ourselves to. Most of all, the mistake of letting it know we're here.

We had forgotten what Ben reminded himself of every day: the Thurman house never allowed itself to be observed without a corresponding price.

Every time you looked into it, it looked into you.

MEMORY DIARY

Entry No. 6

Most days, I'd stop to pick up Sarah so the two of us could walk the rest of the way to school together. It had become habit for me to knock at her side door on the mornings I didn't have one of the Guardians' deadly pre-dawn practices, and for her mom to offer me homemade waffles or bacon sandwiches, something that would have been a Christmas treat in my house. I would decline at first, but I always ended up snarfing down a second breakfast all the same as I waited for Sarah to come downstairs. I liked these stolen minutes, the anticipation of Sarah's face, me telling her mother something that made her laugh too loudly for a woman so petite and religious. Sarah's father had already left for work. Now that I think of it, maybe he'd planned it that way. Maybe he'd designed these moments in the kitchen to say *Nice, isn't it? Make an honest woman of my daughter and all this could be yours.*

But on the morning of the day after Ben told us he'd witnessed—or *felt*, or *dreamed*—the coach carrying Heather Langham into the Thurman house in the middle of the night, I walked past Sarah's place without stopping. The world that she and I inhabited together—the hand-holding walks, the drives out to Harmony, the thrilled admissions of love beyond the football field's endzone—had been soiled by the speculations of the night before. Not irrevocably. Not yet. There was, on that February Wednesday, still a chance for certain courses to be avoided.

But they wouldn't be. Even as I drifted by Sarah's house and realized she wasn't walking next to me only after I stepped out onto the playing field's 40-yard line, I could tell there would be choices coming my way. What they would involve I couldn't guess. All that was clear was that Sarah would have to be shielded from their outcomes.

We had opened our minds to their darkest possibilities. There was no going back from that. But such liberties came with obligations. Like the walls of the Thurman house, we would have to try to keep the darkness inside.

Grimshaw Collegiate sits atop the highest hill within the town's limits, which isn't saying much as hills go. A pocked mound of stone and thistles just steep enough for toboggans to reach a speed that might coax a whoop out of six-year-olds. Still, in a town free of topographic features worth mentioning, the cubist mess of the school building—brick gym from the 1890s, colour-panelled '60s wing of classrooms sticking out the rear, the cinder-block science department added on the cheap—appeared with enhanced importance on its piebald throne, looking down over the mud playing field, the river gurgling next to it, the parking lot surrounded by trees that provided shade for the small crimes entertained within students' cars.

One offence we frequently committed was a "hot box" before morning attendance. This involved me, Ben and Randy cramming ourselves into the two-door Ford that Carl's dad left behind, rolling the windows up and sharing a joint Randy would produce from the baggie he kept hidden in the lining of his Sorels. With the four of us inhaling and passing and coughing, the cabin of Carl's sedan soon became thick with smoke, the air moist and opaque as a sauna. A hot box offered the most efficient use of a single joint, a technique that "seals in all the grassy goodness," as Randy said in his *Price Is Right* voice. When we were done, we would open the doors and stand around in an unsteady circle, watching the plumes escape the car's confines, rise through the pine boughs and into the sky above like a signal to another, faraway tribe.

So while I know what Randy has in mind when he waves me over and makes a toking gesture obvious enough to show he doesn't really care who knows, there's something subdued in his expression, worried quarter moons of darkness under his eyes that tell me there's more going on in Carl's Ford than a bunch of guys getting high before chemistry.

"We're having a meeting," Randy says as we make our way through the rows of cars. "Ben has something he wants to say."

"Is this more bullshit about what he said he saw?"

"He wants us all together first."

"But you've guessed."

Randy pauses at the car, his fingers slipping under the passenger-side door handle. "I've just got a feeling I'd rather be stoned when I hear it, that's all," he says.

We pile in. Carl behind the wheel, Ben hugging the glovebox to let me and Randy slip into the back.

"Ready?" Randy asks.

"Ready," Carl answers, clicking the power window buttons, making sure we're sealed in.

As Randy pulls the baggie out of his boot, Ben shifts around in the front seat, taking each of us in, one at a time. A kind of silent roll call that would be funny if attempted by anyone else. But laughing is out of the question. It intensifies the one sound to concentrate on: Randy, who clinks his Zippo open and sucks the joint to life.

"We have to go in," Ben says.

None of us say anything. It's as though Ben had not uttered the sentence we'd all just heard. Or perhaps we were trying to pretend it was a sentence that didn't properly belong to the moment, a glitch in the soundtrack.

Then he says it again.

"We have to go into the house."

"*What* house?"

"Nice try, Randy," Carl says.

Randy shrugs, passing up to Carl while waving a hand to sweep the smoke that escapes his nostrils back into his mouth.

"I don't see why we have to do anything," I say. "It's not our issue."

"You're right. It's not an issue," Ben says. "It's a human being."

"You're saying Heather's still in there? You saw something new last night?"

"I watched. Stayed up till dawn watching," Ben says. "But no. I didn't see anything."

"So how do you know she's in there?"

"I'm saying she might be. And if she is, she needs help. Our help."

Randy rubs the elbow of his shirt over the window, clearing a circle from the condensation. He stares out at a group of girls in designer jeans climbing the hill toward school, their backsides swaying with each step, before they disappear behind the returning mist of his breath.

"Here's the thing I don't get," Randy says. "What does this have to do with us? Maybe *you*, Ben. But I wasn't the one up in your room spooking myself shitless. I didn't see a thing. So where do I come into it? Where does anyone but you come into it?"

Ben nods. "You didn't see what I saw. But now you *know* what I saw. Which amounts to the same thing."

"It does?" Randy says. "Yeah, I guess it does."

"No, it doesn't," I say, taking the joint Randy offers me. "We're *not* involved. And that's how it should stay.

We go into that house and if—and this is a big mother of an if—*if* something's happened in—"

"Don't bogart that thing," Carl warns. I take a perfunctory haul and pass it on.

"What I'm saying is that if we go in there and find something bad, we're part of it. We're implicated, or whatever."

"Implicated," Carl says. "Very good, Trev."

He waves the joint by Ben. Ben only rarely partakes on these smoky mornings, so he surprises us by expertly nabbing it before it's out of reach. A quick hit and his eyes turn glassy, the whites bleached clear.

"She's missing," Ben says. "And we have a piece of information nobody else has. It's a question not of whether it would be right to act on it, but of how wrong it would be if we didn't."

"Fine," I say, exhaling a blue cloud against the windshield. "You've established that as far as you're concerned, you are duty bound to do something. So go tell the police about it."

"As if they're going to listen to me."

"Why wouldn't they? You're a witness."

"Not really. Not in a court-of-law way."

"So if the pigs aren't going to take you seriously," Carl says, pinching the roach, "why should we?"

Ben turns all the way around to look at us in the back seat. His face shrouded in curls of smoke.

"You're my friends," he says.

And that was it. Our *undoing*, as the Coles Notes described what followed from the dumb decisions of kings and princes in the Shakespeare we never read.

Why? We were good guys. Unquestioned loyalty. A soldier's duty. This is what the coach, our fathers, every hero we'd ever watched on the Vogue's screen had taught us. It was certainly the highest compliment in a dressing room, as in "Carl was a good guy out there tonight when he put that fucker on a stretcher for spearing Trev." Standing up for the fellow wearing the same uniform as you, even if it made little sense, even if it meant getting hurt. This is how it was supposed to go in hockey games, anyway, and in war movies, and in the lessons handed down from our baffled, misled fathers.

But here's the thing we found out too late to make a difference: our fathers and movie heroes might have been wrong.

"When?" I asked.

"Tonight," Ben said.

[6]

IN THE CITY, churches are giving up. Dwindling congregations leaving their places of worship to be converted into condos, daycares or yoga studios. But judging from the streets Randy and I drive through in a cab on our way to St. Andrew's Presbyterian, the churches of Grimshaw are hanging on. Every third corner still has a gloomy limestone house of God in need of new windows and a Weedwhacker. To the faithful this might seem an encouraging indication of resilience, the heartland's refusal to let the devil go about his business unimpeded. But to me, there is something chilling in all the broken-down bastions of the divine, as though it will be here, and not in the indifferent, thrumming city, that the final wrestling of goods and evils will take place. And it won't be as showy as Revelation promised either: no beast rising from the sea, no serpent to tell seductive lies. When the reckoning takes place it will be quiet. And like all the bad done in Grimshaw, it will be known by many but spoken of by none.

———

Randy and I shuffle up the steps at St. Andrew's, flipping up collars against the cold drizzle. We're the last ones in, and while the nave is not large, the pews are no more than a sixth full. I suppose I was expecting more of a crowd, something along the lines of a high-school memorial assembly, as if Ben were the seventeen-year-old victim of a tragic accident and not a forty-year-old suicide.

As the minister plods through the program of murmured prayers and hymns, I try to identify some of the other mourners. There's Todd and Vince, as promised, along with a couple of other Guardians, a startlingly obese Chuck Hastings next to Brad Wickenheiser with home-dyed hair the colour of tar. Aside from Mrs. McAuliffe (a shrunken version of herself, inanimate and collapsed as a puppet after you pull out your hand), nobody looks particularly familiar. I search the rows for Carl. Though I know he's not here, I can't help feeling that if I look hard enough I'll find him.

The minister delivers the brief eulogy. A sterile recitation of Ben's stalled résumé: his "lifelong commitment" to his mother, his love of fantasy books and the "excitements of the imagination," the loss of his father. There is no reference to the surveillance he conducted from his attic roost, nor to the vacant house across the street he believed to be the devil's *pied-à-terre* in Grimshaw.

After the service, everyone files past Ben's mom, the old woman offering a hand to be clasped. Yet when Randy and I reach her, she blinks us into focus and touches our cheeks. I ask if I can come around to the house in the morning to look over Ben's legal papers or do whatever an executor is supposed to do.

"Come anytime, Trevor," she says, straightening my tie. "I'll make tea."

"I'll call first."

"If you like," she says, shrugging. "But I'll be there whether you call or not."

We take another cab down to the Old Grove. Ben's grave is next to his father's. The McAuliffe name engraved in stone at the head of both their places, their tombstones citing only their dates of birth and death, the latter events both at their own hands, whether counted as such on the official record or not. Even fewer have gathered for the burial than at the church, a clutch of shiverers shifting from foot to foot, the soft earth sucking at their shoes.

The minister is here again, though he does little more than run through a memorized "Ashes to ashes, dust to dust" before they lower the casket into the ground.

"That's it," Randy says next to me, and when I turn to him I see quiet, clear-eyed tears that mix with the spitting rain so that, from the other side of the grave, he would appear merely in need of an umbrella. "That's *it*."

"It makes it real, I know. Seeing him go."

"Real? It's like *I'm* the one at the bottom of a hole. I can hardly *breathe*, man."

I guide Randy a few feet away to the shelter of a maple. The two of us stand there watching the others drift back toward their cars. Some look our way as they go, perhaps recognizing us from some prehistoric geography class or peewee hockey team. Only one looks not at us but at me.

My body remembers her before I do.

A woman my age wearing a lace-collared blouse and beneath it a skirt that displays the powerful legs I have always associated with fresh-air-and-fruit-pie farmers' wives. Almost certainly a mom. Filling out her Sunday best with a few more pounds (welcome, to my eyes) than the day she bought it a couple of years back. A good-looking woman who belongs to a vintage I recognize (the same as mine), but not any particular person I know.

And yet, her eyes on me—friendly, but without invitation or promise—starts an immediate rush of desire. Not mere interest, either. Not any casual appraisal of a stranger's form, the kind of automatic sizing-up a man performs half a dozen times walking down a single city block. This has nothing to do with *finding someone attractive*. I smile uncertainly back at her and there it is: the almost forgotten clarity of lust. The only word for it. It is lust that races my breath into audible clicks, unlocks my knees and throws my hand out to Randy's shoulder to keep my balance.

"Is that Sarah?" I ask him. Randy looks over at the woman, her eyes now averted so that she stares into the dripping trees.

"I believe it is."

"Sarah. Good *God*."

"Look at you," Randy says. "All moony like it's grade nine all over again."

"It *is*," I say, and take a deep breath. "It *is* grade nine all over again."

I start over to her with my hand extended, but she doesn't take it, kissing me once on each cheek instead.

"They do it twice in the city, right?" she says.

"You've got all the bases covered."

She pulls back to take a full, evaluating look at me. "So this is how my first love has turned out."

"Must make you glad I wasn't your last."

"I don't know about that. This is Grimshaw. For women over

thirty, men with a pulse who don't smack you around are objects of desire."

There is a whiff of divorce about her. The leeriness that comes from wondering if every kindness is a trick, coupled with the lonely's willingness to hear out even the most obvious lie to the end. She's tough. But it's a toughness that has been learned, a buffer against charm and premature hope.

"I'm sorry," she says, and for an absurd moment I think she's apologizing for our breaking up in grade twelve, before I realize she's speaking of Ben.

"Thank you. It's good that you're here."

She laughs. "I live three blocks from St. Andrew's. I'd say it's good that *you're* here."

"It's been a long time."

"Too bad it took something like this to bring you back."

"I loved the guy."

"I know you did. You all did."

"We went through . . . we were best friends."

"I know."

She opens her arms and I step into them. My hands clasped around the strong trunk of her body, her hair a veil against the grey cold.

"You sure you're going to be okay?" she asks, pulling away sooner than I would like.

"I must look pretty wrecked."

"Just a little lost, that's all."

"Can I tell you something, Sarah? I *am* a little lost."

A pained smile works at the corners of her mouth. "It's strange. Hearing you say my name."

"I can say it again if you'd like."

"No, I'll remember just fine."

I'm doing it before I can stop myself, though I don't think there's much in me that wants me to stop digging in my wallet for my card.

"I have to help Ben's mom with some stuff," I say, clapping the card into Sarah's palm. "Are you in a position—that is, would you like to join me for dinner before I go? Lunch? A shot of tequila?"

Sarah looks down at my card as though it bears not a name and number but the false promise of a fortune cookie. We are paused like that—her reading and thinking, me watching her read and think—when I see the boy.

He is standing behind a tombstone at the crest of a rise maybe a couple of hundred yards away. An old maple sprouts from the hill's highest point, so that the boy is shaded from the day's already diminished light, leaving him an outline coloured in graphite. He stares at me in the fixed way of someone who has been staring for some time, and I have only now caught him at it.

"You can't be here," I whisper.

But I am, the boy whispers back.

"Trevor?" Sarah says, searching.

But I'm already starting up the rise toward him. A walk that loosens my knees into a wobbly jog. Clenched hands held in front of me as though prepared to wrap themselves around the boy's neck and start choking.

Trevor the Brave, the boy laughs.

My shoes skid out from under me on the wet sod, and for a second I pitch forward, knuckles punching off the ground to keep me up.

When I'm propped on my elbows and able to look again, the boy is gone.

I scramble up to the tombstone where he was standing. Search the descending slope on the other side for where he might be waiting for me. And instead of the boy, I find a man. Running into the scrub that borders the cemetery.

"Carl!"

I glance back to see Randy starting up the slope.

Behind him, her hand to her mouth, Sarah watches as though a parachute was failing to open. An unstoppable, fatal error taking place before her eyes.

MEMORY DIARY

Entry No. 7

The Thurman house was no different in its construction than any of the other squat, no-nonsense resi-
dences it shared Caledonia Street with, two rows of
Ontario red-brick built at the last century's turn for
the town's first doctors, solicitors and engineers. So
why did it stand out for us? What made it the one and
only haunted house in Grimshaw for our generation?
Its emptiness was part of the answer. Houses can be in
poor repair, ugly and overgrown, but this makes them
merely sad, not the imagined domicile of phantoms.
Vacancy is an unnatural state for a still-habitable home,
a sign of disease or threat, like a pretty girl standing
alone at a dance.

But it hadn't always been empty. This—knowing
that real people had once occupied its cold and barren

rooms—was what lent the place its sinister aura. This, and the implication that they had left. There was something wrong about a house people chose not to live in. Or something wrong about the last people who did.

Not that I recall thinking any of this as we made our way onto the Thurman property that night. All I was thinking wasn't a thought at all but a physical aversion that had to be fought off with each step, along with a murmur in my head that would have said, if it could speak aloud, something like *Turn back*. Or *It's wrong that you're here*. Or *You are about to step from the world you know into one you don't want to know*.

In short, I was afraid.

I think all of us wanted to stop, to sidle no farther along the thorny hedgerow that shielded us from the pale streetlight, the wan half moon. If one of us had said, "I think we should go," or merely turned and headed back toward the street, I believe the rest would have followed. But none of us said or did anything other than proceed along the side of the house, inching closer to the two tall windows set too close together like crossed eyes. Both fogged with dust, through which someone on the inside had long ago dragged a finger to spell *fuckt* against the glass.

I'm not sure we discussed the best way to get in. I suppose each of us assumed there would be a window left open or gaping cellar doors that would make it obvious. We never thought to try the front door.

"This is where he went," Ben whispered, and the sound of his voice reminded us how long we had gone without saying anything. From the time we gathered at Carl's apartment and made the three-block walk to stand opposite the McAuliffe house, looking into its warm interiors from which we had so often safely peered out at the Thurman place across the way, we had travelled in silence. It was a journey that required no more than ten minutes but felt much longer than that. The whole time all of us walking in a defeated pack, as though escaped prisoners who had decided freedom was too much work and were returning to our cells.

And then, still recovering from the sound of Ben's words, we paused to grapple with their meaning.

The coach. This is what Ben was telling us. *It was over this ice-crusted grass that he carried Heather Langham the night before last.*

In the dark, the backyard was impossibly enlarged, a neglected field of weeds poking through the snow and swaying in a breeze that rushed the clouds across the moon. A see-saw stood in one corner of the lot, the seat of the raised end poking up from a cluster of saplings like the head of a curious animal. *Little kids used to play on that*, I remember thinking. And then: *What kids? When would any child have run around on this ground? Who could ever laugh into this air?*

I wondered about that long enough to be surprised when Carl nudged me from behind.

"It's not locked," he said.

I followed his pointed flashlight to see Ben standing in front of the open back door.

We followed him inside. All of us making our way through a mud room into the kitchen. An old gas stove stood in one corner, the face of its clock cracked, the time frozen at a quarter to twelve. An undoored fridge. The wallpaper a photographic mural of a country scene: a pondside with a forest beyond, and a single deer lowering its head to drink. But then you looked again, looked closer. The forest was cloaked in shadow that seemed to darken as you watched. And the deer wasn't drinking but lifting its head, startled by a cry from the woods. Something about the composition of the picture suggested that whatever was about to emerge out of the trees meant to hunt the deer, to spill its blood on the grass. And that the deer knew this, was frozen by the knowledge that it was about to die.

We were all gazing at the wallpaper now. All of us listening. For the thing in the woods. The thing that was here.

And with our listening came a count. One, two, three, four—our lungs, our in-and-outs of air. Along with a fifth. The idea of another's breath somewhere within the house.

Ben shook his head. A gesture that signified the denial of a request, although none of us had asked anything of him. Then he walked on, and we followed, through the archway that opened on the main-floor hallway running the length of the house to the front. Ben pulled open the sliding doors to the living room.

I hadn't expected all the things left behind. Not just

by previous inhabitants—a sofa exploding its white stuffing, amputated dining-room chairs, a rug patterned with cypress trees—but by visitors. I must have imagined the interior of the Thurman house to have been set-decorated in the manner of a Transylvanian castle: cobwebs thick as shredded T-shirts, a candelabra set atop a grand piano, rooms the size of soundstages. Instead, it was merely filthy. A heap of brown glass shards in the fireplace where a thousand beer bottles had been smashed. You had to watch your step for the used condoms and needles on the floor.

Along with the messages on the walls. Most of it what you'd expect: the graffitied declarations ("I LUV U PENNY!!") and invitations ("Need yur cock <u>SUCKED</u>? 232 4467 ANY time") and pride ("Guardians Rule—Elmira Eats Poo") and slander ("Jen Yarbeck is a WHORE"). The primitive spray-painted penises and anuses, a long-haired woman with enormous breasts and a dialogue balloon shouting "Moo!" over her head.

Then the strange ones. Phrases much smaller than the others. All in lowercase. Utterances that sought the corners and baseboards of the room, that made you, upon finding one, look for another.

stay with me

no such thing as an empty house

i walk with you

I don't know if the others read these or not. The next thing I remember, we were walking away from each other. We must have spoken, though I can't recall what was said. Or maybe we separated without discussion, knowing the quickest way to search the house, find it vacant and get out of there was to split up. In any case, I went to the staircase by the front door knowing I was on my own.

At the landing, I looked back. There was a railing over which the foyer floor lay fifteen feet below, a bulb hanging on a wire where some more elaborate fixture would once have hung. I squinted down the hallway, a spine with two doorways on each side that, if configured the same way as the second floor in my house (as it probably was, this house so much like an unloved version of the one in which I lived), opened onto three bedrooms and a bathroom at the end.

I started toward the first door on the left with shuffling, elderly steps. It had been easy for me to take the stairs up, but now my body fought against moving. My shoes tearing the old newspapers strewn over the floorboards, a carpet of Falklands War headlines and ads for used-car lots, including Randy's dad's place (*Kum Kwick to Krazy Kevin's!*), his clown nose and lunatic grin floating over the rows of Plymouths.

A comics page got stuck to my sole. I bent to peel it off, wondering, with a turn in my stomach, what could be gummy enough to act as glue on the floor of this place, and when I raised my eyes again he was there.

A boy.

Eyes fixed on me. I recall little else about his appearance other than the impression that we were the same age, nearly men but not quite. He could have been Carl, or Randy, or Ben—there was a millisecond flash when I assumed it *was* one of them—but there was a threat in the way he cocked his head that I'd never seen in them, or in anyone.

The boy said nothing. I remember no detail of his face that could be described as an expression, the outline of his body still, ungesturing. So what was it that prevented me from thinking of him as a fully living boy? How could I tell he wanted to show me something?

I remember attempting to speak to him, though what I intended to say I have no idea now. What I do remember is the panic, the claustrophobia of being bound and hooded. Buried alive.

Oh yes, the boy said but didn't say. *You're going to like this.*

A wet click of breath in my throat and he was gone. Not with a puff of smoke, nothing uncanny or ghostly. Simply gone in the way a thing confirms it was never there at all.

I registered the squeak a moment later. The grind of a rusty hinge.

This was what made the boy disappear, what proved he was a misreading of reality. The bathroom door at the end of the hall had been wrenched open, a full-length mirror screwed to the inside. And now, with a nudge of draft, the door moved an inch, shifting the angle of the mirror's reflection. Removing me from view.

There was the explanation for what I'd seen, rational, conclusive. It was *me*. Me, summoning a dark twin to return my gaze.

But even as I continued down the hall with calmed breaths, I didn't believe it. *That wasn't me.* A line of thinking I wrestled down but couldn't completely silence. *You know it wasn't.*

It strikes me as strange now—and it must have then as well—but once the boy could no longer be seen, the feelings he brought with him could no longer be felt either. I was certain that Heather Langham was not going to be discovered tied to the radiator in any of the bedrooms I leaned into, or slumped in the shower stall whose glass door I swung open to a party of skittering roaches. It smelled bad up here, but only in the way of smells I had already encountered, of piss and damp and long-discarded fast-food bags.

I had pulled the bathroom door closed and was leaning against it, suddenly winded, when I saw someone standing where I had been when I noticed the boy. Another figure of dimensions similar to my own drawn in a sharper outline of darkness.

Carl took a step closer. A dim veil of moonlight glazing his face.

"Randy found something," he said.

We descended to the main floor in silence, and I noticed that the house was silent too. Had the others already left? Carl said Randy had found something, but I remember doubting this. Not only because the house was so quiet it seemed impossible that three other breathing, heart-pounding boys could still be within it but also because of the lingering sense of change that followed the appearance of the boy. The world had been altered now that I'd seen him—the mirror me that wasn't me—and the solid grip I'd had on my perceptions before tonight was something I thought might never return. I had the idea that I could no longer count on anything as true anymore, every observation from here on in holding the potential of trickery. Which included my friends. Included Carl.

He led me down the front hall into the kitchen. Only once we came to stand side by side on the bubbled linoleum, listening to the stillness as though awaiting whispered instruction, did I change my mind about the house's vacancy. There *was* something in here with us. Not Randy or what he'd discovered. Not even the boy. But something else altogether. A presence that had yet to let itself be known, but was aware of us. Saw endless possibilities in our being here.

Carl nudged me closer to the top of the basement stairs. I wondered if he might push me. I could feel my skin ripping on the steps' nail heads, the crack of bones loud as felled trees. At the bottom, something sharp.

Carl turned on his flashlight, and a yellow circle spilled over the stairs to collect in a pool on the hard soil of the cellar floor. I expected him to start down first but he waited, looking down the stairs with the distracted expression of someone working to recollect a half-forgotten name.

His lips moved. An inaudible gulp. He turned his head and looked at me.

"It's different," he said.

"What? What's different?"

He gave his head a shake. Two pouches, brown and tender as used tea bags, swelled under his eyes.

"You go first," he said.

And I did. My oversized shadow looming and lurching as I made my way down the narrow steps. A plumbing pipe screwed into the wall for a handrail. One that threatened to give way any time you called upon it.

At the bottom of the stairs, another flashlight found me. As it approached it blinded me to whoever stood behind it.

"We need to make a decision."

I could see Ben only after he pointed the light up into the pipes and frayed electrical cords running through the wood slats of the ceiling.

"You need to be a part of it, Trev," he said.

"Okay. What's the question?"

"What do we do now?"

"How about we get out of here?"

"No," he said, pursing his lips. "I don't think that's an option."

Ben started away into the cellar's broad darkness. I turned to Carl behind me, but he only waved his flashlight against his side like an usher impatient to show me to my seat before the show starts.

Ben stopped. Directed the light down to the floor.

How to describe the scene it revealed in the cellar's

far corner? I don't think I could say what it was like to take it in whole.

The elements, then:

Randy standing with the help of one hand against the stone wall, his other hand pinching wads of red snot from his nose. Blood dripping off his chin and pushing dark dots through his Human League T-shirt.

Carl staring behind us. Terrified. Not of what lay in the corner and he'd already seen, but of what he alone saw in the dark.

Blood on the floor. Not Randy's. Older-looking smears, formless as spilled paint stirred around with bedsheets, along with more recent spits and spots. Handprints, toes. Clawed trenches in the earth.

Heather Langham. Or a life-size doll of Heather Langham, her face looking away from me, knees and elbows bent at right angles the way a child draws a running stick figure. She lay on the floor, so flat it was like she was partly buried, deflated as the long-ago poisoned mice I'd once discovered behind hockey bags in the garage.

I said something. I must have, because Ben asked me to repeat it. Whatever it was I couldn't remember, then or now. So I said something else.

"We have to go."

"I told you. We can't do that now."

"The fuck we can't."

Carl's hand was on my elbow, a grip that held me within the flashlight's circle.

"Randy moved her," he said.

What's that got to do with anything?

"Randy moved her," I repeated.

"I don't know why. But he did."

"So let's move her back."

"It's not where she *is* that's—"

"What are you saying? What are you saying? What are you *saying*?"

I believe I was shouting. And I don't know how many times I asked this before Ben stepped in front of me.

"They'll know we were here," he said.

"Who?"

"The police. After they find her. And they'll find her. Somebody will."

"How will they know?"

"They'll look. And dead things—they start to stink or whatever, and—"

"Not her. *Us*. How will they know we were here?"

"The blood," Ben said. "Randy's blood. On *her*."

Past Ben's shoulder Randy was nearly doubled over, as though the mention of his name was a boot to his guts. Then I took a peek downward. Saw the new, shiny drops of crimson atop the older, brownish crust on Heather's skin.

"Our fingerprints too," Ben said, scratching his jaw. "Along with the witnesses who saw us come here."

"Nobody saw us."

"I'm not so sure about that."

"The street was empty."

"But not the houses."

I remembered us standing across from the McAuliffes' maybe a half-hour earlier and wished we were there again, outside in the night air. A wishing so strong it was a physical effort to sustain, already slipping out of my grip, like holding a medicine ball against my chest.

"Your mom," I said. "In the living-room window. Looking out between the curtains."

"I'm not sure she even saw us. But she might have."

"This is insane," I said.

"That's not stopping it from happening," Ben said.

"We *have* to stop it."

"How?"

"We tell."

"Tell who?"

"Our parents. The police."

"I'm not sure you're quite getting this." Ben came to stand inches from me. He looked seasick. "She was murdered."

"I can see that."

"No, you can't. Look at her."

So I did. And as I kept my eyes on Heather, Ben spoke into my ear.

"This isn't the time you threw the football through Mrs. Laidlaw's window. This isn't letting Randy drive your dad's car into a mailbox. She's *dead*. And they don't just forgive people for that. They need someone to pay. And that is going to be us, unless we make it go away."

I stepped back to get away from him, the sharp tang of his skin.

"How did Randy bleed all over her anyway?" I asked.

"I hit him," Carl said.

"You punched Randy?"

"A few times."

"Why?"

"For being so *stupid*. Moving her? I didn't know he'd bleed all over the place, though."

"We can clean it up."

"It's all *over* her," Ben said. "No matter what we do, if they look for it, they'll find it. And if they find somebody's blood other than Heather's down here—blood on her *body*—"

"They'll know who to look for," Carl finished.

Randy moaned. A childish, stomach-ache sound.

"Shut up," Carl told him.

Randy stood straight. I'd seen people in states of shock before, concussion cases who'd gone head first into the boards left to wander the rink's hallways after the game like zombies, unable to recall their phone number or the colour of their eyes. But Randy's condition was different. He knew exactly who he was, what was happening—he knew too much, and it was crushing him.

"He told me to touch her," he said. It was something less than a whisper.

"Didn't quite catch that," Carl said, and looked as though he was about to charge at him.

"He *told* me to," Randy said again.

"No, I didn't! Why would I do that? Tell you to drag her over the goddamned floor?" Carl looked to us. "You think I'd be that stupid?"

"Wait. *Wait*," Ben said, stepping closer to Randy yet not too close, as though to avoid contagion. "*Who* told you to?"

Randy raised his eyes. Met mine.

"Nobody. Nothing. I'm just—everything's fucked up, that's all."

"*That's* true," Carl said, slapping his hands together. "Fucked up? Right on the money there, Rando."

We fell into a collective silence. Remembering to breathe and little else.

I was the first to move. Even though it was the last thing I wanted to do, I found myself lowering to kneel beside Heather Langham's body. I'm not sure what drew me closer to her, but it wasn't curiosity. The physical fact of her being dead was something I could grasp only at the edges, fleetingly, before forcing my thoughts to some smaller, more manageable detail, like the papery meeting of her grey lips, or her eyes, the lids slightly parted as though caught in a fight against sleep. Perhaps I needed confirmation that this was all as it appeared to be: she *was* dead, there *wasn't* any walking away now. Perhaps I was sorry that she had become a problem of ours, that everything that made her so vibrantly human had left her in this sour-smelling cellar, and now she was, for us, a logistical puzzle, a stain.

Or perhaps I had to see for myself how she had been murdered.

Part of her lay on a blanket. No, not a blanket: a canvas drop cloth of the kind used by painters. The way it was smoothed out beneath her, buffering her from the hard dirt, gave the impression of a makeshift bed. The cloth told a history of a thousand mistakes: splashes of turquoise and yellow and off-whites fallen from brushes or sloshed over the side of a kicked can. Now, as close as I was, I could see the more recent colours. Randy's bright nosebleed. Beneath it, the brown-red sprays and tracks emanating from the back of Heather Langham's skull.

Only then did I notice the screw. A fiercely bevelled four-inch screw that had been pounded through a plank, sharp point up, which lay an arm's length from Heather's splayed fingers. Nearly half of the wood's length had been discoloured by blood. Maybe Heather had managed to pull it from the wound herself and toss it to where it now rested. Maybe someone else dropped it after seeing the job was done.

I leaned over. Bent so far across her body I had to brace myself on palms laid on the floor on the other side of her. For a second, my finger was hooked on the gold chain around her neck, pulling the heart-shaped locket she was wearing to rest like an egg in the soft dimple at the base of her throat. I shook my hand free and the chain made a small, watery sound as it settled over her skin. Then I lowered my head to the floor to look at her face.

Her eyes weren't fully open as I would later dream them to be (the horrific clarity of marbles, twinkly and blind), but they weren't closed either. The lids empurpled, a colour of eyeshadow worn by only the sluttiest girls at school. The result was an expression I initially confused with seductiveness. It made me think that maybe this *was* Heather's twin, the one who liked to do all the naughty stuff Heather would never do. But then I saw the teeth knocked out of her mouth, the white, bloodless gums. The liquefied nose. I saw that she had been alone as the life emptied out of her, and that this aloneness was a thing worse than dying.

A hand came down on my shoulder. A touch that lifted me away from the particulars of Heather Langham's body to look at her again from a standing height. Now, from only the added distance of a few feet, she had lost the Heather-ness I could still find in her face as I bent over her. She was merely lifeless again. A sickening leftover of violence.

The hand left my shoulder. I turned to see it was Ben's.

"Ideas, gentlemen?"

We buried her. Right there in the cellar floor. Miss Langham, all future, being rolled by the toes of our boots into the three-foot trench we managed to axe and heave from the copper-smelling earth on which the Thurman house stood.

It's a struggle now to remember much of what must have been the hour or two we spent at this task, other than the work itself: the selection of tools found in the cellar's corners and hanging on its rusted hooks, the shifts of labour kept short enough to maintain a near-frantic pace, the space's encroaching shadows we held at bay with swings of the flashlight's beam. We did our best to keep her body in the dark.

We stopped only twice. Once when Carl started to cry. The second time when Randy ran upstairs.

Carl's tears were somehow more disturbing than the fear that Randy had rushed straight to his dad to tell him the terrible things his friends where doing over at the Thurman place. I suppose Randy's not being able to stick it out was the lesser surprise of the two. In any case, once he was gone we continued to axe and dig, waiting to hear the approach of sirens. Maybe fifteen minutes after he'd gone, though, Randy made his way back into the circle of light to pick up a shovel and take his place in the deepening trough.

When Carl started to cry, we tried our best to ignore it. Each of us had taken a break at one point—me to throw up in the corner, Ben to sit on the ground with his head between his knees—and we expected Carl to recover on his own as we had. Instead, he got louder. Curled up with his back against a support post, wailing. If it was anyone else, we probably would have stayed at it. But the alien sound of Carl's grief sapped us of our strength, so that we could only kneel around him, our hands on his elbows, the sides of his head, as though we were holding him together.

It wasn't our fault.

This would be our unspoken refrain for years to come. But how many accused have said this and convinced none, not even themselves, of their innocence?

We couldn't have murdered Miss Langham. We loved her. Yet we knew intuitively that love in such close proximity to violence made, in itself, a strong case for culpability. In the crime stories picked up off the wire in *The Grimshaw Beacon*, it was the ones who claimed to least wish harm upon a victim who usually turned out to be the ones who'd done it.

And there was the evidence too. Randy's blood. Ben's mother, who might have seen us slipping into the town's one forbidden place.

We may have discussed all this aloud at the time. But our decision was ultimately based not on any sober deliberation. It was a reaction we were locked into from the moment Randy's light found our music teacher's body in the darkness. Our instinct to cover up, to hide, to pretend we were never there was instant and inarguable. It was our first real summoning of the masculine talent for non-disclosure. We were becoming men. Becoming gravediggers.

[7]

HE ASSUMES IT was only a side effect of grief, a Parkinson's hallucination, some aftertaste of Halloween graveyard imagery brought back from a tale told with a flashlight under one of our chins thirty years ago. Whatever it was, Randy doesn't believe I saw Carl. If I mentioned I also saw the boy from the Thurman house, a ghoul who spoke directly to my thoughts (an observation I make a point of *not* making), he wouldn't have believed that either. If I'd told him about the boy, he might now be taking me to be admitted to Grimshaw General's psych ward and not walking through the town's streets, dusk falling around us like tiny charcoal leaves.

"Why would he run?" Randy asks for the third time.

"I didn't get a chance to ask."

"But whoever you saw wasn't just avoiding you. He was, like, *gone*."

"Maybe he didn't want to see us. Maybe he's sick and he doesn't want anyone to know. Maybe he's not himself anymore."

"Or the law is after him."

"There's that too."

Randy carries on to the corner and rounds it. For a moment, it appears that he is about to slip away into nothing just as Carl—or the boy—did.

"Where you going?" I call after him.

"Where do you think?" he shouts back from the other side of what was, at one time, Brad Wickenheiser's hedgerow.

"You don't think Carl is—"

"Not *there*," he says, not giving me the chance to say "Caledonia Street" or "the Thurman place." "I'm going to Jake's."

"I'll get the first round."

"And an extra one for Ben."

"That's right," I say when Randy comes back to loop an arm over my shoulders. "An extra glass for the watchman."

"Ben was part Irish, wasn't he?" Randy asks as we head into Jake's Pool 'n' Sports, shaking the rain off our coats.

"I think his dad was. Or his grandfather. Or something."

"It'll do."

"For what?"

"A wake."

Tracey Flanagan is our waitress again. From across the room she gives us a comically triumphant thumbs-up as we assume our positions at what is now "our table," the two of us hopping atop the same stools as the night before. She giggles at Randy, who mimes thirst, his tongue out and hands clutched to his throat.

"I took the liberty," she says as she comes to us, pitcher in one hand, mugs in the other.

"I believe we'll be requiring the assistance of Bushmills shots as well today, Tracey," Randy says in a leprechaun accent.

"I'm sorry," Tracey says, with genuine sympathy. "Mr. McAuliffe was a friend of all yours, right? On the Guardians?"

"He was a hockey friend of your dad's," I answer. "But to us, he was a brother. Maybe even closer than that."

Tracey purses her lips, correctly reading that I'm not pulling her leg. I've just told her something intimate, and she acknowledges the honour with an eyes-closed nod.

"I'll get those whiskeys," she says.

After we toast Ben, the conversation moves to the topic of Sarah.

"She looked good," Randy observes. "Then again, she always looked good. You see a ring on her finger?"

"Like a wedding ring? As if that would stop you."

"We're not talking about me."

"I don't remember."

"Bullshit."

"Okay, she *wasn't*."

"It's open season, then."

"She's not an elk, Randy."

"I'm just saying you're here, she's here. Old times' sake and all that. It's sweet."

"I'm here because Ben died, not for some shag at the class-reunion weekend."

"What? You can't walk and chew gum at the same time?"

The bar is even busier tonight. A Leafs game on the flat-screens, an excuse to get out of the house in the middle of the week for some draft and half-price Burn Your Tongue Off! wings advertised on the paper pyramids on the tables.

Among the customers is Tracey's boyfriend. A good-looking, dark-haired kid who comes in wearing a Domino's Pizza jacket to give her a full kiss on the lips. Here's what you can see right away, as surely as you could see it when I kissed Sarah Mulgrave outside the Grimshaw Arena on game nights: these two are in love. And you can see that the Domino's kid knows how special a young woman Tracey Flanagan is. That he is trying to figure a way to not blow it with her and go all the way, out of Grimshaw and beyond. A whole life with Tracey. That's what this kid wants, and is right to want.

"That yer fella?" Randy asks after the Domino's kid has left and Tracey returns to our table. He's decided to use his Irish accent again.

"Sure is," she says. "You better watch yourself."

"No need to be warned about those pizza-delivery guys. They don't mess about."

"Gary played for the Guardians too."

This declaration changes things. And it makes Randy drop the dumb accent.

"What position?"

"Right wing."

Randy slaps me on the back. "That's where Trev played! Though that was many moons ago."

"So my dad tells me."

"Your Gary, does he have a last name?"

"Pullinger."

"Rings a bell," I say.

"Bowl-More Lanes," Randy says, clicking his fingers. "Didn't the Pullingers own that place?"

"Gary's dad. But it burned down about ten years ago."

"The Bowl-More burned down?" Randy slams his fist onto the table in real outrage. "Had many a birthday party there as a youngster. You remember, Trev?"

"I remember."

Randy raises his mug. "Here's to Tracey and Gary. May you find love and happiness."

"Already have," she says.

The night goes on to gain a comfortable momentum, buoyed by Bushmills and the Leafs going into the third period with an unlikely two-goal lead over the Red Wings. They will ultimately lose, of course. But for now, Jake's is a place of hope and mild excitement and we are part of it.

I decide to quit while I'm ahead. I'm feeling pretty good, considering the grim business of the day—not to mention the strange encounter with the boy, and an observer I guessed to be Carl (though now, on the firmer ground of Jake's, I doubt either was who I thought he was). But much more of what's making me feel this way will only be pressing my luck. I'm tired. From the long day, from burying a friend, from fighting to keep the Parkinson's hidden from the world. And tomorrow I have to assume my duties as Ben's executor. A first-class hangover would make that unpleasant task only doubly so.

I head up to the bar to give Tracey my credit card.

"Wrapping up?"

"Just me," I say. "I wanted to pick up the tab before my friend and I wrestled over it. Though Randy is usually willing to lose that particular fight."

She swipes my card and taps the terminal with a pen, waiting for the printed receipt. It gives me a handful of seconds to study her profile up close. No doubt about it: something of Heather Langham lives in this girl.

She looks up at me.

"Sorry," I say. "It's rude to stare."

"Were you staring?"

"Honestly? I was thinking of someone else. Someone you remind me of."

"A girlfriend?"

"No. Just a person I looked up to."

"Are you flirting with me?" she says.

"Is that what this sounds like?"

"A little. But then, I don't really know you. And you're—"

"An old man. Old as your dad, anyway."

"So I don't know how guys like you go about things."

"Well, let me tell you. I'm not flirting. I'm confessing. A man who thinks he can see someone in someone else, but is only dreaming."

"Memory lane."

"That's it. That's where I live these days." My right hand fidgets at this, impatient at being still for the length of this exchange. "Trust me, I'm harmless."

"Trust you?"

"Or don't. Just know that a fellow doesn't get to meet a true lady too often anymore."

She considers me another moment. Then, out of nowhere, she punches me in the shoulder. Hard enough that it takes some effort on my part not to let my hand fly to the point of impact to soothe the hurt.

"Dad said you were pretty good. Back in the day." She laughs.

"Oh yeah? Good at what?"

She laughs some more before ripping the receipt from the machine and sticking her pen between my trembling fingers.

MEMORY DIARY

Entry No. 8

Over the days that followed the night we found Heather Langham in the Thurman house we repeatedly reminded each other to act normal, a direction that raised questions in each of our minds as to what our normal might be. However I ended up resolving this, I considered my act a fairly accomplished performance. It certainly convinced my parents, classmates and, for stretches as long as a couple of hours at a time, even me.

Sarah, on the other hand, was a more skeptical audience. Right off she noticed something had changed. I assumed her main concern was that my feelings for her had waned, in the way Carl's did for the girls he cast aside. With the benefit of honesty, I assured her that I loved her, that I was aware of how lucky I was to have her, that nothing had come between us.

"This isn't an 'us' thing," she said. "Something's wrong with you."

I recall one lunch period when we drove out to Harmony with plans for what Sarah called, in a singing voice, an "afternoon delight." But to my astonishment, my normally enthusiastic teenage manhood offered no response to her attentions in the Buick's folded-down back seat. There were now two secrets I had to keep: I couldn't tell Sarah about finding Miss Langham, and I couldn't tell my friends about failing to get it up with a naked Sarah Mulgrave.

I don't remember us talking about it, huddled under a blanket of parkas, studying the patterns of frost our breath made over the windows. The significance of our skin against skin, dry and cool, was clear enough. Something had turned. And even though I was the one who knew what she couldn't know, I couldn't say how this knowledge had found power over us here, in our place, in Harmony.

"You guys ready?"

Her question, the first words spoken since I rolled onto my back in defeat, so clearly matched the current of my thoughts I worried I might have been speaking them aloud.

"Ready?"

"The playoffs. First game's on Friday, right?"

"Seaforth. Sure."

"Seaforth sucks."

"Shouldn't be a problem."

"I said hi to the coach today at school. It was strange."

I propped myself up on an elbow. "How do you mean?"

"I don't know. I'm standing there, and he stops and looks at me like I've grown a second head or something. Made me feel like a freak."

"Sounds like he was the one being freaky."

"It was just weird."

"He's a weird guy."

That's not true, I heard Sarah reply through her silence. *He's the most not-weird grown-up we know.*

I pulled my pants on. The denim hard and unyielding as wet canvas left to freeze on the clothesline.

"We should get back."

"Back to what?" she asked, and we both laughed. What was funny was how only two days ago we both would have been certain of the answer, and today we weren't sure.

I can't recollect exactly what people said over twenty years ago, even if I repeat their words into this Dictaphone as though I can. These moments are memories, and shifty ones at that, so what I'm doing is the sort of half-made-up scenes we used to watch on those *That's Incredible!* TV specials, shows that "investigated" the existence of UFOs and the Loch Ness Monster using dramatizations of witness accounts. It wasn't the truth, but the truth as someone remembered it, and someone else wrote into a scene. So that's me. A *That's Incredible!* dramatizer.

One thing I do remember, however, was Sarah's description of the coach's gaze when she stopped him to say hello. I may have made up the "grown a second head" part, but I definitely remember her saying how his look made her feel like a freak, because it was precisely the same thought I had at practice after school that day, when the coach entered the dressing room and, in looking at us, his team, wore an expression of suppressed shock, as though he had opened the wrong door and been confronted with chattering sasquatches.

The moment passed so swiftly I don't think any of the older players noticed. They weren't looking to see if the few days since Heather Langham's disappearance had had any effect on the coach. But *we* were looking. And we believed we saw something in the way he had to work up an effort to scratch some plays on the blackboard, remind Chuck Hastings to stay high in the slot on the penalty kill and praise Carl for the blocked shots he took to the ribs in the season-ender against Wingham.

What was more, the coach seemed to notice our noticing. For the rest of practice I thought I caught him studying Ben or Carl or Randy or me, watching us in the same furtive way we watched him.

And then there was the coach's asking Ben how he was doing.

Was there anything odd in that? We didn't think so either. So when Ben told us that night, as we tossed twigs onto a small fire we made in the woods behind the Old Grove, passing a flask of Randy's dad's gin between us, that there was evidence to be gleaned from the coach's inquiring after him, we shot him down.

"He called me son," Ben said. "'Hey there, Ben. How're you doing, son?' It was fake. Like he was reading a line someone wrote for him."

"Are you saying he knows?" I asked.

"How *would* he know?" Ben answered. "Unless he was watching the place. Unless he was there."

"You think he was in the cellar?"

"Didn't it feel like *somebody* was?"

This stopped me for a second. It stopped all of us.

"All I'm saying," Ben said, "is if you'd done something wrong—something really, really wrong—and you didn't want that wrong thing to be found out, you might keep a pretty close eye on the business."

"Return to the scene of the crime," Randy said thoughtfully, as though he'd just coined the phrase.

"That's right," Ben said. "And there was no better place to watch over Miss Langham than down there."

It was strange how over the period of less than a week Ben had gone from the dreamiest of our group to the voice that carried the greatest authority. Our overnight leader.

"If he knows it was us," Carl said, "then he knows we might talk."

"That would also follow if he was aware that I saw him from my window."

"Wait," I said. "Now all of a sudden you're *sure* it was him?"

But Carl didn't let Ben answer. "He sure looks aware of everything to me. And if we're right about that, he's not going to want us blabbing."

"No," Ben said.

"He might try to stop us."

"He might."

Randy unzips, pees into the fire. A wet sizzle that sends up smoke, momentarily enveloping us all in shadow. "The coach wouldn't fuck with us," he said.

"He fucked with Heather," Carl said.

"We still don't know that," I said.

"We don't?" Ben asked, the flames returning to life as Randy finished his nervous dribbles. "You saw the coach today. Do you really think somebody else did that to Miss Langham? Can you honestly say you think he doesn't know that we know?"

Three faces, facing me. Even in the near dark I could see their certainty, their glitter-eyed excitement. The good news was we weren't alone. This was the comfort I could see my friends offering to me. We were in danger, the holders of terrible knowledge, but all could be borne if we stayed together. And we would.

"You're right. He knows," I said, my conviction instantly as real as I tried to make it sound. "And we're the only ones who know what he did."

"So what are we going to do?" Ben asked, though we could tell he knew the answer already.

Heather Langham failed to show up for our music class on Tuesday, and we found her body at the bottom of the Thurman house on Friday. But by the time the next Tuesday arrived, and because there were no new developments to report, the story of her continued missing status in that morning's edition of *The Grimshaw Beacon* moved off the front page for the first time. The town's speculation over Heather Langham had already been replaced by the chances of the Guardians going all the way to the provincial championships.

Which is not to say that people had stopped caring about the missing teacher, just that her story had nowhere to go. She had no family in Grimshaw, no one to make impatient urgings to the police or write letters to the editor. Despite the appealing photo of her that appeared with each article and TV news clip we saw, Heather Langham remained an outsider. There were no Langhams other than her in the phone book, none listed on the granite war memorial that named the local men who died overseas. She came from elsewhere, an unattached woman who lived alone in a rented room. She offered little foundation to build a mystery on.

Perhaps it was for these reasons that most of us were forced to accept the dullest of explanations: she had quit and left town. Besides, there were no lashings of blood in Heather Langham's dormitory in the nurses' residence as was first rumoured, no suicide note, no sign of an evil twin sister stirring up trouble. Some concrete suggestion of foul play was required to get the town excited about the Langham story after the first few days of nothing to report.

Over that first week, we—Ben, Carl, Randy and I—were kept busy perfecting our "normal" act. You might think one of us would have cracked, blabbed, broken into guilty sobs against our mother's breast. We had buried someone, after all. We carried news of murder. Wouldn't this find its way to the surface? Didn't we come from a world so cushioned and flat that the secret of what lay in the Thurman cellar would be more than we could bear?

The answer was in the *us* of it. Alone, we would have run screaming from the house and told all. But together we held it in. As *us*, we could believe what was happening wasn't entirely, wakingly real.

Sarah wanted to go to the movies. I remember because it was a return engagement of *Flashdance*, which we'd both seen when it first came out months earlier, and because I didn't really believe she was interested in seeing it again. She wanted what I wanted, something that only a couple of hours in the back rows of the Vogue could deliver: the two of us together in a warm place without any of the talk that had become so troubled between us.

The house lights dimmed, and we were enveloped in shadow and Love's Baby Soft. As Jennifer Beals tumbled and flew across the screen, Sarah and I drew close. We weren't making out—there was no grappling with bra hooks or belts. Our hands were communicating, skin on skin. And what did our touches say? Some combination of *I'm sorry* and *Here I am* and *No one could ever be closer to me than you.*

Then the movie ended, and we were forced back out into the cold. We stopped a half a block from her house, in the side lane next to Patterson's Candy & Milk that was our goodnight-kiss spot. Not that we were kissing.

"I'm not going to ask you about it anymore," she said.

"Ask about what?"

"You're a terrible liar."

Snow fell in fat clumps over our heads. It made the night feel smaller, surrounding us like the walls of an old barn, solid enough to keep out all outside sound but not the cold.

"You think you're doing this for me," she said.

"It's not your problem."

"Look at me."

It was a hard stare to meet. Partly because her hurt was so much clearer than my own. And because it made her even more beautiful.

"I'm looking," I said.

"And what do you see? Just another girl who can't handle the serious stuff."

"That's not it."

"Does Randy know what you're not telling me? Do Carl and Ben?"

"They know because they have to know."

"Well, maybe I do too."

"Can't you just let it go?"

"You think this is because I'm *curious*?"

"Aren't you?"

"I would be if I thought it was just you screwing some other girl. But it's not that. It's not something we can hide away."

"Why not?"

"I could if you could. But you can't. And it's killing you. You can't see that yet, but it is."

I started away in anger, but Sarah grabbed me by the arm and spun me back to face her.

"I had a dream the other night with you in it. In fact, there was nobody else," she said. "This old man walking along a beach wanting to say, 'Look at that sunset' or 'Those waves are coming in high' but never opening your mouth because there is nobody there to say it to."

I thought she was about to cry. But it was me, already crying.

"I know you, Trevor."

"Yeah."

"Then you have to trust me. And if not me, I hope you find someone else."

I watched her walk to the street, where she paused. It was an opportunity for me to go to her. A held hand might have done it. Matched footsteps for the last hundred yards to her house, where I could have told her I'd see her tomorrow. But by the time I decided which of these felt more right she'd started off on her own, and there was no way of following.

We lost the first game of the playoffs to Seaforth. For most in Grimshaw this was a disappointment. A handful might even have found it an outrage. But for us, it confirmed that the coach was Heather Langham's murderer.

Most of the other players wrote off the coach's screwed-up line changes and listless pre-game talk as an off night. But we saw more than mere distraction in his struggle to remember our names, the out-of-character insults at the ref for making a tripping call on Dave Hurley (who was guiltily on his way to the penalty box anyway).

Even more telling, he put Ben in net.

Halfway through the third period, our team behind 3–1 but still with enough time for a chance to tie the game up, the coach summoned Vince Sproule to the bench and tapped Ben on the shoulder.

"You want this?" he said.

Not *You're in* or *Shut 'em down* or *McAuliffe! Get in there!* but a question.

You want this?

Spoken through the cage of Ben's mask so that he was the one player on the bench who heard. A whisper that could be understood only as a warning or a challenge.

Ben played well, by Ben standards. But by then the team had been thrown off by trailing a "bunch of dung-heeled inbreds" (as Carl called the Seaforth squad) and the coach's odd decision of sending our backup goalie in to finish the game, and we slowed, coughing up pucks, leaving Ben to fend for himself. He let in another two before the buzzer.

"That's it. That's *it*," I remember Ben muttering as he came off the ice to the rare sound of boos echoing through the Grimshaw Arena. The others assumed he was voicing his frustration at being hung out to dry by his teammates. But we knew he'd come to a conclusion.

There was a new clarity in Ben's eyes I saw even as he skated out from his net, a look he shot toward the bench that our fellow players saw as anger and we saw as stern resolve, but that now, in hindsight, might have been the first hint of madness.

[8]

I'VE BEEN UP for a couple of hours when there's a knock at my door. *Tap-slide, tap-slide, tap-slide.* The way the boy might ask to come in.

I'd dreamed about him all last night—dreams of me wandering through the Thurman house, sensing something just ahead or just behind, until a pair of cold hands drape over my eyes and I can smell the rancid breath of his laugh before he sinks his teeth into the back of my neck—and awakened to the threadbare sheets of my Queen's Hotel bed glued to me with sweat. A shower of brownish water helped remind me that these were only Grimshaw nightmares, and would retreat as soon as I was able to leave. Yet when the three evenly spaced knocks at the door come—*tap-slide, tap-slide, tap-slide*—all such comforting thoughts skitter away. And in place of my own voice in my head, there is the boy's.

Can Trev come out and play?

I go to the door because he will never go away if I don't, and it is the only way out. And because the answer to his question is yes. Trev has nothing better to do. He can come out and play.

The doorknob is a ball of ice in my hand. This, I tell myself, is likely only another quirky symptom of Parkinson's I've noticed of late, the exaggerated hots and colds of things. Yet my fingers remain frozen to the brass, unwilling to turn the knob, unable to pull away.

Open up, the boy says.

The door swings back. So unexpected its edge slices into my shoulder, knocking me back a half-step.

"Jesus," Randy says, slouching in the hall, his T-shirt and jeans crosshatched with wrinkles. "You look worse than I feel."

"I'm fine."

"Whatever you say."

"Is that coffee?"

Randy looks down at the two paper cups screwed into the tray in his hand as though a stranger had asked him to hold it and had yet to return.

"It appears it is," he says, then tries to look past my shoulder. "You got company?"

"No. Why?"

"You look all blotchy and flustered, for one thing. And for another, you're not letting me in."

"I thought there was someone else at the door."

"Who?"

"Nobody."

"Funny. I thought there was nobody knocking at my door this morning too."

Randy comes in, stands with his back to me as I take a seat at the desk, steadying my hands by gripping its edge. "You up for some breakfast?"

"I'll just grab something on my way to the McAuliffes'."

"Right. Trevor the Executor."

"Care to join me?"

"Me and you folding Ben's underwear and filing his *Hustler*s? I'm good, thanks."

Randy notices the Dictaphone I've left on the desktop.

"What's that?"

"A tape recorder," I say, slipping it into my jacket pocket. "Except it doesn't use tapes. So I suppose it's not really a *tape* recorder. It's digital."

"I know what it *is*. I'm wondering what you're using it for."

Randy stares at my hands, white knuckled and ridged, both returned to clutching the edge of the desk.

"I'm keeping a kind of diary," I say.

"Really."

"One of my doctors said they sometimes help."

"Help what?"

"People with diseases like mine."

"Yeah? How's that work?"

"It's supposed to make you feel less alone or something."

"I'm just trying to picture you sitting here talking into that thing, counting up how many beers you had last night and the crap you took this morning and how many hairs you pulled out of the drain after your shower."

"It's not like that."

"No? What's it like?"

"I'm not keeping a diary of the present, but the past."

This loosens the teasing grin from Randy's face, so that he appears vaguely pained, as though waiting for a stomach cramp to release its hold.

"The past," he says finally. "How far back you going?"

"Guess."

"The winter when we were sixteen."

"That's not a bad title for it."

Randy sits on the end of the bed. Rests his hands on his knees in the way of a man who thinks his body might be about to betray him in some unpredictable way.

"You think that's a good idea?" he says.

"In what sense?"

"In the sense of anyone reading or listening to this diary of yours?"

"Nobody's ever going to read it."

"Because we *promised*. You too. You *promised* never to tell."

"I'm not telling. It's just for me."

"To be forgiven."

"That's asking too much."

"So what's it about?"

"I just need to hear myself say what I've never let myself say."

"Because we never talked about it even then, did we?" Randy lowers his head to be held in his cupped hands. "We never said a goddamn thing to each other."

"We were trying to pretend it wasn't real."

"But it was," Randy says, his freckled face the same self-doubting oval that looked out from his grade ten yearbook photo. "It *was*. Wasn't it?"

I step out of the taxi in front of the McAuliffe place, pay the driver through the window and make my herky-jerky way up the steps to the front door, all without looking at the Thurman house across the street. Not as easy as it sounds. I can feel it wanting me to turn my eyes its way, to take it in now in the full noontime light. To deny it is as difficult as not surveying the damage of a car accident as you roll past, the survivors huddled in blankets, the dead being pulled from the wreck.

And this is how the house wins. Mrs. McAuliffe takes a few seconds too long to come to the door after I ring the bell, so that, even as I see her shadow approaching through the door's curtained glass and hear the frail crackle of her "Coming! Coming!" I steal a glance. At the same instant, the sun pokes out from a hole in the clouds. Sends dark winks back at me from the second-floor windows, a dazzle of false welcome.

"Trevor," Mrs. McAuliffe says, and though I can't see her at first when I turn back to the door, my vision burned with the yellow outline of the Thurman house, I can feel the old woman's arms stretched open for a hug, and my own arms reaching out and pulling her close.

"I'm so sorry about Ben, Mrs. A.," I whisper into her moth-balled cardigan.

"I'm not a Mrs. anything anymore to you. I'm just Betty."

"Not sure I'll ever get used to that."

"That's what you learn when you get old," she says, pushing me back to hold my jaw in the bone-nests of her hands. "There's so much you never get used to."

The house looks more or less as I remember it. The dark wood panelling in the living room, the lace-covered dining table, the brooding landscapes of the Scottish Highlands too small for the plaster walls they hang on. Even the smell of the place is familiar. Apparently Ben and his mother carried on with their deep-fried diets well into his adulthood, judging from the diner-like aroma of hot oil and toast.

"You look well," Betty McAuliffe tells me as I shakily replace a Royal Doulton figurine of a Pekingese to the side table where I stupidly picked it up.

"I do?"

"Tired, maybe," she says, ignoring my struggles. "But handsome as always."

"It's just a little dark in here, that's all. Pull back the curtains and you'll see the wrinkles and bloodshot eyes."

"Don't I know! It's why I keep them closed."

In the kitchen, Mrs. McAuliffe shows me the neat piles of papers that are Ben's will, some of his receipts, bank statements. His death certificate.

"It's not much, is it?" she asks. "A whole life and you could fold it into a single envelope and mail it to . . . well, where would you mail it?"

"To me."

"Of course. Mail it to you. Though there'd be no point in that because you're here now, which I'm glad of. Very glad of indeed."

I turn back to find the old woman standing in the middle of the kitchen, looking to the fridge, the sink, her shoes, me, then starting over again. Her hair white and loose as dandelion fluff.

"Mrs. McAuliffe. Betty. Are you—?"

"Would you like a cup of tea?" she asks, and I can see that making a pot for a guest might just be enough to save her life.

"That would be great. And a biscuit, if you have one."

She busies herself with these tasks, and I do my best to busy myself with mine. But aside from confirming the filing of Ben's past few tax returns (he'd earned next to no income), there seems little for me to do. Then I discover the package on the chair next to mine. A brown bubble-wrapped envelope with my name on the front.

"What's this?" I ask Mrs. McAuliffe as she places an empty mug and plate of butter cookies in front of me.

"Ben didn't leave a note. Nothing aside from a white rose he left on my bedside table. And that."

"You haven't opened it?"

"Ben was sick," she starts. "But he had . . . *interests*. And I respected that. So no, I haven't opened it. Because whatever is in it, he felt you would understand and I would not."

There is an edge to these last words, a buried grievance or accusation.

She fills my mug to the brim. Stands over me, the teapot wavering in her hand, as though uncertain whether to carry it to the sink or let it drop to the floor.

"Where are you staying?" she asks.

"The Queen's."

"Horrible place."

"In the dark, it looks like any other room."

"Perhaps you'd like to stay here?"

It takes me a second to interpret what she's just said. *Stay here?* The idea causes a shudder that has nothing to do with Parkinson's.

"Just for a night or two," she goes on. "Until you're finished looking through Ben's things."

"It's very kind of you. But I wouldn't—"

"Be no trouble."

"You must be very—"

"I'd *like* you to stay."

Mrs. McAuliffe puts the teapot down on the table. Uses her now free hand to wipe the sleeve of her sweater under her chin.

"Of course," I say. "Thanks. I'll bring my things over this evening."

"Good. *Good.*" She breathes, a clear in and out. "You can have Ben's room."

———

That, Betty, is never going to happen.

This is my first thought as I push open the door to Ben's attic room and look up at the splintery beam from which he'd tied the noose.

I am never going to spend the night here.

At the same time, even as I enter with the sound of my shoes sticking to the recently waxed floorboards (was this done after Ben died? Perhaps to clean away the blood? if there *was* blood?), I can already feel myself sliding between the sheets of the freshly made bed against the wall and turning out the light. A moment at once unthinkable and unstoppable.

The room is clean, but preserved. Even if I didn't know of Ben and the wasted years he'd spent up here, I could discern the not-rightness of its former inhabitant through the teenage boy things that hadn't been replaced or stored away. So there was still the Specials poster over the dresser. Still the Batman stickers on the mirror, the neat stacks of comics and Louis L'Amour novels against the wall. Still the Ken Dryden lamp on the bedside table.

I sit on the edge of the bed, and the wood frame barks. A sound Ben would have been so used to he'd long ago have stopped hearing it.

The package he left for me sits on my lap. His square letters spelling my name. So carefully printed it suggests the final act in a long-planned operation. The licking of the envelope's fold a taste of finality, of poison.

I tear it open in one pull.

So it was you and me both, Ben. A thick, black leather journal slips out. *Diary keepers.*

It's heavy. A cover worn pale through repeated openings and closings, its inner pages dense with ink.

The entries are mostly brief, all written in chicken-scratched print, as though the paper he wrote on was the last in the world. The book opens with an unintentionally comic record of non-event:

> *March 19, 1992*
> *Nothing.*
>
> *March 20, 1992*
> *Nothing.*
>
> *March 21, 1992*
> *Nothing.*
>
> *March 22, 1992*
> *Same.*

Then, after several more days of this:

> *March 29, 1992*
> *The front door handle.*
> *Something on the inside. Trying to get out.*

No names, hardly any mention of the neighbours' comings or goings. Just the house. And, at certain points, the apparent sightings of characters so familiar to Ben he didn't waste the letters to name them, as in "He was at the downstairs window" or "She shouted someone's name" or "They moved together across the living room like ballroom dancers."

May 18, 1992
Kids coming home from school. Stop to stare at it.
*   I shout down at them, "Save yourselves! Keep moving!"*
*   They tell me to go fuck myself. But they don't go in, don't go*
any closer.

I flip ahead, scanning. Five hundred pages of lunatic surveillance and shouted warnings. I close it after reading only the first dozen pages, my mind aswirl. Why did Ben bother keeping such a record in the first place? How did he think his observation was protecting anyone? Why kill himself now, leaving his post vacant?

And the kicker: Why had he left this to me?

I attempt to read on. But a minute later, I'm struck with a rare headache. A pair of marbles growing into golf balls at the temples.

I lay the journal down on the bedside table and sit in the chair by the window. Here it is, the full extent of Ben's world: a tar-veined Caledonia Street climbing up the hill to the right, and through the branches of the neighbour's maple, the Thurman house, colourless and unnumbered. For all the seriousness Ben brought to his role as watchdog, it doesn't look threatening from up here in the neutral daylight so much as ashamed of itself. Was there ever a day when Ben doubted himself and saw it as I see it now, weak and forsaken? Did he ever run up against the boredom of waiting to see something in a building that had nothing to show?

I suppose he had his memories of being inside it to keep certain possibilities alive. He could look down at the Thurman house from this roost and visualize the floor plan in his head. It must have been a kind of anti-love, unrequited and undying, that kept him here. Instead of a girl, he had been altered by an experience that had left him frozen, compelled to relive the past as sentimental lovers do.

Yet there *was* a girl. Maybe she is why Ben stayed. Someone had to honour her by carrying her memory, even as her name faded year by year. In recalling the sight of Heather Langham walking up Caledonia Street, indifferent to the leer of the house's darkened eyes, Ben was saving her from becoming nothing more than another Terrible Story.

I try to summon this very image of her now, but it's beyond my reach. There is only the moan of a car accelerating up the slope, the screech of a backyard cat fight, the house. So I wait as Ben waited. The morning unmoored from time. It might be meditative if it wasn't for the accompanying fear. The growing dread that I'm not the only one watching.

Poor Trev. First day on the job and more scared than Ben ever was.

The boy appears at the second-floor bedroom window in the time it takes my eyes to move from the attic shutters, down to the front door and up again.

But there's nothing to be afraid of. All you need is a rope. A chair.

He is looking at me with the same open-mouthed, dumbfounded expression I feel on my own face, a mimicry so expert that, for the first second, I try to see him as me somehow, a telescoped reflection, some smoke-and-mirrors tomfoolery. But in the next second, I realize the gap of years between us: the boy remains sixteen, and I am forty.

All you need to see is that none of it's worth holding on to, because it's already gone.

I was wrong. The boy cannot be me. And the persistence of him in the window confirms his reality with each passing second he remains there. He is trapped inside, but not necessarily forever. I can see that—*feel* that—in the strength he gains even as he charts the depths of my weakness. There are ways out by bringing others in. And with this realization—as though hearing my thoughts just as I can hear his—the startled mask slips off, and he laughs.

"Trevor!"

Mrs. McAuliffe's voice, cheerfully calling up the stairs. A voice that makes the face in the window pull back into shadow.

"Your friend is here!"

Randy stands on the McAuliffes' front porch, arms crossed, refusing to cross the threshold.

"Hey, Trev," he says, a little surprised to see me, even though he knew I'd be here. Maybe a part of him was expecting Ben to come down the stairs, not me, a joint-stiffened man with sweat stains the size of pie plates under his arms.

"What's wrong?"

Randy looks past me, at Mrs. McAuliffe, who remains standing in the hall.

"I'll leave you boys to your business," she says finally and shuffles away through the kitchen door.

Randy still says nothing. Wipes his nose in a slow sweep of the back of his hand.

"Why don't you come in?"

He glances over his shoulder. Almost turns his head far enough to take in the Thurman house, but not quite.

"It's like it's watching us," I say.

"Bricks and wood and glass. That's all it is."

"I'm talking about the inside." I take a step closer, lower my voice. "Don't you feel it?"

"No."

"It's a good thing you never got married. You're a lousy liar."

"Listen, Trev. I didn't come here to talk about an empty house." Randy shakes his head. Physically jostles one line of thinking out of place to make room for another. "The waitress," he says. "Todd's kid."

"What about her?"

"She's missing."

MEMORY DIARY

Entry No. 9

I used to think—or at least I did before the winter of 1984—that one could read the capacity for badness in a face. The mugshots of drive-by shooters and child molesters that were reprinted in the National section of *The Grimshaw Beacon* revealed a similar absence, the groggy complexions that told of cigarettes and nocturnal scheming. I believed that when it came to discerning between the truly evil and the rest of us everyday sinners, *you can just tell.*

But I've come to learn that evil's primary talent is for disguise: not letting you hear the cloven hooves scratching on the welcome mat is how the devil gets invited inside. It's how he can become your friend.

I was thinking this, or something like this, when we pulled over to the curb and asked the coach if he wanted a ride home, and he stopped to look into Carl's Ford. At us.

Carl was at the wheel and Ben in the passenger seat, with me on my own in the back. We had been driving around, arguing over the costs of doing something versus nothing in discovering the truth of the coach's role in Heather Langham's death. That is, I was arguing with Carl and Ben, and they mostly ignored me, studying the houses we cruised by as though considering buying one.

"Where *is* the freckly fuck?" was all Carl would say every few minutes, referring to Randy, who wasn't home when we called.

"We can't do anything without him," I said. "We have to be together on it."

But Carl and Ben just kept looking at the houses. They made me feel like I was riding in a baby seat, watching the backs of their heads as though they were my parents.

"There he is," Carl said. He took his foot off the gas and the Ford rolled on, gently as a canoe after taking the paddles in.

"Who?"

Because they could both see the answer to this on the street ahead, they ignored me. It forced me to slide over between them and peer out the windshield.

The coach. Walking along the sidewalk with his back to us, a stiffening of his stride that suggested he'd heard a car slow behind him. This was his street. A street we had driven up more than any other over the last half-hour. Carl and Ben had been hoping to come across the coach making his way home. And now that they had, they drew even with him and pulled over to the curb.

He stopped. I don't know if he knew who it was before he turned to see, but it seemed there was a half second's pause as he gathered himself.

"What's up, guys?" he asked, glancing up the street toward his house a half block on.

"Need a ride?" Carl asked.

The coach squinted. We knew where he lived. Why would he need a ride? So: this was an invitation. And not necessarily a complicated one. Boys on the team came to him all the time. They told him things, sought advice. There were always Guardians wanting to hang out with him, asking if he needed a ride.

"You think I'm that out of shape?" he said.

"We're just driving around. Killing time before practice."

"You want something to eat? My wife makes this baked spaghetti thing that's not half bad. I'll be eating it the rest of the week if I don't get some help."

"Thanks." Carl glanced around the car at Ben, back at me. "We're not too hungry, I guess."

The coach stood there. Unmoving except for his breath leaking out in feathery plumes.

"How about it?" Ben asked.

"I've got some time," the coach said, pulling back the sleeve of his coat to show the watch on his wrist, though he didn't look at its face. "A little spin? Why not?"

———

Less than two hours before we had driven up to the coach on his walk home, we'd had another hot box meeting in the school's parking lot. It's hard to recall who said what, or the positions we started out defending (I think I changed my mind half a dozen times during each circling of Randy's joint). What was agreed on by all was that *something* had to be done. We alone knew Miss Langham was murdered, the where and how it was done. Maybe, if this was *all* we knew, we would have found a way to justify trying to forget about it. But the thing was this: along with the where and how she was killed, we now felt sure we knew the who.

Why not go to the police? A good question. As good today as the afternoon we asked it in Carl's Ford, coughing it out through the blue haze. Why *not*? There were some halfway reasonable answers to this, and we voiced them at the time:

1) The police would never accept our slim evidence of Ben's nighttime sighting.

2) We had found and moved and bled on and buried her body, which meant the odds were greater that we had done it than anyone else.

3) Pointing a finger the coach's way too early would only allow for his escape.

But the real reason was one none of us spoke aloud.

This was our test. Heather Langham's memory had been adopted as our responsibility.

It was Ben who was the last to speak. Last, because he used words almost as powerful as his reminder of friendship that had led us into a haunted house. Words that have, in different contexts, ushered soldiers onto killing fields.

"We need to find the truth," he said. "We have to. For Heather. For justice."

Truth. Justice. These were the opened doors through which we saw a way to save Heather Langham in death as we had longed to save her in life.

We talked about hockey at first. Or the coach did, repeating the ways we would have to exploit the weak links on Seaforth's defence. He sat next to me in the back but spoke directly to the window, as if rehearsing a speech. He reminded me of a dog who didn't like cars: sitting straight and still, but every muscle tense as he waited for the machine to stop and the doors to open so he could leap out.

"We saw you," Ben said.

This is how the conversation turned. Ben swivelling around in the passenger seat to face the coach. And it was "we."

"You did?" the coach said. He looked at me, at Carl in the rearview mirror, at the toothpaste stain around Ben's mouth.

"Last Monday. Going into the Thurman house."

"Monday?"

The coach looked as though he was trying to remember his mother-in-law's middle name or the capital of Bolivia.

"Just over a week ago. Monday *night*."

"Okay. Monday night. Why would I be going in there, Ben?"

"Why would you? Why *would* you?"

The coach continued to look at Ben for a moment, then turned to me. "What is this?"

"Answer the question," I said.

"I don't know what you're asking me."

"Have you been inside the Thurman house at any time in the last week?"

"No. Now you tell me. What the hell is a Thurman house?"

He chuckled at this, and I was sure we'd got everything wrong. The coach's awkwardness had come not from secret knowledge but from us. He had detected a worrying turn in his youngest players and was trying to guess what was wrong. We were acting weird, not him.

"The empty place on Caledonia," Carl said. "You don't know about it?"

"Where you guys go to smoke pot or whatever? Yes, I'm aware of it."

"Have you ever been inside?"

"I just told you."

"So you haven't?"

"Hold on here. I mean, seriously, what is this shit?"

It was an understandable question. One minute he's on his way home to his wife's spaghetti casserole and the next he's being interrogated by three kids in a car. He had every right to be impatient. But what all of us heard—what dismissed my earlier impression that we'd got everything wrong—was his *shit*. It was the first time any of us had heard him swear.

Carl pulled over. I thought he was going to ask Ben

to pop his seat forward to let the coach out, and so did the coach, who gripped his hands to the back of the headrest, ready to go. Instead, Carl rolled his window down. That's when I noticed Randy out front of the Erie Burger.

"Get in," Carl said.

Randy bent down to see me and the coach in the back. If he was surprised he didn't show it. When Carl leaned forward, Randy lined up to get into the back with us.

"One here, one there," Carl said.

After a second, Randy got it. He came around the other side so that the coach was sandwiched between us.

Carl drove on, making sure to stay off the main streets. For a while nobody said anything. There wasn't much room in the Ford now, and breathing was something of an issue, particularly in the back seat.

"Okay, so what are we doing?" Randy asked earnestly.

"We're just talking," Carl said.

"That's not quite true, Randy," the coach said. "Your friends want to know if I've had a hand in your music teacher's disappearance."

Randy shifted around like something was biting his bum. "No shit?"

"None at all," the coach said.

"So let's hear it, then," Ben said. "What do you know about what happened to Heather?"

"Happened? What *has* happened to Heather?"

"You said it yourself. She's disappeared."

"You seem to know more than that."

"This isn't about me."

"No?" the coach said. "You're the ones who've seen things going on in empty houses. You're driving around with your hockey coach and won't let him go, which is a crime in itself. I'd say it's definitely about you, Benji."

Benji. That was new too.

"We're just asking some questions," Ben said, less certain now.

"Okay. Here's an answer." He reached forward to tap Carl on the shoulder. "Pull over."

"Don't think so," Carl said.

"Give me a break! You hairless nut sacks think you're the fucking Hardy Boys or something?"

"No need to be insulting," Randy said.

"Insulting? *This* is insulting. Kidnapping is insulting. Being forced to waste an hour of my life with you pimply-faced cocksuckers is insulting."

"Just tell us where you were last Monday night."

"That, along with my whereabouts on any night for the last thirty-eight years, is none of your business."

"It's our business now," Ben said. "And it would have been Heather's too. But she can't speak for herself anymore, can she?"

The coach's brief show of anger slipped out of him with a sigh. Then he took a deep breath and inhaled something new. A taste that seemed to make him sick but that he swallowed anyway.

"I'm serious," he said. "You boys have to take me home now."

"You were with her that night, weren't you?"

"Stop the car, Carl."

"Tell us."

"Stop the car."

"Tell us the truth."

That's when the coach surprised us. Or surprised me, anyway, when he lifted his hand from his lap, curled the fingers into a white ball and drove it into my face.

A white flash of pain. The car swung hard, left to right and back again. Knees and elbows clashing as everyone seemed to be trying to trade seats all at once. A voice that may or may not have been my own shouting *Sonofabitch!* over and over.

Eventually, Randy folded one of the coach's arms behind his back and I got hold of the other. Once settled, he faced me. Not with apology or accusation. He looked like he wanted nothing more than to knock the teeth he'd loosened clean out of my head.

"You know something?" Ben said. "I don't think any of us are making practice tonight."

Outside the Ford's windows Grimshaw floated by, dull and frostbitten. The few pedestrians scuffing over the sidewalks' skin of ice with heads down against the wind.

If they had raised their eyes to watch our car rumble past, how many years would it take them to guess that the conversation among its passengers concerned one of them pounding a four-inch screw into the back of Heather Langham's skull? Had they looked, could they even have seen the coach among his youngest players, shaking his head in denial?

I remember seeing the streetlights come on, and wondering why they bothered.

Ben asked most of the questions. Trying to lead the coach through a narrative of what happened the night Miss Langham died. Where did they meet? Had she been subdued somehow? Was it always the plan to kill her in the Thurman house? Had there been a plan at all, or, given the makeshift weapon involved, was it a spontaneous attack? If so, what brought it on?

Randy was the only other one to add a query of his own. Always the same one, asked through barely withheld tears. *Why?* The look on his face a contorted version of the one he wore when an opposing team's goon elbowed him into the glass. *Why'd you do it?*

The coach answered none of them. He merely reminded us of how far out of our hands the situation was. The trouble we'd be in if we took this any further.

Carl turned onto Caledonia Street. And there it was. Although we'd been circling the blocks around it for the past half-hour, we had yet to pass it. Now we eased by the Thurman house, slow as Heather Langham once did as she walked up the hill to the nurses' residence. It was dark by then. The blue light of televisions filling living rooms with ice water. Etchings of smoke rising from chimneys.

All of these houses, the ones that sheltered microwaves announcing dinner with a beep, spousal debates, toddlers learning to use the potty while sitting in front of *The A-Team*—houses with life within them—looked *inside* at this hour. Everyone was home. There would be no going out again until morning, the February night left to seethe through the leafless boughs.

The Thurman house alone looked out. Looked at us.

The Ford slid around the next corner and started down the laneway that ran between the backyard fences between Caledonia and Church. Nothing to see by other than the headlights that, a few yards along, Carl extinguished. For a moment we drifted blind between the lopsided garages before stopping next to a wooden fence that leaned against a row of maples. On the other side, the dim line of the Thurman house's roof.

"What's going on here?" the coach asked.

Nobody answered. Maybe none of us knew.

After a time, Carl reached into his parka's inside pocket. This, along with the expectant, open-mouthed expression he wore, made me think he was about to pull out a Kleenex to capture a sneeze. But he didn't sneeze. And when his hand came out of his parka it held a gun.

His dad's. All of us, including the coach, knew this without asking. It was Carl's dad's revolver, just as it was his car, his apartment, his cartons of cigarettes left in the crisper in the fridge. The gun was part of the inheritance he left to his son after being chased out of town by debts, warrants for arrest, demons of his own making found at the bottom of President's Sherry bottles. Now Carl pointed his father's departing gift at the coach's chest.

"You know something? I'm tired of you bullshitting us," he said, opening his door and gesturing for Ben to do the same. "I don't want to hear any more 'You know what trouble you're in?' *You're* the one in trouble. And just so there won't be any confusion later on"— Carl nodded at Ben, who produced a handheld tape recorder from his jacket pocket—"we'll make sure we know just who's doing the talking."

Ben and Carl opened their doors at the same time. They sat there, looking back at us, oblivious to the subzero air that swirled into the car.

The only one I could look at was Ben. His head fixed upon his slender neck but its features alive with half-blinks and flared sniffs. It was impossible to tell if he'd known about Carl's gun or was just going with it, his formerly zoned-out self replaced by this twitchy, miniature thug in a Maple Leafs tuque his mother had knitted for him.

We waited for Ben to speak. And when he did, he used the coach's signature call before opening the dressing-room door. Words that, only days ago, ushered us out onto the ice to play a game.

"Shall we?"

RANDY HEARD THAT Tracey Flanagan had failed to come home from work the night before from the waitress who brought him his scrambled eggs in the coffee shop of the Queen's Hotel earlier this morning. The waitress, apparently, is a neighbour of Todd's, and was among those he called to ask if his daughter had been seen or heard on their street the night before. The police were already involved, she told Randy, treating the circumstances as suspicious on the grounds that Tracey was not one to stay out without letting her dad know her whereabouts. Volunteer search parties were being whipped together to spend the afternoon stomping through the Old Grove and sloshing around the edge of the Dale Marsh. Randy asked her why they chose those two places in particular. "Because they're just *bad*" was her answer.

"I forgot how small a town this is," I tell Randy, the two of us now slumped at the McAuliffe dining table.

"Small? It's like word got out through string tied between old soup cans. If this was Toronto, and your twenty-two-year-old didn't show up from a bar last night, they'd tell you to take a Xanax and get in line."

"I'd worry too, if I were Todd."

Randy nods. "I guess she's about all the family he's got."

"And every cop in town knows him and Tracey. They're just pulling out all the stops."

"She's probably already at home, wondering where everybody is, and they're all out in the woods with bloodhounds."

"They check with the boyfriend?"

"They're still looking for him."

"I bet the two of them are under a sleeping bag in a parked car somewhere."

"Maybe they should look out by the walnut trees in Harmony."

"That where you used to go too?"

"I was talking about you."

"Me and Sarah."

"Anybody else I might know?"

"How'd you know we'd go out there?"

"You *told* us," Randy says, shaking his head. "We told each other pretty much everything back then."

Randy looks down the length of the table as though expecting to see others seated around us.

"Think we should go see him?" I ask.

"See who?"

"Todd."

"Me and you popping by after half a lifetime to say sorry for your missing only child? I don't know, Trev. Let's just wait on that one."

Randy moves to stand, but then his eyes catch on the hands I've planted on the tabletop. The hands still, but the elbows vibrating like a pair of idling engines.

"Don't say it," Randy says.

"Say what?"

"What you're thinking."

"You're a mind reader as well as an actor now?"

"I don't need to read minds. Not about this. And not with you."

"So tell me."

"This missing girl. Heather. The house. How it feels the same all over again."

"For the record, you were the first to say it out loud, not me."

Randy draws his sleeve over his forehead as though to wipe away sweat, but his skin is dry, the cotton rasping.

"How's the executor duties going?" he asks, both of us happy to change the subject.

"I'm not sure actually."

"You need some help?"

"No. Thank you, though."

"It must be kind of strange. Going through Ben's things."

"He kept a diary."

"Yeah? You read it?"

"Enough to know he wasn't well."

"I think we knew that."

"He thought there was something in the house across the street. Something he believed was trying to get out, and *would* get out—"

"If it wasn't for him."

"That's right."

"You said it. He wasn't well." Randy's not looking at my elbows now, but squinting severely right at me.

"Or he was right," I say.

"About what?"

"That the Thurman place needed to have an eye kept on it."

"Well, let's see," Randy says, lifting his hands to count off the points he makes on his fingers. "One, nobody lives there, so there was nobody to keep an eye on. Two, Ben was an anti-social shut-in with delusional tendencies—and that was him in *grade eleven*. Three, even if there was something in there that was trying to escape, how would staring at the front door stop it from getting out? Four, Ben was talking about ghosts. And people with full decks don't believe in ghosts."

"You haven't used your thumb yet."

"Okay, then. Five, you're grieving, whether you think you're immune to that particular emotion or not. And grief can make you stupid."

"Aren't you grieving too?"

"In my way. God knows I raised my glass to his memory enough times last night."

We laugh at this. In part because we need to in order to move on to the next chance for normal to settle over us again. In part because Randy's mention of the word "ghost" feels like it invited one into the room.

"What about some dinner tonight?" Randy says, rising.

"Sounds good."

"I was thinking the Old London."

"Is it still there?"

"Was when I walked past it last night."

"Perfect."

"I was going to hit the coin laundry this afternoon. Want me to grab some stuff from your room and throw it in too?"

"I'll use the washer here if I need to. I'm staying here tonight anyway."

Randy turns around on the porch. "Here? Overnight?"

"Betty asked if I would. I think she needs the company."

"Where you going to sleep?"

"Ben's room."

"That's fucked. Got to say."

"I think it was your point number four, wasn't it?" I say, pushing the door closed. "People with full decks don't believe in ghosts."

The next couple of hours are spent back up in Ben's room, fitting his belongings into boxes and stuffing the clothes from his closet into bags for the Salvation Army ("Take whatever you and your friends might want," Betty McAuliffe had invited me). I put aside a pair of ties, though I did it just to please her.

They are activities that keep my fidgety hands occupied, but not my mind. Over and over I return to Tracey Flanagan. Odds are that she's fine, and that Randy was right: starting an official search after less than a day was nothing more than the over-reaction of small-town cops. Yet the news struck me as hard as it seemed to have struck Randy. Maybe it was the way she reminded us of Heather. Maybe it was Randy saying how, now that we'd let it see us, the Thurman house knew we were back.

And then there's the house itself.

By mid-afternoon the clouds had not quite lifted but thinned, so that, from time the time, the sun found a square to poke through. It would flash across the Thurman windows and reflect into Ben's room, beckoning me to turn and look. Each time I did I'd have to close my eyes against the light, and when I opened them again, the sun was gone, the glass dull. The effect was like a leering wink from a stranger, so swift and unexpected you couldn't be sure if it was a signal or just a twitch.

It happens again. The sun, the blink of light.

Except this time, as I'm returning to the pile of Ben's clothes at my feet, something changes. Not in what I can see in the house, but in my peripheral vision. Something in the room with me.

I spin around to face it. And it *is* a face. Mrs. McAuliffe's, her head popping up another foot where she's come halfway up the stairs.

"Phone for you," she says.

"I'll take it up here, if that's okay."

I start for the phone on Ben's bedside table, but Betty McAuliffe waves me over. Tugs on my pant leg until I bend down, my ear close to her lips.

"It's a *girl*," she whispers.

Once Mrs. McAuliffe has started back down I pick up. Wait to hear the click of the downstairs receiver.

"Trevor?"

It's Sarah. Sounding nervous, her voice slightly higher than yesterday. The way my own voice probably sounds.

"Hey there."

"I tried you at the Queen's," she says. "When you weren't there, I figured I'd see if you were at Ben's."

"What was your next guess?"

"A bar somewhere. Maybe the back row of the Vogue. The entertainment options haven't changed much around here."

"I can tell you that folding up Ben's underwear isn't too entertaining either."

"Want some company?"

"Sorry?"

"I've got the afternoon off. Just wondered if you thought it might be easier with an extra pair of hands."

She wants to see you. A distinctly external voice, not the boy's. Mine. *She's been thinking of you as much as you've been thinking of her.*

And then a different voice.

Ask her over, the boy says. *Take her across the street. We can all have a good time.*

"I'm fine. But thanks for offering," I say.

"It was a dumb idea."

"No. I'd like to see you, Sarah."

"Really?"

"What about dinner. Tomorrow?" There's a pause, and the foolishness of what I've done hits me square. "Listen to me. It's like I'm sixteen all over again, calling you up for the first time."

"I called you."

"Which I appreciate. And I'm sorry if I've made this awkward. You're probably married or have a boyfriend. I didn't even ask—"

"What time?"

"Time?"

"When do you want to come over?"

"You tell me."

"There's a Guardians game tomorrow night. You could come by here first."

"Sounds wonderful," I say, because it does.

The Old London Steakhouse used to be—and likely still is—Grimshaw's one and only so-called fine dining restaurant. We would come here, my parents, brother and I, for special birthday dinners, squeezing ourselves into itchy dress shirts and affixing clip-on neckties for the occasion. When I find the place now and push open its door, I see that nothing has changed. Not even the lightbulbs, apparently: the place is impossibly underlit, not to create a mood (though this may have been the intention when it opened forty or so years ago), but to hide whatever crunches underfoot on the carpet.

I have to wait something close to a full minute for my eyes to adjust to the near darkness. There is nobody to welcome me, so I must endure the muzak version of "The Pina Colada Song" alone.

"You'll be joining your friend?" a voice eventually asks, the low growl of a chain-smoker. And then the outline of a man in a shabby tux, backlit by a fake gaslamp.

"I guess he's already here?"

The maître d' has stepped close enough for me to see the grey cheeks in need of a shave, the bow tie pointing nearly straight up, like a propeller snagged on the bristle of his chin.

"Your friend," he says with a sadness that seems connected to the ancient past, the suffering of ancestors in a lost war, "he is having a cocktail. A Manhattan."

"I'm not one to rock the boat."

He leads me into the dining room—or dining rooms, as the space is divided into a warren of nooks and private booths separated by hanging fishnets and "log cabin" walls with peekaboo windows. Other bits of maritime and frontier kitsch are scattered throughout, but aside from the framed print of the Houses of Parliament glowering over a moonlit Thames set above the stone fireplace, there is nothing "Old" or "London" about it. Not that this stops Randy from speaking in a particularly bad cockney accent through the first drink of the evening.

"'Ello, gov!" he calls out, and there he is, waving me over to an enormous round table. "Set yourself down and warm your cockles!"

"What's a cockle, anyway? I've always wondered."

"I don't know," Randy answers thoughtfully, pushing his empty glass to the table's edge. "But mine are certainly warmer now than they were five minutes ago."

The maître d' returns with our drinks in the time it takes me to pull out one of the throne-like chairs and sink into its over-stuffed seat. Everything is slowed in this dark—every search for the men's room, every reach for water goblet or butter dish. It is like being able to breathe underwater.

The Manhattans and joking at the expense of the escargot appetizers pass pleasantly enough, a testimony to how much, despite everything, we enjoy being together, particularly given that the initial conversation concerns updates on Tracey Flanagan's disappearance. No sign of the girl. Todd refusing to leave the house in case the phone rings or she comes home expecting him to be there. The boyfriend claiming he didn't see her after work last night, now taken in for questioning and described by police, in their first press conference, as a "person of interest." And to reconstruct a narrative of her evening, authorities are asking all patrons of Jake's last night to come forward to provide their accounts of the bar's comings and goings.

"I guess we should go down there tomorrow," I say.

"I've already spoken to them," Randy answers. "They're expecting us at eleven."

"It *does* kind of remind you of Heather. Doesn't it?"

"So what if it does? People go missing sometimes. Even in small towns," Randy reasons. "If it's two missing persons over thirty years, Grimshaw is probably below the per capita national average."

"Not just two missing persons. Two women, early twenties, look kind of similar. Fits a profile."

"Listen to you. 'Fits a profile.' You auditioning for some crime show?" He reaches for his wineglass. "Actually, *I* auditioned for a crime show a few weeks ago."

"You get the part?"

"Are you trying to hurt my feelings?"

When the maître d', who took our order, is also the one to pour the first bottle of "Ontario Bordeaux," it becomes clear that he is the only front-of-house staff on tonight—and that he is the only one needed, seeing as we're the only customers. This fact, combined with the Old London's velvety gloom, gives us the sense of cozy seclusion. Anything might be said here and it will never pass beyond these stuccoed walls. It seems that Randy shares this impression, because soon he is turning the talk toward topics we would be better off avoiding, yet here, for the moment, feel are merely intriguing, the sort of thing you light upon in reading the back pages of the paper and harmlessly ponder over the morning coffee, protected by the knowledge that it has happened to someone else, not you.

"Don't you think it's weird?"

"This is Grimshaw, Randy," I answer, employing my full concentration to guide a chunk of rib-eye past my lips. "It's *all* weird. And if you're talking about Tracey Flanagan and how—"

"I'm not talking about her. And I'm not talking about Grimshaw. I'm talking about how we've been here for almost two days now and we haven't even mentioned it."

"You're going to need to be—"

"The coach. The coach. The *coach*!"

I stop chewing. "There's good reason we haven't brought that up."

"But it's just the two of us, in the same place at the same time, for the first time in forever. Who knows when we'll be together again like this?"

"I get it." I swallow. "Seeing as we're sitting here enjoying ourselves, we might as well bust out all the bad memories for the hell of it?"

"I'm not sure I deserve the sarcasm."

"I'm just trying to understand you, Randy."

"Understand me? Okay, here's a start: I'm scared. Haven't slept a good night's sleep since before I could shave. And it's only going to get worse now that I've seen that house again and know it's still there."

"Do you want to talk about it? I mean, do you feel you need to?"

"*Want* to? No. *Need* to? Maybe. It's a lot to carry around all the time, all on your own, don't you think?"

"I've done my best to pretend it's not even there."

"And how has that worked for you?"

"Couldn't say. It's the only way I've ever known how to be."

"But that's not true," Randy says, lowering his fork to the table with an unexpected thud. "Once upon a time, you were yourself. We all were. But since then, we're something else. We got so good at holding on to what we knew that even coming back here—even what Ben did to himself—won't let us bring it up."

Randy looks around to make sure no one is listening, though in the Old London's murk there could be a guy six feet away holding a boom mike over our table and we wouldn't be able to spot him.

"What we did was a crime," I say.

"You're the one blabbing about the past into a Dictaphone. So why are you talking to a machine about it and not me?"

"That's different."

"Really? Haven't you ever wondered if we all would've been in better shape if we'd just shared what we were going through instead of trying to bury it?"

"I'm not sure sharing something that could send us to prison is great therapy. I'm wondering if you forgot that part."

"I haven't forgotten."

"Good. Let's not start forgetting it now. We're supposed to give a statement to the police tomorrow about being in the bar last night. Once that's done, and so long as Betty doesn't need more help in clearing up Ben's things, I plan to get the hell out of here."

"Isn't that tidy?"

"I happen to *like* tidy."

We busy ourselves with our steaks. Hoping for our tempers to even, for the bad wine to bring back its initial good feelings. We just chew and swallow. Or in my case, chew and spit a mouthful out into my napkin. It turns Randy's attention my way. And I am about to explain that with the Parkinson's, grilled meat can sometimes be a challenge to choke down. But instead I say, "I saw something."

Randy continues to look at me precisely as he had a moment ago, as though I have not said anything at all.

"Back then," I go on. "And then, just yesterday, I thought I saw it again. When I was looking at the house from Ben's window."

"What was it?"

"Me. I thought it was only a reflection in a mirror the first time. And then, I guessed it was only you, or Carl, or Ben, because he was a boy about our age, looked the way we looked. Except it *wasn't* one of us."

Randy blinks repeatedly over the vast distance of the tabletop.

"I saw him too," he says.

"So it wasn't just Carl and me."

"Carl?"

"After we found Heather. He told me he'd seen someone. Or was it that he'd only heard someone? Anyway, he was pretty messed up about it."

"Join the club."

"I mean he was even worse than I was."

"Worse?"

"He held my hand."

"You and Carl *held hands*?" Randy asks, as though this fact is more shocking than both of us confessing to having seen the living dead. "I'd pay a good chunk of change to have been around to see that."

"You had more money then."

"True. Maybe I should give up this acting thing and go back to dealing weed and mowing lawns."

We both want to go back to half an hour ago. I can see it in Randy's face just as he can see it in mine. But now that we've said what we've said, the implications are rushing to catch up, and they're too numerous, too wrigglingly alive to hold on to.

"What happened in there?" I find myself saying. "What *happened* to us?"

"Trev. C'mon," Randy says, reaching his hand toward me, but the table is too wide.

"Was there something wrong with that place? Or something wrong with us?"

A cleared throat.

The two of us look up to see the maître d' standing there, hands clasped over his belt buckle. A vacant smile of blue bone.

"Something sweet, gentlemen?"

We must have thought it would be easy.

Force a man into the cellar of an abandoned house, accuse him of murdering a female colleague in the very same location, then stick a tape recorder in his face and expect him to confess. *It seemed like a good idea at the time.* Except I'm not sure even this was true.

I know now that you can do terrible things without an idea. You can do them without feeling it's really you doing them.

Looking back, I'm almost convinced it was someone else occupying my skin in the cellar that night. Someone else whispering in my head, encouraging, taunting. Telling me that it was okay, that none of this counted anyway.

You've come this far already, the boy said but didn't say. *You don't want to miss all the fun, do you?*

For the first hour or so, the coach didn't answer any of our questions. He just repeated a question of his own.

"How do you think this is going to end?"

We had no reply to this, only more questions. Like why he brought Miss Langham here. How she ended up dead.

"Maybe it was some kind of accident," Randy suggested.

"You're some kind of accident."

"I'm trying to help."

"Help? I need Handy Randy's help?" He turned to Carl. "Please. Shoot me now."

"We're looking for an explanation, that's all."

"Why do you think I owe you that? I mean, *look* at yourselves."

And we did. For the first time since we'd filed down the cellar stairs and made the coach stand with his back to the wall, we let our gaze move off him and to each other. We looked at least five years younger than we pictured ourselves. Carl especially. The biggest one of us reduced to a child who needed both hands to aim the revolver an inch higher than the toes of his boots.

"How do you think this is going to end?" the coach asked again.

I think now that if Ben hadn't taken a step away at that point, if he hadn't made us focus on his scuffling movement instead of lingering on the shrunken, stilled outlines of ourselves in the dark, we might still have avoided the worst yet to come. Argued a defence based on the stupidity of teenage boys (at least we hadn't killed ourselves by driving drunk into a tree, the more common end for the worst sort of Perth County misadventure). It was the conclusion of our grim, exhilarating ride. And now, facing the coach's question, we found we had run out of ways to fill the next moment, and this gap had let the awakening light of absurdity in.

But Ben plugged the hole up again by moving. By rustling through some orange crates piled up around the worktable and returning to stand within range of Carl's flashlight beam. A length of frayed extension cord in his hand.

"We can use this to tie him up," he said.

We pulled the parka hood over the coach's head and swaddled him with rank blankets discovered in the main hall closet. (Carl wondered if we should gag him as well, but the coach told us nobody could hear him down there no matter how loudly he screamed. "And *how* are you so sure of that?" Ben asked.) Then we made our way up to the kitchen.

After closing the cellar door we felt the house seal shut, the air silty and still. For a time we waited there, as though there was something more to be done but we'd forgotten what it was. Standing on individual squares of the checkered linoleum like chess pieces.

"We can't leave him down there forever," Randy said.

"It's up to him." Ben started toward the back door and pushed it open an inch. "We'll take turns visiting him tomorrow. I'll come first, and we can decide on a rotation at school. When he makes a statement we can use, he can go."

"What if he doesn't?"

"He has to," Ben said, and started out.

Randy followed. I wanted nothing more than to be with them. Outside, breathing the cold-hardened air, sure of where I was. But I stayed. Not out of hesitation over leaving the coach behind. I stayed because the house wanted me to. It *liked* our being here, was warmed by the mischief being performed within it. I could feel the plaster ceilings and panelled walls closing toward me in a suffocating embrace, the too-long hug of a creepy uncle at the end of Thanksgiving dinner.

"Wait."

I spun around, expecting to see the unimaginable behind me. The boy.

"Fuck, man," I gasped. "We gotta go."

"*Wait*," Carl said.

He focused on me. A combined expression of fear and insane amusement, as though he was as likely to run crying into the night as stick his dad's gun into my mouth just to watch how my brains would slide down the wall.

"Can't you hear it?" he said, stepping closer.

"Hear what?"

"Don't *lie*."

And then he did raise the gun.

"Sure. I can hear it too."

"What *is* it?"

I surprised myself by answering instantly. Honestly.

"A boy."

"What's he look like?"

"Like you. Like any of us."

"It would *like* you to think that."

"You've seen it?"

Carl appeared to search his memory. "Have you?"

"Yes."

"Where?"

"Upstairs. The night we found Heather. But it was only me. Me, in the mirror on the bathroom door."

"It *wasn't* you," Carl said, his face looming closer. "And it's *not* like us."

"Maybe we should—"

"It's *not*!"

Carl backed away. He looked like he had just lost a long and exhausting argument with himself.

I took his hand. A weird thing to do. The kind of thing Carl in particular would have resisted, taken as an affront to his unshakeable Carlness. But once we were connected, he held my hand as much as I held his.

We let go only once the night opened wide around us outside. Thankful that the others had already headed home.

It should go without saying that I never mentioned the hand-holding part to anyone ever again. Until today.

[10]

By the time Randy and I walk to Ben's house from the Old London it's later than I'd thought, and my exhaustion from the evening's revelations, as well as the wine, prevents me from asking myself the one question that should have been asked before Randy disappeared around the corner of Caledonia and Church, leaving me standing on the McAuliffes' front porch, key in hand: *Where am I going to sleep?*

All day I'd meant to tell Mrs. McAuliffe that, while I appreciated her hospitality, I couldn't accept her invitation to stay overnight in her son's room. Her *dead* son's room. But whether I was distracted by my tasks as executor or couldn't bring myself to disappoint the poor woman, I hadn't gotten around to it. Now it would be plainly wrong to scuff after Randy and get my old room back at the Queen's. Betty would be expecting me for breakfast in the morning, had likely gone out earlier to buy the makings for her specialties—raisin bread French toast and fruit salad. Indeed, she may well still be awake in her darkened room, awaiting the sound of my steps up the stairs.

I open the door and swiftly close it again once I'm in. A silent oath made with myself: if I am actually going to spend the night in this place, I cannot afford even the briefest glimpse of the house across the street. In fact, it might be a better idea to not go upstairs at all, and simply crumple onto the sofa in the living room. I'm on my way toward it, checking the chairs for a blanket, when I'm stopped by a sound that comes from the kitchen.

A scratch, or the rustle of plastic. The sort of thing that could be confused with a breath from one's own chest.

From the hallway, I can see part of the kitchen. Nobody stands there, knife in hand, as I half expect. There is nothing but the play of moonlight over the cupboards, moving around the tree branches in the September photo on the calendar pinned to the wall.

I'm partway to the kitchen entrance when a chunk of shadow breaks away and tiptoes over the linoleum. A large mouse—or small rat—that, upon spotting me, races behind the fridge, its tail audibly scratching across an edge of drywall.

For a second, the silence suggests we're both working through the same thought.

What the hell was that?

The sheets in Ben's bed have been freshly washed and made even since I sat on them earlier in the day. Betty wants me to feel welcome. And I do. Or at least, I'm grateful for being able to pull the covers up to my chin so that the boy-smells of Ben's room are partially masked by fabric softener.

Sleep, I have found, is like a woman you'd like to speak to across a crowded room: the harder you wish it to come to you, the more often it turns away. So it is that I am left awake and wishing, staring up at something awful (the beam that Ben looped his rope over) in order to avoid looking at something even more awful (the Thurman house, whose roof would be clearly visible if I turned my head on the pillow). Did Ben fight this same fight himself these past years? Was he forced to consider every knot and crack in the wood that would eventually hold him thrashing in mid-air?

It is these questions that lead me into sleep. Into a dream that carries me down the stairs and across Caledonia Street to lie on the cold ground beneath the hedgerow the runs along the Thurman property line. Staring up at the side windows of the house, the glass a blackboard with *fuckt* finger-drawn in its dust.

It starts with a woman.

Standing up from where she had been lying on the living-room floor out of sight below the sill. A woman who places her palms against the glass. And with this touch, I can see she is naked, and young, and not alone.

Another figure calmly approaches from behind her. Male, his identity concealed by the dark, though his form visible enough for me to see that he is naked as well. He stands there, appreciating the full display of her body. For a moment, I feel sure he is about to eat her.

His hands cup her breasts as he enters her. With a jolt, her own hands flail against the window. Fingernail screeches.

They're real.

But they're not. This is a dream. And no matter how convincing, there remains a thread that tethers their performance to the imagination. It's this understanding that allows them to continue without my trying to get in the way, or desperately swimming up toward consciousness. It is a dream, and therefore harmless.

Yet the dark figure who works away at the long-haired woman seems more than capable of harm. Harm is all there is to him. It looks like sex, this thing he's doing, but it's not. There is no explicit violence, no shouted threats—it may well be mutually voluntary what the two of them do. But for him, it has nothing to do with wanting her, or even with the pleasure of her body. He wishes only to disgrace.

I'm expecting the male figure to reveal himself to me first, but instead it's the woman. Lifting her chin and throwing her hair aside.

Not Tina Uxbridge's face, or Heather Langham's. It's Tracey Flanagan's.

Her eyes emptied of the humour they conveyed in life. But otherwise unquestionably her. Mouth open in a soundless moan. Her breasts capped by nipples turned purple in the way of freezer-burned meat.

For some reason I assume it is the coach standing behind her. It is more than an assumption—the anticipation of him showing himself to me, the *ta-dah!* moment that is the waking trigger to every nightmare, is so certain I am already recalling his face from memory, so that when he appears, I won't be wholly surprised. It *will* be the coach. Released from the cellar to carry out this perversity, this pairing of the apparently living with the probably dead.

But I am wrong in this too.

I am already scrabbling out from under the branches when the boy leans to the side to reveal his face over Tracey Flanagan's shoulder. Enflamed, gloating. He is more interested in me than whatever mark he means to leave on Tracey.

Hey there, old man. It's been a while.

The boy's lips don't move, but I can hear him nonetheless.

You want a piece of this? Come inside.

It's his voice that prompts me to move. To get up and run away. But I'm not sixteen, as I thought I was. This isn't the past but the present, and I am a man with a degenerative disease, fighting to get to my feet. Three times I try, and each time I am stricken with a seizure that brings me down. All I manage to do is roll closer to the window, so that Tracey and the boy loom over me.

Look at you, the boy says as I claw at the house's brick, his voice free of sympathy, of any feeling at all. *You're falling apart, brother. Ever think of just cashing out? Keep little Ben company?*

My hand manages to grip a dead vine that has webbed itself up the wall. It allows me to get to my knees. Then, with a lunge, to my feet. Instead of waiting to see if I can maintain my balance, I try to run to the street, but the motion only crumples me onto the ground once more. Eyes fixed on the boy's.

Poor Trev. I'm not sure you could manage this if I pulled your fly down for you and pointed you in the right direction.

The boy laughs. Then he thrusts against Tracey a final time before holding himself inside her, his knuckles gripped white to her hips, his shoulders shuddering with the spite of his release.

I was right about breakfast.

By the time I make it downstairs, Mrs. McAuliffe is in the kitchen, bathrobed and slippered, eggy bread in the pan and a bowl of fruit on the table. At the sound of me entering (my fingernails dig into the doorframe for balance), the old woman lights up.

"Sleep well?" she asks, returning her attention to the stove to flip the slices.

"It's a good mattress."

"Posturepedic. Ben had a bad back."

"I didn't know."

"It was all the sitting."

"That'll do it."

"I'm glad to see it's given somebody a good night's rest."

As I stagger to the kitchen table I wonder how I could possibly be mistaken for someone who's had a good night's rest. And then it comes to me that this is only Betty McAuliffe's wish: that I be comfortable and enjoy her cooking, that I use the things her son will never use again, that I stay a little longer. She sees me as well rested and affliction-free because her life with Ben had trained her in the art of seeing the sunny side, of pushing on as though their lives were as sane as their neighbours'. We have this in common, Betty and I. We've both had to work at our normal acts.

I'm bending my chin close to the bowl to deliver a wavering spoon of mango to my mouth when there's a knock at the door. As Betty goes to answer, I'm sure it's the police. They've finally come for me. The charges may be related to the present or the past. They've come, and I am ready to go.

But it's not the police. It's Randy, now taking the seat across from mine and accepting Mrs. McAuliffe's offer of a coffee and shortbread.

"You look terrible," he says once Betty has excused herself to get dressed.

"Should have called before dropping by. I would have made a point of putting my face on."

"Don't bother. I can see your inner beauty."

"Do lines like that actually work on your dates?"

"Acting has taught me this much, Trev: it's not the line—it's how you sell it."

Randy crunches into his shortbread. Crumbs cascading down onto the doily Mrs. McAuliffe had placed before him.

"What are you doing here?" I ask.

"I'm your escort."

"To the police station? I think I know where it is, thanks."

"I'd like to stop somewhere else along the way. You've got to see something."

"What?"

"A website. There's an internet café on Downie Street. They've got terminals and little privacy walls between them so you—"

"What website?"

"You know, one of those places where boyfriends submit photos of their girlfriends."

"Jesus Christ, Randy. You're hauling me downtown so I can be your porn pal?"

"First of all, it's not *really* porn," Randy qualifies, popping the rest of the shortbread into his mouth. "And second, it's Tracey Flanagan."

If my memory's right, Insomnia Internet used to be Klaupper's Deli, the latter selling Polish sausages and German chocolates to the Grimshaw immigrants who couldn't shake their taste for home. Now there are racks of hyperviolent games where the meat counter used to be, and rows of computers where I recall walking the aisles with my mother, searching for the imported butterscotch candies Klaupper's sometimes carried. When Randy and I enter, I imagine there is still a trace of fried schnitzel and Toblerone—and unexpectedly, my mother's Sunday-only spritz of Chanel No. 5—in the air. But then, on the next sniff, it is replaced by the fungoid aroma of teenage boys.

"Back here," Randy directs me, waving me to a terminal he's already secured in the rear corner.

I'm worried at first we'll be observed by the kids who machete and Uzi their way through the carnage on their screens. But as I pass, not one of them turns to look at the shaky old guy who makes his way to the back. And though some of them are apparently engaged in some communal game involving others in the room, they don't acknowledge their fellow players in any way, aside from an occasional cry of "Backup! Need backup!" and "*Why* won't you *die*?"

"Have a seat," Randy says, pulling over a wheeled chair from the next cubicle. I watch as he takes his wallet out and, from within it, a slip of paper with a web address written on it.

"Who told you about this, anyway?" I ask.

"I went by the Molly Bloom for a nightcap on the way back to the hotel last night. Had one with Vince Sproule. Who tells me about this."

"This?"

"Mygirl.com. Where Tracey has her own page."

"How does Vince know about it?"

"The boyfriend, Gary Pullinger, let the cat out of the bag. Told one of his buddies that he uploaded some snaps, and then the friend told some other friends and . . . well, it's a small town."

"Are the police aware of this?"

"It's part of why they're still grilling Gary so hard. They're trying to see if these pictures are part of a motive somehow."

"Motive for what?"

Randy types in the address and clicks Enter. Only then does he turn to look at me. "She's *missing*, Trev. Odds are she's not coming back. And you always start with the boyfriend. Or the dad."

"They think Todd has something to do with this?"

"I don't think he's at the top of the list. The Pullinger kid holds that spot. But you never know. Do you?"

I'm searching for an answer to this when suddenly Tracey is there on the screen.

There are no toys, props, costumes. No leather or rubber or lace. Just a young woman without any clothes on. Standing in front of a cluttered bookcase or sitting on the edge of an unmade bed in a basement bedroom, a towel on the floor around her feet darkly wet from a recent shower. Her hair clinging to her shoulders, framing her breasts. Water dripping off the ends and leaving a map of streaks over her belly, fading sideroads all converging on the dark curls between her legs.

She is smiling in most of the shots. The same expression of welcome she offered us when we first wandered into Jake's Pool 'n' Sports. In a couple of pictures she attempts a pouty look of wanton invitation, but it is play-acting that fails to convince either the photographer or her, judging from the laughter that follows.

In all of the photos, even the silliest ones, she is beautiful. Beautiful in her nakedness, but equally for the fun she is having, the goofing around that has as much to do with pretending at being a seductress as with the provocation of real desire. She is a young woman showing herself not to the camera's vacant lens but to the man behind it.

"Close it," I say.

"God. You've got to admit. She's *something*, isn't she?"

"Randy—"

"You wouldn't guess, under that dumb referee outfit they make them—"

"Turn it off."

Randy looks over his shoulder at me. "What's your problem? We're not peeping through her keyhole or anything. The whole world can find this if they want."

"I'm not talking to the whole world."

He presses his lips together in a combined expression of puzzlement and pain, as though he'd let his hand linger over an open flame but was unable to figure out how to pull it away.

"She's a kid," I say.

"Okay."

"She's our friend's kid."

"*Okay.*"

Randy closes his eyes. Blindly, he slides the mouse over the pad. Clicks it—and Tracey disappears.

"Doesn't it rattle you at all?" I ask, leaning in close enough to whisper. "The way the whole Heather and Tracey things overlap?"

"Sure. I'd say it rattles me a fair bit."

"It's like someone is copycatting or something."

"That might be taking it a little far."

"Maybe. But on the same day we roll into town?" I shake my head. Part Parkinson's, part avoidance of this line of thought. "We'll be gone soon."

"I'll stay as long as you have to."

"I'm fine, really."

"Oh yeah. You're just dandy."

"Nothing a decent night's sleep won't fix."

"And you're going to get that in Ben's bed?"

"Don't worry about me."

"What, me worry?" Randy smiles, looking very much like Alfred E. Neuman. "All the same, I think I'll stick around so we can head out on the same train. How's that?"

"We Guardians stick together."

"Goddamn right." He pinches my cheek. Hard. "You are goddamn right there, brother."

From Insomnia, we make our way to the Grimshaw Community Services building, otherwise known as the cop shop. We present ourselves to the receptionist as patrons of Jake's Pool 'n' Sports a couple of nights ago, here to answer questions.

"Regarding Tracey Flanagan," Randy says when the woman doesn't seem to register either us or what we've just said.

"I *know* what it's *regarding*," she replies. "Have a seat."

When two officers finally emerge, it's a Laurel and Hardy pair, a slim fellow with jug ears and a short waddler heaving a basketball around inside his shirt. The big one introduces himself to Randy and takes him down the hall to an interview room, leaving the tall one standing over me, nodding as though something in my appearance has just settled a wager and he'd won.

"Trevor," he says. And then, when this fails to remove the puzzled expression from my face, he taps the name tag pinned to his shirt. "It's Barry Tate."

"Barry. I think I remember."

"I was a year behind you. We even had a couple of classes together."

"Hairy Barry," I say, and then he's all there. The only kid in school with a handlebar moustache that, unbelievably, actually suited him. "You played hockey too, right?"

"I took your number the season after . . . after you stopped playing."

"Did it bring you luck?"

"Eighteen goals."

"Not bad."

"Some goon broke my wrist in a game against Kitchener the next year, and that was it for me."

"Now you're one o´ Grimshaw's finest."

"Pension, dental, paid holidays. And you get to drive a car with lights on the roof."

Barry starts down the same hallway, but I have a little trouble lifting myself out of my chair. It brings him back to grip my elbow and heave me up. "You okay?"

"Just a little stiff in the mornings."

He gives me a look that says he's not buying that for a second, but hey, a man's body is his own business. I'm expecting him to make a joke instead, something to brush away the awkwardness, but he just stands there with his hand on my arm.

"I'm sorry about Ben," he says.

"Me too."

"I used to see him up there in that window of his. Thought about calling on him, but never did."

"I'm not sure he would have come to the door."

"Even so. I feel lousy about it."

Barry guides me down to an interview room next to the one I can hear Randy giving his statement in (". . . delivery guy. Just a boyfriend giving his girl a kiss. Didn't see much more to it than that . . ."). Next door, we take our places on opposite sides of a metal table, Barry slapping a notepad onto its scratched surface.

"Okay, then," he sighs. "Tell me about your night at Jake's."

It takes only a minute. Me and Randy having drinks after Ben's funeral. Todd Flanagan and Vince Sproule there watching the game. And Tracey bringing us pitchers and whiskeys. Other than the pizza-delivery guy, who dropped by to say hello to the girl, nothing to report. And judging by the way Barry Tate flips the notepad closed when I'm finished, he didn't expect there would be.

"That's great, Trevor. We appreciate you stopping by."

He rises, extends a hand to be shaken, but I don't move.

"So unless you have any questions of your own . . ." Barry says, now pulling his hand away and using it to open the door.

"It's not really a question so much as a suggestion."

"Oh?"

"Maybe you guys should check out the Thurman house."

He looks like he might laugh, as if he's not sure if I'm being serious. "Why would we want to do that?"

"It's just a thought."

"Have you seen or heard something that makes you have such a thought?"

"Not really. I just thought I spotted some movement in one of the windows last night."

"You happened to be walking by?"

"I'm staying with Ben's mother for a couple of days. I'm the executor of his estate. She's a little lonely, so I'm staying in his room."

"Which has a view of the Thurmans'."

"That's right."

"Where you saw . . . ?"

"A flash. Something passing behind the glass."

"Male? Female?"

"I don't know if it was even a person."

"Well, I have to tell you, that's not going to be enough for a search warrant."

"You think you need one of those? Even if you got one, who would you serve it on? The place has been empty more or less since you and I were shooting spitballs in Mrs. Grover's French class."

Barry Tate crosses his arms over his chest. Considers me. Perhaps wondering whether the years have left old Trev as bonkers as Ben McAuliffe was.

"Hell of a business," he says finally. "What they pulled out of that place back when we were kids."

This is a surprise. It shouldn't be, but it is. Even though all of Grimshaw remembers the bad news of the winter of 1984, it feels as though it's private knowledge, something shared by me, Randy and Carl alone.

"No doubt about it."

"You think that's got something to do with you wanting us to take a look in there?"

"How do you mean?"

"The mind, the way it works sometimes. It can get rolling along certain tracks and not want to stop," Barry says, touching his now neatly trimmed moustache as though it was helping him find words. "What happened to Ben, and now you're staying in his house and everything. Could be that you're just a little spooked."

"I'm spooked silly, to tell you the truth. For me, this whole town is crawling with ghosts. I'm *forty years old*, for Chrissakes."

"I hear *that*."

Barry coughs, though between men, it is a sound to be understood as a kind of muted laugh.

"Okay. I'll try to clear some time in the afternoon," Barry says, pulls the door open a foot more.

"Thank you."

I get to my feet. It takes longer than I'd like.

"My dad had the Parkinson's too," Barry says.

"No kidding?"

"Sorry to mention it. It's just—"

"It's getting hard not to notice, I know. How's your dad doing?"

"He died four years ago."

I nod. We both do. Then I make my way down the hall to where Randy waits for me by the exit.

Once we're outside he says, "That was Hairy Barry Tate, wasn't it?"

"Certainly was."

"What were you two talking about in there?"

"Hockey. He played for the Guardians too. A Kitchener guy broke his wrist."

Randy shakes his fist skyward, raging at heaven in his not bad Charlton Heston voice. "*Damn* those Kitchener guys. Damn them to *hell!*"

Randy walks me back to Ben's, offers to hang around as I "alphabetize his *Archie and Jughead*s or whatever you're doing up there." I tell him there's little point in both of us being bored senseless.

"Any plans for tonight?" he asks. "Sounds like you're pretty close to wrapping up. Could be our last evening in town to check our the culinary offerings."

"I'm grabbing something with Sarah, actually."

Randy bugs his eyes out. "Are we talking date?"

"She mentioned we might go to the Guardians game."

"That's as close to 'Come up and see my etchings' as you get around here."

"She's just being nice."

"I could go for some of that kind of nice."

Up in Ben's room, I tape up some of the boxes I've been tossing stuff into, marking them "Books + Mags" and "Hockey" and "Misc." I'm not sure if there's much point to even this basic sorting—what is Betty going to do with it once I'm gone, other than let it rot in the basement or drop it off at the Salvation Army to be piled into their Pay What You Can bin?—but it gives me the idea that I'm helping, bringing some kind of expertise to the job. A job I'm nearly done now. The closet empty, the clothes bagged, the room emptied of knick-knacks and clutter. Randy was right: there's no reason we can't be on the train out of here tomorrow.

I pick Ben's diary off the bed. I've already decided this will be the only keepsake I will take with me. Not because I feel any special warmth from the thing—the Ben who authored it wasn't the Ben I knew—but because it can't be left behind.

I sit in his chair by the window and I've just opened it up when a Grimshaw Police cruiser rounds Church Street and eases to a stop. My first instinct is to hide. I slide off Ben's chair to kneel on the floor, nose pressed to the sill so that I'm able to peer down at the street.

Barry Tate and his roly-poly partner step out of the car and stand on the sidewalk. For a time they stare up at the Thurman house with their hands on their hips, speaking to each other in words I can't make out, though their tone seems doubtful, as if wondering aloud if they have come to the right address.

Barry makes his way to the front door first, tries the handle and, finding it locked, starts around toward the rear, his partner following. After five minutes, they have yet to reappear.

I slip down and let my back rest against the wall. Open Ben's diary again. For another dozen pages there is his continued notation of wasted hours and days. Over time, it becomes so repetitious I play the game of scanning for the flavours of soups he heats for his lunches. A prisoner's menu of split peas, minestrones and chicken noodles.

Among the banal details, there are occasional episodes of Ben making sure that none entered the house. Shouting down at kids making bets over who had the guts to open the front door and place both feet over the threshold. Threatening to phone their parents, pretending he knew their names. Another entry told of a "half-drunk girl" being led by her boyfriend around the side of the house at night. Ben rushed downstairs, ran across the street to the back door in time to haul the girl out of the kitchen, telling her she didn't know how bad a place it was, how much danger she was in just being there. She ran away crying, whereupon the boyfriend suckerpunched Ben in the mouth.

Sometimes, when older high-schoolers had slipped inside, Ben called the cops. The diary would note how many trespassers were hustled out by the officers, who seemed to arrive later and later with each report Ben called in; the police would have let the Thurman house go unmonitored were it not for the McAuliffe head case who was conducting a permanent stakeout on it. Not that Ben cared what they thought. His duty was to keep the empty house empty.

Then there's a longer entry. June 22, 2002. The date underlined in red ink.

Something today.

Just after noon the door handle turned. I have seen it rattle before. But this time it <u>turned</u>: a slow circle, like the person doing the turning was figuring out how it worked. Or didn't want to be seen doing it.

Then the door swung open. It was Heather.

> *Blinded by the daylight, terrified. Filthy. No clothes.*
>
> *Then the door slammed shut again. <u>Slammed</u>. If anyone had been listening—anyone other than me—they would have heard the wood cracking the frame. The click of the lock . . .*

Voices from the street pull me from the page. It's Barry Tate and his partner, the former finishing up an anecdote that brings a chortle from the latter's chest. Before they reach the cruiser Barry looks up to the window. He doesn't seem surprised to see me here, my chin resting on the sill. In fact he waves. And I wave back.

"Nothing," he says, or at least shapes his mouth around the word without speaking it. Then he shrugs.

I watch the two of them take their time getting into the car, enjoying being out of the office. Even once the engine's started they linger, taking notes. Then, having run out of excuses to let the clock run on, Barry shifts into drive, rolls up Caledonia and out of sight.

I'm watching the front door by coincidence. Or I'm watching it because I was directed to, just as Ben was on the twenty-second of June, 2002. Either way, within a heartbeat of Barry Tate's cruiser rolling away, the doorknob turns.

The motion is tentative. And there is part of me even in this moment that recognizes that this is merely an echo of Ben's hallucination, my own imagining of an earlier imagining. It's why I let the doorknob turn a full circle without looking away.

A click.

And then, before I can turn away, the door swings open.

A young woman. Naked and shaking, her hair a nest of sweat-glued clumps. She tries to run, to attach the motion of pulling the door to her first step of escape into the daylight, but her limbs are too unsteady, and she wavers dizzily on the threshold.

It isn't Heather. It's the woman from the photos Randy showed me, the one I tried not to let myself see, to memorize, though I was too late in that. Just as I am too late to close my eyes against the dirt-blackened hands that come down on Tracey's shoulders and pull her back into the house before the door slams shut.

The morning after we left the coach overnight in the Thurman house, we waited for Ben at our table in the cafeteria, drinking the watery hot chocolate spat out of a machine that made even worse tea and chicken soup. There was little talk. We were boys of an age when sleep came easy, and were new to the emptiness that followed a night spent troubled and awake.

When we saw Ben through the window making his way across the football field we knew that he had found no more sleep than the rest of us, and that his visit to the coach had not gone well. He looked like he was reprising his role as one of Grimshaw's founding fathers in the annual school play: stooped, bent at the knees, arms rigid at his sides.

"You think he's dead?" Randy asked, and for a moment I thought the question concerned Ben himself. But of course Randy was asking about the coach. Whether he had survived the night's cold.

And then, as Ben entered the cafeteria and started our way, a second interpretation of Randy's question arrived. Had Ben going alone to see the coach had a purpose other than eliciting a confession? Was he now the coach's killer, just as the coach had been Heather Langham's?

Ben sat, reached for my hot chocolate. As he swallowed, he raised his brow as though impressed by its wretchedness.

"We should bring the coach some of this," he said. "If he figures it's the only breakfast he's going to get, he'd say anything."

It took what felt like five full minutes before any of us realized Ben had just told a joke.

Eventually, Ben told us he'd gone into the house just before dawn. The coach was "okay, physically." He wasn't admitting to any crimes, though. In fact, the only things he was saying weren't making much sense at all.

"How do you mean?" I asked.

"I don't know. It might be an act."

"Is he pissed off?"

"More like he's scared."

Ben noticed some other kids, a bunch of grade niners, looking our way. He directed a stare back at them so intense it made them scuttle off to mind their own business.

"He kept saying he'd had an interesting conversation last night. Then he's looking over his shoulder, like I'm not even there."

"What else?"

Ben thought for a moment. "He said we would have to be guardians."

"We are."

"I don't think he meant the team. He kind of switched personalities again—not a scared kid anymore, but himself, more or less. He got, I don't know, *fatherly* on me."

"What'd he say?"

"Some bullshit."

"What bullshit?"

"'You have to keep watch.'"

"What's that supposed to mean?"

"You're asking me?"

"Sounds like he's losing it," Randy said.

"It's pretty cold in there," I said. "Maybe he's hypothermic."

"Or possessed," Randy said, and mock-barfed, Linda Blair–style.

Carl was the only one who laughed. A sharp snort that reminded us he was there.

"Don't you get it?" he said. "It's a warning."

"About what?"

Carl looked around the table. *He's going to tell them*, I thought. *He's going to say there's a boy in the house who can talk inside your head if you give him half a chance.*

"Us," he said. "He's saying we have to guard against ourselves."

Now it was Randy's turn to snort. "Ooooh. That's *deep*, Carl. You've just *blown my mind*."

Carl just kept grinning. Trying to look like he was still able to kid around with Randy as he always had. Sitting there, aware of our eyes on him, we saw how our hockey brawler, our square-jawed tough who was alone among us in being able to fool liquor store clerks about his age, had lost twenty pounds overnight. Chilled and frail, hugging his arms across his chest like one of the wheelchaired ladies who lined the halls of Cedarfield Seniors Home.

I wondered if Todd Flanagan detected anything strange about us as he made his way over to our table. Todd was a Guardian too. I could only hope he was writing off our oddness to nerves about that night's game two against Seaforth.

"Morning, ladies," he said.

Todd was blue-eyed and dark-haired ("black Irish," as my father called his family, though I never knew what this meant) and essentially decent, though he fought hard to keep up his minimum obligations in the bullying and mockery departments. I always thought he'd rather have been our friend than his senior-year teammates', but such transgression between grades was unthinkable. What also set Todd apart was that he was a dad. An eighteen-year-old father to a daughter born at the beginning of the season. We envied him—not for this, but for his girlfriend, Tina. A tight-sweatered vixen whose brief career in boy-trading had been cut short with the arrival of Tracey, the drooling, howling bundle she sometimes brought to games.

"Anybody seen the coach?"

"No," Ben said, taking another gulp of my muddy hot chocolate. "Why?"

"Laura called me this morning."

"Laura?"

"His *wife*, dickwad. Said he didn't come home last night. Wondered if he was hanging out with somebody on the team."

"All *night*?"

"I know. It's weird."

"He'll turn up," Carl said. "Has the coach ever missed a game?"

Todd shook his head. "Seaforth pussies," he said half-heartedly before backing away.

Over morning classes, news of Laura Evans spotted in the principal's office was circulated in different versions, from her showing up with a pair of cops to her bawling uncontrollably until the school nurse gave her a pill. We didn't believe any of these stories necessarily. But what we did know was that the coach's absence had now been officially reported. Combined with Heather Langham's disappearance, it was a story that had nowhere to go but into wilder and wilder speculations. Primary among these was that Heather and the coach had run off together. The other theory concerned a more macabre take. A monster who had crept into Grimshaw to claim its teachers, one by one.

"I hope he takes Dandruff Degan next," I remember Vince Sproule saying. "Save me asking for an extension on my cartography assignment."

Among the Guardians there was an added concern about whether that night's game could go ahead without the coach. There was a critical, morale-sapping difference between the man behind the bench being reported missing and him coming down with the flu. Nothing actually wrong was known to have happened. And yet the mystery about his absence, the foreign whiff of the uncanny that had drifted over Grimshaw's imagination, seemed to undermine the importance of a hockey game, even if it was the playoffs.

But without a coach to call it off, and without any evidence of adultery or more serious wrongdoing to bring before league officials, the game was an at once unbelievable and unstoppable event shadowing our day. For us, the four Guardians who knew where the coach was, the idea of lacing up and charging around the ice in just a few hours made us almost as sick as thinking of how he had got there.

It wasn't until I saw Sarah waiting for me at my locker that I realized I'd been running from her all day. Taking different routes between classes, avoiding the cafeteria at lunch, pretending I didn't see her on the one occasion she waved over the heads of other students at the far end of the hall. But now there was no escape. Nothing to do but try to work up a smile and taste her grape ChapStick with a kiss.

"You sick or something?" she asked. "Because you look a little on the pukey side, gotta say."

"Just nervous about tonight's game."

"Nope. Try again." She came in for another hug, which allowed her hand to cup my crotch. "So tell me," she whispered against my ear, "what's going on here?"

"There's nothing going on."

"You think I'm dumb?"

"You're the opposite of dumb."

"And what's that?"

"Smart?"

Sarah pulled back a few inches so I could see her face.

"I love you, Trevor," she said. And though I tried to say it back, it wouldn't come.

I remember this exchange so clearly now for a reason I hadn't expected when I first summoned it to mind. It wasn't the worry I had that Sarah would figure out what we had done. It was a flash of knowledge.

What was happening in the Thurman house had already drawn a line between Sarah and me, and though it didn't stop me from loving her, it was draining the idea of *forever* from our love. *There will be others*, I thought for the very first time as I kicked my locker shut, spun the lock and started away, lying that I had to get to a team meeting. *She is only a girl among girls.* It was cruel, however private a thought it remained. *Soon, a whole day will pass when you don't think of her once.* Thoughts whose meanness was all the harder to bear because their truth placed them out of reach, beyond forgiving.

———

My turn to visit the coach was scheduled to follow the last bell of the day, and I was late already. At that time of year, losing fifteen minutes can mean a lot when it comes to light, the after-school dusk easing ever closer to night. It made my walk to the Thurman house feel longer. And when it came into view, it was halfway to losing the vulnerable details—the bubbled paint, sagging porch—that in daylight denied it some of its power. The house preferred darkness for the same reason old whores do. It allowed for the possibility of seduction.

The between-class report from Randy, who'd gone in before me, told of a coach whose mental condition was deteriorating faster than his confinement alone should have given rise to. Ben had tried giving him a pen and piece of paper on which to write whatever he needed to say that he couldn't say aloud, and the coach had simply signed his name at the bottom and told Ben to fill in the rest any way he wanted. He hadn't eaten the food we delivered to him. He wasn't complaining of the cold, or of being falsely accused, or even of being lashed to a post in a sunless cellar. What he kept saying was that he wasn't alone in there.

This was what kept me frozen on the sidewalk. I pretended that I was making sure nobody was looking before I crept along the hedgerow, but in fact I was wondering how much money I had left in my account from a summer of pool cleaning, and if it would be enough for a train ticket to Toronto.

He's not alone in there.

As if on cue, there was the sound of a distant train

whistle, beckoning me. Followed by a flash of movement in one of the side windows.

Pale skin. A blur of long, tossed hair from a head twisted from side to side. A blink of struggle.

It was the impulse to help, to save—it was a *woman* I'd seen—that crunched my feet onto the frozen grass. Sliding under cover of cheek-poking branches. When I drew square with the house I fell to my knees.

It was the same window where I'd noticed the hopeless *fuckt* the night we discovered Heather Langham's body. The word still there, a legible blue against an interior of black.

Up the hill of Caledonia Street, the streetlights were flickering to life, one by one. That's what I'd seen. Not a woman but the bulb in the streetlight behind me popping to brightness.

Yet even with this mystery solved, I stayed where I was. The twilight, the dirty panes, the lightless interior: even if something was there, anything that could be observed through the window would be obscured if it showed itself again. It made me squint. There was the sense that, above all, the house wanted me to stick around, to witness. Better yet, to come inside.

Which I wouldn't do. What difference would it make? The coach wasn't going to tell me anything if he hadn't already told Randy or Ben. And they were coming by later for another visit anyway. It needn't be me going in there now, alone.

I crawled out from under the hedgerow. Rose to my feet, started sidestepping back toward the sidewalk.

That was the right thing to do. Here's the wrong:

I looked back at the window. And saw a woman's face come to the glass.

I fell back against the branches. If the hedge hadn't been there I would have collapsed, but it held me up, pinned to its nettles like a plastic bag blown against a fence.

When I looked at the window again, there was only an orb of streetlight. And the *fuckt*. Though wasn't the *t* slightly smudged from the moment before?

I started toward the back of the house, adding details to the face I'd seen. A woman. That was all I had to start with. Along with the idea that she was in desperate fear. And that she was naked. That she wasn't alone.

Tina Uxbridge.

I'd been thinking of her ever since Todd had come by our table in the cafeteria. In the back of my mind I'd been flipping through my (partly made-up) mental snapshots of Tina hip-swinging down the school's hallways, Tina breastfeeding, Tina and Todd and the different ways they might have gone about conceiving their daughter. The truth is, I'd pictured her, dwelled on her, before. Because she was pretty and I was sixteen. Because I was a sixteen-year-old boy.

I opened the back door.

For a time I stood in the kitchen, listening. I think I half expected to hear the coach's voice, cackling my name from the cellar or pleading for release. The house's quiet should have brought relief, but didn't. I was waiting and listening. Which meant something else was too.

And then it *told* me it was.

We're waiting.

The faintest whisper, no louder than a midge's wings.

I didn't go down to the cellar to check on the coach. He might have escaped, might have been dead, I didn't care. His fate meant nothing to me as I shuffled down the hall and came to stand just inside the living room. It was the woman I needed to see.

There was the *fuckt* on the window. The smudged *t*.

The house had wanted me to watch. And all there was to see was the way the shadow of the backlit tree limbs tried to nudge a beer can over the rug. Yet I stayed. Wishing for the woman or any other dead thing not to appear, and impatient for it at the same time.

Within what was probably less than three minutes, I slid from the heights of fear to boredom. This is what a haunted house was: a place where nothing happens, so you have to make something up. It's the same impulse that makes us tell lies to a stranger sitting next to us on a plane, or pushes the planchette over a Ouija board to make it spell your dead cousin's name.

Yet I stayed. I told myself this was foolishness, and knew that it was.

The light outside the back deck of the house next door flicked on. It barely added any illumination to the room, but it was enough to change its chemistry, to hasten the draft that swirled through its space. Details—stray threads over the length of the sofa's piping, moisture stains seeping through the wallpaper—found more particular focus. And the messages on the walls. *stay with me. i walk with you.* It was enough to bring the fear back.

Along with a formless shadow moving over the floor. One that, over the course of seconds, cohered into a human form lying on the rug.

"Tina?"

The shadow rose to its feet. Went to the window I'd first seen her face in. Performed the same act of pressing close to the glass, looking out.

Except this time she turned.

Her eyes a pair of glistening buttons. The glint of froth on her lips.

Heather.

I must have turned away. I must have found the back door, shouldered out into the cold.

But even this was already a memory. I was past Ben's house and at the top of the Caledonia Street hill, breathless but still running, before I could say I'd seen anything at all.

When I made it home my mother had two phone messages for me. One from Ben, the other from Sarah.

I returned Ben's call first. He asked how my session with the coach went, if I remembered to turn on the tape recorder while talking with him, if he seemed any closer to confessing. It was a question I'd prepared an answer to.

On the rest of the walk home, part of me argued that I should tell Ben what I'd seen in the window, that what was going on was out of our control, that we had awakened some long-slumbering presence with what we'd done and it would win any fight we might attempt to wage on it. It might not kill us if we went into the Thurman house again, but we wouldn't come out wholly alive either.

In the end, though, I merely lied.

"The bastard's still not saying anything."

"Okay . . . okay. *Okay*," he said. "After the game. You and me."

I called Sarah next. Faked a girl's voice and squeaked "Wrong number" when her dad answered.

Sarah sat in the stands in her usual spot opposite the teams' benches. Offered me a good-luck wave during the pre-game warm-up, though I didn't look her way. Didn't wave back.

When I came out of the dressing room for the start of the first period, she was gone.

We lost. Coachless, tentative, winded. 5–1. Though even that makes it sound closer than it was.

I scored our only goal. A Trev classic: an in-the-crease flip over their fallen goalie's shoulder, my stick a spatula tossing a rubber burger into the net. Not pretty, but it counted.

The rest of the game is out of memory's reach now. I must have looked down the bench and locked eyes with Carl, or Randy, or Ben, but whatever their faces revealed was something I failed to take with me. It felt only like the end of things.

Which, in a sense, it was. That night's loss turned out to be the final game of the Guardians' season.

As for me, I never put skates on again.

11

IT TAKES SOME TIME—a minute? a half-hour?—to fully convince myself that I had not just seen a naked Tracey Flanagan attempting to escape out the front door of the Thurman house. So what *had* I seen? A reimagining of what I'd read in Ben's diary, surely, except for him it was Heather—a long-dead Heather Langham—who had been pulled back into the dark. It was nothing more than the power of suggestion.

Still, I had to remind myself that Officer Barry Tate and his partner had just searched the place and found nothing. That what Ben had claimed to see was an impossibility. That hallucinations are on my Parkinson's symptom list ("Not long, but often quite weird," one doctor warned).

Working my way through these arguments prevents me from calling the police. I don't do anything but have a shower, get dressed and call a taxi to take me over to Sarah's.

But that's not to say that I don't return every five minutes or so to the image of Tracey Flanagan opening the Thurman house's front door. Or that I don't allow myself to wonder: Whose hands pulled her back?

Sarah lives in a boxy, aluminum-sided place out by the fairgrounds, a structure shaped much like the house tokens in Monopoly. When I give the cab driver the address he calls it "the new part of town," which is how it was regarded even when I was growing up, even though all the properties were built in a rush immediately after the war. Aside from a few stabs at additions—a blown-out kitchen here, a carport there—it's a neighbourhood that looks about the same now as it must have in the late '40s, and serving the same purpose too: entry-level homes for the blue-collared, the secretarial and, more recently, the refugees of divorce.

Sarah's is the nicest on its block. Perennials lining the front walkway, shutters freshly painted green, a vase of cut flowers displayed in the living-room window. I wonder, as I haul myself out of the cab, if they've been put there to welcome me. Me, as razor-burned and over-cologned as a teenager, and about as nervous too.

Is this, as Randy had asked, an actual date? I'm surprised, clearing my throat and knocking at the door, how much I want it to be. Some nostalgic simulation of courtship might be just the thing, sweet and reassuring and laced with the suspense that comes with wondering if there will be a goodnight kiss at the end. I'm thinking the question will be answered by Sarah's choice of wardrobe, and I am hoping, as the door opens, for some show of leg or collarbone. But instead I am met by a kid. A boy I'd guess to be around eleven years old.

"Is your mommy home?"

"You mean my *mom*?"

"If they're the same person, then yes."

He stands there. Patiently absorbing my details, which at present include two fluttering hands at my sides that I attempt to subside by having one hold the other across my waist. If this trembly stranger at his door asking for his mother disturbs him in any way, he doesn't show it. In fact, he ends up standing aside and, with an introductory sweep of his arm, mumbles, "You want to come in?"

It smells good in here. It's the flowers in the window, but also recent baking and perfume.

"You're Trevor," the kid says, closing the door behind me.

"That's right."

"My mom's boyfriend."

"From a long, long time ago."

"That's just what *she* said. Except she had one more 'long.'"

A teenage girl wearing train-track braces emerges from the kitchen with a plate of oatmeal cookies.

"My babysitter," the kid says with a shrug, then takes a cookie. "These are good. You should try one, Trevor."

"Don't mind if I do."

"You want to see my room?"

"I think I'm supposed to take your mom—"

"She's still getting ready. She said I was supposed to entertain you."

"Okay. Any suggestions?"

"I've got Transformers."

"Why didn't you say so?"

His name is Kieran. Sarah's only child. The father supposedly lives out east now, though nobody really knows for sure. He doesn't show up even on the holidays he says he will, and he never sends the money from the jobs he says he's going to get. I learn all of this on the walk up the half flight of stairs to the kid's room.

"Trevor?" Sarah calls out from behind the closed bathroom door. "I'll be out in three minutes."

"Take your time. Kieran's giving me the tour."

"Go easy on him, Kier."

"He ate a whole cookie almost as fast as I did!" Kieran shouts with the excitement that might accompany the witnessing of magic.

I sit on the edge of Kieran's bed and collect the toys and books he shows me, noting the cool sword of this warrior-mutant, the wicked bazooka of that marine. Our conversation is sprinkled with off-topic questions ("Did you have soldiers when you were a kid?" from him; "Do you have friends in the neighbourhood?" from me), through which we learn what we need to know of each other. He is nearly breathless with pleasure at showing me his stuff, which is of course not really just stuff but entryways into a boy's world, his secret self.

The kid's hunger for this—the company of a grown-up man in the house, shooting the breeze—is so naked it shames me. Shames, because it is something I too wanted at his age, but only partly, occasionally received. Though Kieran's case is worse than what I remember of my own. Companionship with a dad type has been missing so long in him he doesn't bother hiding it anymore. He isn't picky. Even I'll do.

He asks about my shaking only once. "What's wrong with you?" is how he phrases it.

"It's a disease."

"Does it get worse?"

"Yes."

"It's not so bad right now."

"No. It's bad. But what can you do?"

He nods just as Randy or Carl would have. Because all of us know it: What *can* you do? His unhandsome circle of a face confirms this. There are a good many things he can do nothing about too.

Sarah appears in the doorway. I am glad to see both collarbone and black-nyloned legs.

"You think I could borrow Trevor for a few hours?" she asks.

"Okay. But take this." Kieran drops a toy Ferrari, his favourite, into the palm of my hand. "You have to bring it back, though."

"I promise."

Kieran nods. Spins around to give his mother a kiss. As Sarah and I head downstairs and out the door he tells us to have a good time.

"What about dinner?" I ask Sarah as we slip into her car.

"They had pretty good hot dogs at the arena last time I was there," she says, pumping the gas until the Honda's engine coughs to life. "Mind you, that was over twenty years ago. Give or take."

"You just went for the hot dogs?"

"Course not. There was a cute boy who played right wing at the time."

"Bit of a hot dog himself, if I remember correctly."

"Nah. He was just a boy. And they're *all* hot dogs."

The Grimshaw Arena hasn't changed much since the days we charged around its sheet of ice, cheered on by parents and sweethearts and fans who saw good value in a night out that consisted of a four-dollar ticket and seventy-five-cent hot chocolates. The tickets are double that now, and the stands, when Sarah and I find our seats behind the penalty box, feel dinkier than in my day. There is still the cold of the place. A refrigerated air that huddles Sarah close to me for warmth.

For most of the first period we just watch the game—surprisingly exciting, though the players are smaller than I was expecting, just a bunch of cherry-cheeked kids trying to look tough behind their visors—and eat hot dogs that, as Sarah recalled, aren't half bad. It feels to me not just like an old-fashioned date but like an old-fashioned *first* date: no low lighting, no alcohol. The opposite kind of thing I'd do with the girlfriends I dated during my Retox days, if you could call them dates. If you could call them girlfriends.

At the intermission, we catch up on the last couple of decades of each other's lives in broad strokes. Sarah tells me about her "okay job" as assistant office manager of a contracting firm in town; the handful of women friends she goes out with once every other week to get hammered and "complain about our marriages, or how we wished we still had one;" how she feels that while her life isn't necessarily great, she's not miserable either, like she's "floating on this black ocean without sinking into it, y'know?" I talk about the deals I hustled to rise from restaurant manager to hedge-fund pusher to owner of my very own nightclub, where I would hire and fire and in the evenings feel ten years younger (and in the headachey mornings feel ten years older). I speak of the Parkinson's indirectly, referring to it as "this disease thing of mine," as though it's a vaguely ridiculous side project I'd been asked to be a partner in and now can't get out of.

"Who's taking care of your nightclub while you're here?" Sarah asks.

"It's not mine anymore. I sold it."

"Why?"

"I figure I'll need the money later, when this disease thing of mine gets worse."

Sarah nods in precisely the same way that Kieran had earlier.

"Kieran strikes me as a fine young fellow," I say.

"That he is."

"He tells me his dad hasn't really been in the picture for a while."

"Kieran's father is a liar and third-rate criminal, among other things."

"It must be a drag. For both of you."

"Not for me. He's just *gone*. But Kieran doesn't fully understand that yet. He doesn't get how some people are just rotten."

You mean me? I want to ask.

And then the image of Tracey Flanagan returns. Standing blind on the threshold of the Thurman house's front door.

"What about you?" Sarah asks.

"Me?"

"A family. Wife? Kids?"

"No wife. No kids, either. As far as I know."

"I suppose those were things you didn't want anyway."

"I was preoccupied. *Wilfully* preoccupied."

"Sounds kind of lonely," Sarah blurts, then rears back. "Oh my God. That came out wrong. I didn't mean to assume—"

"Yes. I think I've been lonely. And not terribly happy either, though I never let myself slow down long enough to realize I wasn't. Until recently, that is."

"Your illness."

"That. And Ben. And coming back here. Seeing you."

This last bit isn't flirtatious, it just comes out in the uncrafted way of the truth.

The second period starts, and Grimshaw begins to pull away from the tough but unskilled Elmira boys, our forwards buzzing around their net but unable to put one away. It is the sort of game where things can go wrong: you're winning as far as the performance goes, but the scoreboard only shows the goals. It makes me think that this is what moving to the city from a small town is all about. It's not about the quality of life you live, but about putting up the hard numbers for all to see.

"You ever feel like you missed out on something?" I ask. "Staying here?"

"Missed out?"

"The opportunities. Professional options."

"No, you didn't mean that. You think the people you left behind were just too scared to go where you did."

"I never saw it as leaving anybody behind."

"No?"

"Listen, I didn't—"

"You think I was avoiding life by staying," Sarah says, icy as the Grimshaw Arena's air. "Did you ever think you were doing the same thing by leaving?"

I'm thinking, for the minutes that follow, that this is pretty much it. We had both done our best to avoid the past, the vast body of unsaid thoughts between us, and now we had been shown to be fools. Sarah still wanted the answers she'd sought the winter we were in grade eleven, and I still couldn't give them to her. There was nothing now but to wait until the game's end—or earlier, if she decided to get up and leave—and return the buffering distance between us.

But then she surprises me. She holds my hand.

"Let me tell you what I know," she says, leaning close to my ear, so that I am filled by her voice. "Something happened to you when we were kids. Something awful. You think you escaped it, but you never did. You see me as one of the casualties, the cost of running away to the circus. But I don't need to know. I'm grown up, just like you. Borderline old, if you judge a thing by how you feel most of the time. We can talk about the serious stuff if you want, or not. But we're both way too banged up to worry about scratching the paint. Know what I mean?"

Sarah leans away from me again, and the sounds of hockey return—the cut of skates, the thunder of armoured bodies against the boards—leaving me light in my seat. No tremors anywhere, no fight to remain still. I watch the game, but all of my attention, every sense available to me, is concentrated on the woman in the seat next to mine.

"Close game," she says.

"It only looks that way."

After the game, Sarah drives us back to her house, where she relieves the babysitter of her duties and offers me a drink in the living room. She turns on the stereo and cranks up the song the CD had been paused at the start of. "Hungry Like the Wolf" by Duran Duran.

"Remember this?" she says, passing me my scotch and dancing on her own in the middle of the room, the same cool, feline moves that stirred me as I watched her on the darkened gym floor at school dances. "It's *terrible*, isn't it?"

"I like it," I say, not lying. "Is it going to wake Kieran up, though?"

"*Nothing* wakes that kid up."

I watch Sarah dance. Make a private request of my brain to not show me any scary pictures of Heather or Tracey or the boy or anyone but Sarah until the song is over. Just give me this. Allow the next three and a half minutes to be ghost-free.

When she's finished she sits next to me on the sofa. Her skin pinkened, lips plumped. She is so different from the girl I remember. Yet those are the same freckles I once kissed.

"Poor Trevor," she says. "It must be hard, being a mystery."

"I'm not a mystery. There's just one thing I can't talk about."

"That's what makes it so hard."

She touches the back of my neck. Pulls me in. Her mouth warm and tasting faintly of vanilla.

"We're going to have sex now," she says. "Aren't we?"

"Lordy. Do you think we could?"

We go up to Sarah's room. She draws the curtains and lets me watch her take her clothes off. When my shaking hands struggle with my belt buckle, she helps. And then she proceeds to help me in other ways too.

It is a kindness. But maybe there is even some suggestion of a future in it—an unlikely, difficult, but not wholly impossible future. Something we both could live in, live through. I had assumed that, with my disease, there was nothing I could offer women anymore. But perhaps this was true only of those who saw me as I am now and could envision little more than the decline to come.

Sarah could see this too, but also other things. She could see a past.

MEMORY DIARY

Entry No. 12

Funny what the memory holds and what it decides it can do without. Like a drunk fisherman, it guts some of the least edible fish and tosses its prize catches back into the deep.

For instance, I can distinctly remember the smell of the pay phone receiver I put to my lips in the mezzanine of the arena after our second and final playoff loss to Seaforth, but not why I said nothing when a voice at the other end told me I'd reached Grimshaw Police dispatch and asked, "What is the nature of your emergency?" I didn't speak, didn't move. Just breathed in the receiver's ingrained traces of mustard, Old Spice and whisky sweat.

Perhaps the question posed too great a challenge. What *was* the nature of my emergency? A kidnapped coach?

("Who kidnapped him?" "We did.") A missing teacher's buried body? ("Who buried her?" "We did.")

But no matter which of these crimes I had rushed from the dressing-room showers to confess, it was over for me. And I was surprised. I thought it was more likely to be the clownish Randy, the volatile Carl or—before his recent transformation—the meditative Ben who would break first. In fact, I was counting on one of them to tell.

Here's the thing: I wasn't a bad kid. I was a good kid. We were all good kids. And now it was time for our essential natures to take control again. So I got dressed before everyone else, pulled a dime from the pocket of my jeans and dialled the cavalry.

I remember that perfectly well. Just not why it didn't end there.

But the memory can lie too. Hide things away. Occasionally, it can lie and hide even better than you.

Because there's Ben. Eyeing me through the crowd of disappointed fans lingering beside the trophy cases.

We can't, his look said. *I want this to end too. But right now, you have to put the phone down.*

I opened my mouth to speak to the dispatcher. To put words to the nature of my emergency.

They'll send us to jail. Ben started toward me, his face growing in detail as he approached. *A grown-up biker-gang-and-rapist jail. We'll be their girlfriends in there. For years. And when we get out, we'll be fucked all over again.*

I returned the receiver to its cradle.

"Sarah not home?" Ben said, lying for us both.

―――

I remember dropping my equipment off after the game, telling my parents I was going over to Ben's house and walking along to the McAuliffes' with a bad feeling. I'd had bad feelings about what was going on since our first hot-box meeting, when it was decided something had to be done. But that night, the ragged nerves took a turn into full-blown illness. Light-headed, tingly-toed. I had the idea that the Thurman house wasn't haunted as much as it carried contagion, and I was showing the first signs of infection.

This idea was followed by another. A premonition of the life ahead that turned out to be largely true. Feeling sick, worrying about becoming sick, fighting and carrying sickness: this is what it meant to grow up, grow old.

By the look of Ben's blotched cheeks when I met him under the railway trellis, he'd caught the virus too.

"It has to happen tonight," he said.

When Ben opened the door to the cellar, I couldn't tell if he heard the voices down there or if it was only me. A whispered conversation (too soft to make out any words) between the coach and someone else. No, not a conversation—it was too one-sided to be called that. The coach murmuring with excitement, and his audience offering only a hissed *Yes* in response.

But how could I have heard all that within the few seconds between Ben's opening the cellar door and placing his boot onto the first step, its protesting creak instantly silencing whoever was down there? Because I'd been hearing them *before* the door was opened. Whatever the coach was saying had been growing louder in my head from the moment we'd stepped onto the Thurman house's lot. A few seconds more and I might have clearly made out the words.

We turned on our flashlights and started down. There was a smell I hadn't detected on previous visits. A sweetness. It reminded me of the orange I had left in my lunch box over Christmas holidays, and it turned my stomach.

Our lights found the coach at the same time. His teeth, in particular. Bared in a comic exaggeration of mirth.

"Come closer," he said.

With his attention on Ben alone, I took the revolver out of the workbench drawer and came forward to aim it at the wall two feet off the coach's side. (It is harder than you'd ever guess to hold a gun steady on a man's chest. The snout keeps slipping off its target, resisting, like trying to press two magnets of the same charge together.) Now the coach watched me. Still showing me those teeth of his, but with his head back, so a red throat glistened in my flashlight beam as well.

Ben untied his hands. Offered the coach a ham sandwich, which he took but didn't eat. Instead, he stuffed it into the front pocket of his parka to join the last two sandwiches we'd brought him.

"You have to eat something," I told him.

"I've lost my taste for meat."

"We'll bring you something else, then."

"No, no, no," he said agreeably, in an I-don't-want-to-be-any-trouble voice. "This will do fine."

That's when he bit Ben.

Launched forward without any change in expression or posture, not a twitch. He was sitting on the floor, rubbing his wrists. Then he was on his knees, snarling, clamping down on Ben's knuckles.

Ben screamed. Someone else screamed too. Not me, I don't think.

The blood startled me. Quick and forceful. The rhythmic pulses, like jumping up and down on a hose. How the coach swallowed it without letting go.

"*Don't!*"

It took my voice for him to spit out Ben's hand. Then he leaned back against the post. Crossed his arms over his chest, his teeth outlined in crimson.

Ben was already wrapping his hand in a rag from the floor.

"Didn't your mother ever tell you to keep your fingers out of the monkey cage, Benji? Or maybe that was your daddy's department. Wait. Wait! Your daddy did himself in, didn't he?"

"Shut up," Ben whispered.

"Checked out early. Benji's dear old dad."

Shut up, Ben's lips said again.

"Can I ask you something? Nobody actually believes he drove into a hydro pole doing a hundred by *accident*, do they? So what do you think his problem was? Didn't have the stomach to see how useless his only son turned out to be?"

None of us ever mentioned Ben's father's suicide. I was surprised the coach even knew about it. But then it occurred to me: Ben was the one who had told him. He'd confessed this to the coach in the same way we had confessed our own secrets, and for the same reason. We thought the coach was the only adult we could wholly trust.

Yet the coach wasn't the coach anymore. And it was impossible to know whether what he was saying came from him or the vile other that was halfway to claiming him.

"But I suppose something good came out of your dad hitting the gas instead of the brake," the coach said to Ben. "That cute little group hug you and your fairy-boy friends had upstairs."

Ben's eyes widened. "I didn't tell you about that."

"I didn't say you did."

"Then how do you know?"

The coach grinned in a way that changed his face. Stopped it from being his.

"No more," I told him.

"But I *like* this game," he said, turning to me. "Now, let's see, what about you? Oh yes. Peeping Trevor."

"What are you talking about?"

"Our moonlight chicken-choker. Our wanking voyeur."

"I don't—"

"Hiding behind trees on the hospital grounds to look into lovely Heather's window at night."

"That's bullshit!"

"It's only what you told me."

"I *never* told you that because it isn't *true*."

"No? What do you think, Benji? You think Trev here likes to get his rocks off watching ladies changing into their nighties before lights out?"

Ben looked at me.

"He's lying," I said.

"Am I?" The coach's voice was no longer his, but the boy's. "Isn't it true that Randy dreams of graduating from class clown to great actor? Has he told you that? 'Like Pacino in *The Godfather*.' Pathetic, isn't it? Poor Handy Randy."

"That's enough," Ben said.

"Or Carl? You want to know his big secret? Oh, it's *good*. It's a *real* surprise."

Ben held out his good hand for the gun. When I gave it to him he walked up to the coach and swung the side of the revolver against his cheek.

"I don't want to hear any more of that," Ben said. "I only want to hear what you did."

Ben clicked on the tape recorder in his pocket. Started reciting the same questions he'd been asking all along.

Tell us the truth.

The coach's eyes rolled white. A line of blood making its way to his jaw. Then he was smiling again like the madman he was, or we'd made him into.

Ben stepped away to lean against the wall. Fatigue bloomed pale and puffy over his face, a weakness that pulled down at his arms as though lead weights were stitched to his sleeves.

"Why Heather?" I asked.

It was the first time any of us had asked this. And for the first time, the coach was prepared to answer.

"Why *Heather*? Have you *seen* my wife?" he exclaimed, and it seemed he was about to follow with the punchline to some well-worn joke, but instead, a second later, he was fighting tears.

"What about her?"

"Laura *saved* me."

"Saved you?"

"Before I came here, I'd done some things. But she stood by me. A beautiful woman. On the *inside*. Heather? She had it on the outside too." He threw us a conspiratorial leer. "I mean, that *ass*? I thought I was through wanting that. God was kind enough to give me a new start over here in old Grimshaw. All I had to do was snuggle in, keep quiet, be good. And I *was* good. Then guess what? Heather Langham shows up."

"So you decided you had to kill her?"

"Kill her?" Those teeth again. "No. I decided I had to, I really *needed* to . . . well, let's not be *crude*. Let's just say that the first night after she introduces herself to all the dried mushrooms in the teachers' lounge, I'm dreaming of her. Bad, bad dreams."

"Then what?"

"Then I play Harmless Married Guy. Share some of my favourite books with her, ask what brought her to the noble profession of teaching, et cetera. 'I'm a good listener,' said I. 'We have so much in common!' said she. I knew it was over when she told me all she needed to be happy in Grimshaw was a friend. Well, that's all I needed too!"

"You brought her here."

"My contribution was the flask of Jack Daniel's out in my car. Loosened things up considerably. 'Where do we go now?' says I. 'I know a place,' says she. A haunted house, she called it. I just knew it as that derelict place where some of the guys on the team went to drink beer. Turns out she was more right than I was."

I remember searching for something hurtful to say to him. Something as disembowelling as his mention of Ben's dad. A way of showing how furious I was at him for talking about Heather this way.

Show him, the boy said but didn't say. *Wake him up.*

Before I knew what I was doing, the toe of my boot met with the coach's mouth. And it *did* wake him up. Eyes aflutter with liquid blinks. Spitting out blood pinked with mucus.

"You can't blame a house for what you did!"

When he focused on me, he seemed pleased that I was here. That it had been *my* boot.

"It was you," I said. "Not a place, not a building. It was *you*."

"You're right. Quite right, Trevor," now the proper English teacher, patiently expanding on a student's rudimentary observation. "All this place gives us is a licence to act. It's a stage, but a bare one. A theatre without sets, without a script. And most important, without an audience!"

He laughed. Not the coach's laugh. Not a living sound at all.

"You hurt her here because you could? Is that it?"

"Here? *Here*?" The coach swung his head around, peering into every corner. "There's no *here* here!"

"What did you do?"

We'd asked him this perhaps a hundred times since he slipped into Carl's Ford half a block from his house. But now the coach looked up at me as though it was a fresh and intriguing query.

"What *did* I do?"

"Just tell us and it'll be over."

"You don't get to decide that."

"We'll let you go."

"Every time you come down here, I leave when you go, piece by piece," he said, his voice flattening. "I'll get out whether you open the door for me or not."

"Who are you?"

"I'm the coach."

"You *were* him. Who are you now?"

"Whoever I need to be."

"To do what?"

"Keep you here."

I took the gun out of Ben's hand. I must have, because there it was, pointed at the coach's forehead.

"I'd like to know what you did to Heather. Right now."

"I brought her here to do what all of you would have liked to do," he said, the voice dead as a dial tone. "To fuck her pretty pink behind."

Pretty. The word my father had used. More than this, it was like he knew that it was.

"Where?"

"In the living room. Standing up, because she thought the carpet was too dirty."

"Were you alone?"

"Alone as two people can be. Our coitus was interruptus, though. Something heavy falling onto the floor above us. And maybe a voice too. No . . . a breath. Who *cared* what it was?"

"You didn't go upstairs to check?"

"I *did*. Nervous Heather asked me to make sure nothing was amiss. So up I went. Nobody there. But by the time I came back down, she was gone. I figured she'd changed her mind and left. On my way out, though, I noticed the door to the cellar was open, and it definitely wasn't when we first came in. Down I go. And there's Heather. Had time to put her panties on, but that's about all."

The coach grinned fondly now, shook his head as though at an amusing turn in a practised anecdote.

"'Hey, doll,' I said. Never called a woman that before. But she *looked* like a doll. Those big glass eyes staring at me but not seeing anything. I didn't want to touch her. She was soiled. I was having a good old time with pretty Heather, and now she disgusted me. Trembling lips, chin all folded up. So scared she was *sickening*. These were the kind of thoughts I had. But they *weren't* my thoughts."

"Whose were they?"

The coach rubbed his chin in a stage gesture of deep thought.

"You're both men, give or take, right? You know those naughty little whispers that you hear all the time, but that you're able to hold down, hold in place? Well, those naughty whispers became all I could hear."

"And they told you to bash her head in."

"They told me nothing really counted. Not here."

"So?"

"There was a piece of wood on the ground. I didn't notice it before. A long piece of wood with a screw in it. I think Heather knew what I was going to do before I did."

"You hit her."

"Once. Maybe twice."

"It was enough to kill her."

"No, it wasn't. Because the next thing I knew—next thing I saw—the wood was on the ground and Heather was alive."

"How did you know?"

"Because she was speaking."

"What did she say?"

"*I have to go home. I have to go home. I have to go home.*"

"Then?"

"I hit her again."

At that, the coach glanced over to the spot we'd buried her. It must have been a lucky guess, because you couldn't tell what we'd done just by looking. Unless you could hear her struggling to get out from beneath the soil. For a moment, maybe we all heard it.

"It's like I told Benji. You have to guard against places like this. Against people like me," he said, and turned away from Heather's grave to face us. He was, as far as I could tell, the real coach again. "That's what's really dangerous, what'll surprise you. The things that have nothing inside."

A noise from upstairs. Heavy thuds, as though someone was kicking the mud off his shoes. I remember the coach closing his eyes, chin raised, as though in anticipation of the first strains of a musical performance.

It is impossible to describe what came next.

Not music. Music's opposite. A noise in which I could discern the slide of a heavy piece of furniture slamming up against a doorframe. An animal grunt. A child's howl of pain.

Then silence again. The cellar's perfect, entombed darkness.

"Nobody knows we're here," I said.

The coach grinned. "Too late for that."

"Keep him quiet," I said to Ben. "I'll go up and see."

I started away, but Ben's flashlight spilled through my legs. When I turned, he was right behind me.

"Don't go."

"I'm not leaving you behind, Ben. I'm just going to see what's up there."

"Maybe we should leave."

"We will."

"So let's do it *now*."

"Not yet."

"Why?"

And then I said something I don't remember thinking, though once it was past my lips it had the familiarity of a long-held belief.

"Because there might be something in here we can't let out."

———

I started up the cellar stairs, the flashlight held at arm's length in front of me as though its beam was a rope I clung to, pulling me higher. Ahead, the door I thought we'd closed was ajar, a half-foot band of moonlight running from the kitchen floor up the doorframe to the ceiling. It felt like it had taken me a full minute—and maybe it had—to travel the thirty feet from where I'd stood with Ben to where I was now, partway up the narrow steps. I was being pulled higher by the light, and then I wasn't.

This way, the voice said.

A darkness swept across the moonlit gap.

A blink of movement so swift it took shape as a human figure in my mind only after it was gone.

I leapt up the remaining steps in two strides, elbowed the door wide. The kitchen was empty. But there was the smell the boy left behind. Something mossy and fungal, like the first breath that came up from the well behind my parents' cabin when we lifted its metal seal at the beginning of the season.

There was a scratching I assumed was the soles of my boots dragging over the floor. But I wasn't moving.

To my left was the main hallway that led to the front door. And halfway along, the boy walked off, dragging his hand over the curled flaps of wallpaper.

You can taste it already, can't you?

That's when I puked. An instant torrent splashing over the linoleum and burning a hole at the back of my throat.

Takes a while to find your sea legs. But you're gonna like it, Trev. Promise.

The boy reached the base of the main stairs. Paused to place a hand on the banister.

I went after him. But what was intended as a charge of attack ended up as an off-balance lunge, palms out to catch a doorframe or coat hook to keep me from falling. Speeding faster toward the boy even as I tried to pull myself to a stop.

I expected him to disappear, but he didn't. As the distance between us shortened he only became clearer, larger. *He looks like me*, I thought again. And then, distinctly, nonsensically: *Me with all the hope drained out.*

The streetlight that came through the stained glass over the front door coloured him in murky orange and blue. It shaded the dimples at the corners of his mouth and revealed the pimples on his forehead, each casting a tiny shadow that doubled the thickness of his skin, a leather hood fitted over the real face beneath it. A face that looked nothing like the one I swung my fist toward.

The brilliant white flash of pain, flaring up my arm. My eyes open to the paint-peeled front door. My cheek against the wood I'd just delivered a punch to.

Come.

I swung around to face the boy, but he was already on his way up to the second floor, shrinking into the dark.

The party's upstairs.

Why did I follow? In a rush, dropping the flashlight as I went?

I wanted to hurt him, to kill him again and again until he stayed dead.

I wanted to see what he wanted me to see.

When the boy reached the landing I threw myself at his back, waiting to feel only the cold air of the hallway, the not-thereness of the space he occupied. Instead, I felt him.

The wool of his shirt. The heat of his body. Fever sweat.

More than this was the shattering glimpse of his pain. Wordless, thoughtless, soundless. But it let me see something. An image I recognize now as a version of that Edvard Munch painting of the figure on a pier, mouth agape, the very landscape distorted by torment. Touching the boy was like touching the inside of a scream.

The boy spilled against the far wall. Hands clasped together in his lap in a schoolboy pose. Amused by the look of horror on my face. But when a door at the end of the hall squeaked open, the grin slid away. Now he mirrored me with a horror of his own.

The boy turned his head to see. So did I.

The bedroom door stood open. Beyond it, so did the bathroom door with the mirror on the inside. But now the mirror was in pieces over the floor, glinting fragments of light over the ceiling. This must have been what we heard in the cellar. A draft that finally nudged the mirror off its hook. The sound of a child's pain only shattered glass, the grunting animal only the mirror's frame clattering to the floor.

Silence. The too-quiet of having water in your ears. I looked back to the boy, expecting the same show of fear as before. But he was already facing me. And he was smiling.

I couldn't meet his eyes. So I looked at the open bedroom door.

Go on, the boy said.

I started down the hall. When I was just short of the doorframe, I stopped. Glanced back. The boy was gone.

I closed my eyes. Stepped forward into the room.

Look!

A chest of drawers against the wall. The only solid thing in an otherwise vacant room, except for a single bed in the far corner. A mattress black with mould. Painted flowers on the cracked headboard.

The rumble of a snowplow turning onto Caledonia Street. I remember the roar of the diesel engine as the driver built up speed to make it up the hill. The idea of someone behind the wheel of the plow—a city employee who probably came to my dad to complain about the deductions on his paycheque—opened my mouth. To cry out for him to stop, wait for me to run downstairs. To ask him to take me home.

Instead, I stood and watched as the blue rotating light atop the plow played over the bedroom ceiling. A false dawn that blinked through the windows to show that it wasn't empty anymore.

The boy was there. Standing over a naked body lying face down on the bed. A young woman. White buttocks glinting. On her skin, the walls, a snaking spray of blood.

The boy raised his head to look directly at me. He looked sad. No, that's not right: his face was composed in a "sad look," but an inch past this he was hollow. He was nothing.

The boy started toward me. Two more of his long strides and I would choke on his breath. His hands squeezing the air, readying their grip.

The snowplow growled up the slope, and its blue light disappeared behind the neighbour's line of trees. It wiped away the boy, the body on the bed. Left me alone again.

I ran the length of the hall. Threw myself down the stairs, both hands riding the railings, pincushioned with slivers as I went.

Without the flashlight, I had to trust my memory of the darkness to make it down to the cellar. I remember descending in flight, a visitor to the underworld who had been discovered and now sought only to collect the living and find his way back to the light.

And there *was* a light. Held by the coach, who shone it at Ben on his knees before him. In the coach's other hand was the gun.

"How was it?" the coach asked without looking my way.

"Don't hurt him."

"Never mind *this*," he said, dismissively waving the revolver at Ben. "What did he show you? I bet it was something good."

"Ben? It's going to be okay."

"Sure, Benji. You'll go home and Mommy will tuck you in across the street from where you buried the pretty teacher, and she'll tell you how Daddy would've been proud."

"How do you know—?"

"Benji told me. Didn't you, Benji?" The coach steadied

the revolver. Trained it six inches from the end of Ben's nose.

"What did you tell him, Ben?"

"Benji's not saying."

"Then you tell me."

"He pointed to that mound in the corner and said, 'That's where she is' and knelt down like a good little altar boy ready for his wafer. 'Forgive me,' he said! To *me*! Can you believe that? Seriously. Can you *believe* it?"

The coach pressed the end of the gun into Ben's cheek. It pushed his head back. Allowed the flashlight to show the broad circle over the front of Ben's jeans where he'd pissed himself.

"Let him go and I'll stay here with you."

"Trevor the Brave."

"I'll tell you what I saw upstairs."

"Tell me now."

"Let Ben go first."

"Fine. I'll stick this up both your asses."

That's when I said what I must have thought before but never spoken, or thought of speaking.

"You've never really had a friend, have you, David?"

The coach kept his eyes on me for a long time. Because the flashlight blinded me, I couldn't tell what he was thinking, if anything. But I felt that he wasn't really considering me at all. He was listening.

The flashlight grew brighter as he approached. He was going to put the gun against my head and blow it off. Then he was going to turn around and do the same thing to Ben. And then he'd walk out of here with the boy whispering ideas in his head, and he'd do as he was told.

But what he actually did was stop right in front of me. Press the handle of the revolver into my right hand, the flashlight into the left.

"I'm glad he chose you," the coach whispered.

I followed him with the light. Watched him walk, hunched, to the post we'd shackled him to. Ben rose to his feet. Blinked at the coach, then back at me, before rushing up the cellar stairs. It left me to keep the light on the coach as he slid his back down the post until he met the floor and stretched his arms back, offering his wrists to be tied.

"I'm tired," he said, his voice the coach's again. "Jesus *H*., am I tired."

There would be repeated questions among us about this later. And because Ben was already upstairs, waiting for me to join him, it was my memory that had to be counted on.

Before I left, I put the gun back in the workbench drawer. I made sure the coach didn't see me do it. Then I tied his hands tight to the post.

I swear it now as I swore it then. That's what I remember.

That's the truth.

12

THE DAWN IS PINK and smells of clean sheets and Play-Doh. The latter scent emanating from the human figures that Kieran had apparently made some time ago, and that his mother had refused to smush back into formless blobs. Smiling sculptures where the clock radio usually sits.

"He calls it his family," Sarah says, stroking the hair off my forehead. "But there's six of them. Aside from his dad, and my mother before she died, he's never met a blood relative, so I'm not sure who he's thinking they are."

"He wants to be part of a clan."

"Too late to give him that."

"He's got you. It's all he needs."

"Really?"

"One good person to look out for you? I'd take it."

"But it doesn't stop him from wishing."

"You can't stop anybody from that."

She kisses me. When my hand has trouble finding her cheek she places it against the soft skin it was aiming for.

"You can stay here," she says. "For as long as you're in town. If you want."

"What about Kieran?"

"It's not his room."

"Would it be, I don't know, confusing for him or something?"

"You can't protect kids from reality. My one piece of wisdom from my time down here in Single Mom Land."

"I might be leaving tonight. I'm not sure."

"It's an invitation, that's all."

I consider this, my hand steadied by the firm line of her jaw. I thought this was the one advantage of Parkinson's, selling Retox, withdrawing from the world's excitements: no more desire, no more crests and troughs to unsettle the ride. And now this sensible, good-looking woman—Sarah, object of my high-school lust and daydreams of death-do-us-part—is inquiring after my wants as though I had a right to them.

"Thank you," I say.

"Don't panic. I'm not asking you to be my date to the prom or anything." She taps a finger against my temple. "We're just falling forwards for a day or two, that's all."

"Falling backwards, in our case."

"Backwards, forwards," she says, rising out of the sheets. "You're saying you can tell the difference?"

I want to outline her lips with a finger but I don't trust any of them, so I remain still. As still as I can manage.

"Sarah?"

"Yeah?"

"Why are you doing this?"

"Doing what?"

"Being nice to me."

"*Nice*? This isn't about *nice*."

"I just don't want you to be here because you think you're doing me some good."

"Like a charity case?"

"Something like that."

"Okay, let's get this straight. I'm here because I want to be here. Because what we did last night felt good. And because I've thought about you a lot for a long time, since you were a boy. I'm curious about the man that boy has grown into. That's all there is to it. I'm in this for *me*, understand?"

My request of the night before had been honoured. I had enjoyed ten solid hours of thoughts uninterrupted by Tracey Flanagan, or the shapes that the terrible hunger that has been awakened within the Thurman house has taken. But as I watch Sarah get dressed for work, the early sun through the window tells me that all bets are now off. It's how Sarah's nakedness interchanges with Tracey's, the two bodies losing their particularity, veering close to becoming a lifeless composite. This, along with the mental stop-starts that throw me from desire to fear and back again in the time it takes a bare arm to slip through the sleeve of an undershirt.

"Are you all right?" she asks when her head pops up through the collar. "You've gone all white."

"I'm nothing without my morning coffee."

"You look like you've had a bad dream or something."

"Except I'm awake."

"Yeah. Except you're awake."

I roll out of bed and do my best to pull my pants on and button my shirt without asking for help, and Sarah knows enough about male pride not to offer it.

"I need to talk to Randy," I say.

"What about?"

"We were at Jake's the night Tracey Flanagan went missing. She was our waitress. I spoke to the police about it yesterday."

"You know something?"

"No. But that hasn't stopped it from freaking me out."

"Heather Langham."

My fingers spasm open. The belt they were holding clatters to the hardwood. "I don't suppose I'm the only one who's thinking about her right now."

"You'd be surprised. Even in a town this small, people forget, or half forget."

"Maybe I'm just not as good at forgetting."

"It's not that. It's that you've been away."

"It doesn't feel that way."

"That's sort of my point. You left after Grimshaw's last big tragedy, and now you're here for its latest one. It's like the time in between got squished together. It was another life. But for the rest of us, we've just got the one, and there's been twenty years in the same place to muddle through."

"I've done my share of muddling."

"You told me. Preoccupations. But in your mind, Grimshaw is frozen in time. It's a museum."

"And I remember every inch of it."

"You feel it more than you remember it."

"Wait a second. How do you know all this better than I do?"

"I *always* knew it better than you did."

I bend to pick up my belt. Surprise myself by threading it through the loops on the first try.

Here's the problem. Here's why I walk through the wakening streets of Grimshaw hearing the birdsong as the nervous chatter of bad news: despite anything I might tell myself, there is a line that runs through the past, the secret history of Heather and the coach and the boy, right up to the more current events of Ben's death and Tracey Flanagan pulled out of the world. I don't know where the line started, or where it might find its end, but it's there, understandable to itself, refusing to let common sense break its hold.

Still, as I walk into the Queen's Hotel and struggle up the stairs to knock on Randy's door, I don't expect him to see this as I do. Indeed, part of me is hoping he doesn't.

"Look at you," he says, wearing only boxers and a threadbare Just Do It T-shirt. "Mr. I Got Lucky."

"You could at least make an attempt to hide your jealousy."

"Why bother?"

"Come to think of it, you always had a thing for Sarah, didn't you?"

"Of course. But I was the horniest teenager in Perth County. I had a thing for Minnie Mouse and Natalie from *Facts of Life* and the lady who did the weather on Channel 12."

Randy digs the sleep from his eyes. Steps closer.

"What's happened?"

"Nothing," I say.

"So what are you doing here when you should be bringing Sarah breakfast in bed?"

"Does the coffee machine in your room work?"

"It spits out brown stuff, if that's what you're asking."

A moment later I'm staring out the window, listening to the water hiss and dribble into the glass pot.

"I told you," Randy says behind me, and I turn to accept his congratulatory handshake. "I *told* you she was into you."

"You're acting like I just made out with somebody in a parked car."

"You did it in Sarah's *car*?"

"How old are you, Randy?"

"Hey now. Let's not be cruel."

Randy hands me a mug of coffee. "Did they find her?" he asks, slumping into the room's only chair. "That's it, isn't it? They found Tracey?"

"I haven't heard anything about that."

"But this has to do with her, doesn't it?"

"Yes."

"So?"

"I think she's in the house."

Randy returns the pot to the warmer, where it sizzles off the coffee that had spilled when he pulled it out. He watches it bubble for a moment as though recording the observations of a science experiment.

"What makes you say that, Trev?"

"A feeling. I've thought I've seen some things, too."

"Like what?"

"It doesn't matter."

"You're relying on your feeling, then."

"And the way there seems to be some kind of pattern. Heather and Tracey."

"Not really much of a pattern. These things just *happen*. I wish they didn't, but they do."

"You're forgetting Ben. He believed his watching the house was keeping something bad inside of it. And then, after he's gone, something bad happens."

Randy sits down on the edge of the bed. "I thought you got the police to go in there already."

"I don't know how hard they looked."

"How hard would they have to look?"

"You can miss places."

"You mean a secret room you can get to only if you pull on a candlestick holder and the bookshelf spins around?"

"I mean a closet, under the floorboards. The cellar."

Randy looks up at the ceiling, as though reading a message in the plaster's cracks.

"You want us to go in there," he says.

"I can't go to the police again. So that leaves us."

"Because you think Heather is inside."

"Tracey," I correct.

"Right," Randy says. "You think Tracey is in the Thurman house."

"I only know that I won't be able to live with myself if I guessed right that someone's in there and I didn't do anything about it."

My intention is to leave, but my legs aren't following orders. I'm standing by the window, arms crossed, waiting for my engine to start.

"You sound just like Ben," Randy says.

"You don't think I know that?"

"And we remember how that turned out."

"Yes. We remember," I say. "But was he wrong?"

Something in the force of these words lubricates my joints, and I'm launched toward the door. But Randy beats me to it.

"You figure Thiessen's Hardware is still open out on King?" he says. "Because I'm guessing neither of us packed gloves and flashlights."

———

Randy suggested we wait to go in at midnight. Yet when I pointed out that it got dark at seven this time of year and asked what was to be gained by waiting around another five hours, he had no answer, other than "Isn't this the sort of stuff you *do* at midnight?"

We're up in Ben's room, passing around a mickey of Lamb's that Randy picked up on the way over. It helps. The rum's warmth lends some humour to the situation. We are nothing more than a pair of grown men contemplating a harmless stunt. The hiring of a stag-party stripper or cocooning the groom's car in toilet paper.

"Did you like it?" Randy asks after a couple swallows. "The whole nightclub business. Was it what you wanted?"

"It was very profitable for a time."

"I'm not asking about that."

"I know you're not." Randy passes the bottle and I take a swallow. "Okay. This is going to sound ridiculous."

"And what we're doing tonight isn't?"

"I think I worked so hard the past fifteen years to build something I could hide behind," I say. "People think anybody who runs a place like mine is in it for the girls or the dope or having people stop to look as you drive by in your Merc with the personalized Retox plates. But honestly, I didn't really care about any of that."

"Doesn't sound too bad to me."

"It wasn't. It was neither good nor bad, nor anything. It was just this thoughtless, gleaming, perfect skin I could wear."

I hold the Lamb's out to Randy, who takes a glug. And then another.

"It's a funny thing," he says. "But I think I was trying to do the exact opposite."

"How's that?"

"All this time I've been working to take my skin *off*. Show what lies beneath. Which might sound like drama school crap, but I believed it."

"You didn't seem to take it too seriously."

"But I *did*," he says, passing the bottle back to me. "'Just act normal.' Remember?"

"Acting was more than just a job for you? That what you're saying?"

"It wasn't a job at all. In fact, it's the job part that I hate."

"Or not *getting* the job."

"Yes. That sucks too."

I try to screw the cap back onto the bottle, but my fingers aren't cooperating, so I take another drink instead and leave it open.

"I've never understood something about the whole drama thing," I say.

"What?"

"Are actors faking being someone else or opening up what they already are?"

"The lousy ones—the ones like me—are just making faces and saying lines they memorized. The good ones *become*."

"Become what?"

"Something new out of something they've always been."

Randy appears reflective, and at first I suspect it is the beginning of a routine, a comic mask of seriousness he's put on to set a mood before delivering the punchline. But when he speaks next, it doesn't sound anything like humour.

"You know what the worst part of getting old is?"

"Old?" I say. "We're only forty, Randy."

"Don't give me that 'only forty' bullshit. Because I *know* you know what I'm talking about."

"Okay, you got me. What's the worst part?"

"Realizing you haven't done a goddamn thing with your life."

"There's only so many Nobel Prizes to go around."

"It doesn't have to be that big. Nobody else even needs to know about it other than you. It just has to be, I don't know, *remarkable*."

"There's still time."

"I don't think so," Randy says, and the lost look in his eyes is suddenly real, a joke-repellent sadness. "That's all I've wanted since I left this place. To do one small, remarkable thing. It could have changed everything."

"Changed you, you mean?"

"Everything."

Outside, the wind blows night over the town. A grey sand that settles on the roof shingles and in the crooks of tree limbs. Randy is watching it come when he asks, for the first time out loud, a question I have asked myself a thousand times before.

"Who is he?" he says.

"I don't know."

"What do you think he wants?"

"I've got a theory on that one."

"Shoot."

"More."

"More what?"

"Whatever it is someone might be able to give him. More of themselves."

"The worst part of themselves."

"Exactly."

"It's like he *pushes* you."

"And he does it by pretending he knows you," I say. "He's almost *sympathetic*, you know? *We're all flawed, all have impure thoughts, no big deal. So let's have some fun.* He makes it feel like the two of you are best friends."

"Except he actually hates you," Randy says. "He hates you, and he wants you to rot and hate in there with him."

It's night now. Dinnertime, though it could be any of the long hours between now and the reluctant October dawn. This, and our talk of the boy, has chilled the previous illusion of good humour and left us stone-faced and cold, wishing for homes we haven't known for half a lifetime.

"This was my idea, so I guess I ought to lead the way," I announce finally, working my way to the top of the attic stairs. For the time it takes me to reach the second-floor landing, I can't hear any steps behind me and figure Randy has decided to stay behind. Yet when I look back he is there.

"Night, Mrs. McAuliffe," I call through her closed bedroom door as we pass.

"You boys try to stay out of trouble!"

"In Grimshaw?"

"Oh, you can find trouble just about anywhere if you're looking for it," the old woman says, and from under the door, the light from her bedside lamp retreats into shadow.

Just as we crossed Caledonia Street with the intention of entering the Thurman house when we were sixteen, we don't even try the front door, and instead prowl along the hedgerow to the back. On our way, I measure the side windows that look into the living room, half expecting to still see the *fuckt* drawn into the dust. But there is no message there at all now except for the streaks of condensation that have left lines over the glass like tear stains.

The backyard is the same as I remember it, if smaller. The rusted swing set and see-saw built for dwarves, the fence around the lot that looks like even I could heave myself over it if I came at it with a little speed.

And then we look up at the back of the house, and it seems to have grown over the second we took our eyes off it. The brick arse of the place looming over where we stand, the windows unshuttered and lightless. The headless rooster weather vane spinning left, then right, then back again, as though trying to decide which way offers the best route for escape.

"It's just the same as every other place along this street," Randy whispers. "So why is it the only one that's so friggin' ugly?"

"Because it's not the same as every other place," I answer, and start toward the back door.

Start, then stop. Wait for Randy to take my arm for a few steps when my legs refuse to carry me any closer.

"You okay?" he asks, and with my nod, he goes in.

Which leaves me on my own. And I'm turning around. Ready to get as far from the bad smell that exhales from the open doorway as my feet are prepared to take me.

Hold on, Trev, the boy says. *You don't want Handy Randy to see the show without you, do you?*

No. I want to see the show too.

From the kitchen, Randy asks where I've got to. Then I'm in too. The sound of Randy's steps pacing over the curled linoleum. Along with the internal cold that signals the arrival of a virus. A sensation located more in the mind than the body. A degradation. The unshakeable idea that, in merely being here, I have shamed myself.

"How do you want to do this?" Randy asks once I feel my way to where he is.

I don't know. But let's stay together, I want to say, but instead say, "I'll take the cellar. You look around on this floor and upstairs."

"Better you than me."

Then he's gone.

It could be courage that has me shuffle over to the cellar door and push it open, staring down into the dark, but it doesn't feel like it. It is merely a surrender to the next moment.

What's suddenly clear is that it wasn't Tracey Flanagan who brought me here. I am here because the house was lonely for me. And in a way I can't possibly explain, I am lonely for it too.

I turn on the flashlight, and an orb of yellow plays over the stairwell's plaster walls.

But there is nothing to see. I'll have to go down there to find whatever might be found. And it's not something I am able to do without someone else going down first. Or being pushed.

Pushed. The last time I stood here I'd wondered the same thing. Wondered if Carl, who stood behind me, was someone else entirely. Someone wearing a convincing Carl suit.

But it *was* Carl, only changed in the way all of us had been changed.

"It's different," he had said at the time, and I hadn't known what he'd meant. Though I do now.

I'm three steps down when I hear Randy's voice. Speaking my name from the other end of the hall. Careful not to shout, as though trying not to disturb another's sleep.

I backstep up the cellar stairs and scuff to the hall. Randy is standing against the front door, so that at first I think he's trying to prevent it from opening. But as I get closer I see that his back isn't touching the door at all.

"Up there," he whispers.

Now the two of us stand at the bottom of the stairs. Nervous suitors waiting for our prom dates to come down.

But when someone appears at the top of the stairs it's not a girl in a chiffon dress. It isn't Tracey Flanagan, and it isn't the boy. It's one of us, unshaven and hunched. Alive but with all the years of regret and negligence written over him like a useless map.

This is what frightens Randy and me, what we can see clearly for the first time:

There is the unreal.

And then there is the real, which can sometimes be the more surprising of the two.

MEMORY DIARY

Entry No. 13

I didn't ask Ben how the coach had managed to get
untied and take the gun from him. We walked out
the back door together without talking of the boy, or
the scene the blue light of the passing snowplow had
revealed to me upstairs. Ben just crossed Caledonia
Street and shuffled up the front steps of his house,
kicked his boots against the wall to knock off the snow
and slipped inside. I looked back at the Thurman house,
half expecting some new display in one of its windows,
but each pane of glass was a hollow iris, taking in me,
the street, the slumbering homes of Grimshaw, giving
nothing in return.

I don't remember speaking to my parents when I
came in (my father captaining the remote, my mother
asleep sitting up on the sofa, a basket of half-folded laundry

at her feet—their usual evening positions). It was strange how, after all that had happened in the house that night, I walked out and didn't speak a word to anyone until the next morning, when I called Carl and, before he could say hello, blurted out "It's over" as if we'd been dating.

"I know."

"We have to let him go, Carl."

"I know."

"And last night, Ben and I were with him, and—"

"Not on the phone."

"You don't understand."

"Fuck you I don't."

"I saw something. There was—"

He hung up.

Ten minutes later we were walking over to the Thurman house together.

Why had I called Carl and only Carl? There was no choice, really. It could only have been him puffing steam out his nose, telling me to shut up every time I tried to explain what happened the night before, his eyes darting between the houses on either side of us, alert to witnessing stares.

It was early enough that there was little traffic on the streets. Still, we approached the house by way of the back lane and slipped through the break in the fence.

As soon as we were through, we both stopped. The house looked different somehow, though it took a moment to figure out how.

"Did you leave the door open last night?" Carl said.

"No."

"Did Ben?"

"I was the last one out."

Carl started toward the back door. His gait—rolling shoulders and old warrior's limp—suggested the weariness of a man charged with completing a serious task, but been thwarted at every turn by his forced partnership with children.

I followed him in. By the time my eyes had adjusted to the dimness, Carl was already heading down the cellar stairs. Neither of us had brought flashlights, thinking (if we thought of it at all) that the morning's sunlight would be sufficient. But there were only two half-buried windows in the cellar. It was barely enough for me to see Carl standing just a few feet from where I had stopped at the bottom of the stairs.

"Oh fuck," he said.

I went forward to put my shoulder against his, peered into the near darkness beyond.

Emptiness. No, not that. Not *only* that. The cords we'd used to tie the coach to the post now a loose coil on the ground.

"We'll find him," I said.

"He's probably at the cop shop right now."

"No. They would have come for us already."

"You think he just went home and asked his wife to fry him some eggs and not to worry about where he's been the last three days?"

"I don't think he ever planned to go home after this."

"Right, *right*," Carl said, his thoughts so rushed it seemed to be causing him pain. "So why bother looking for him? We were going to let him go anyway."

"We need to make sure he's okay."

"Why wouldn't he be?"

"Because he was in here alone."

Carl shuffled closer to the post. Bent to inspect the cords.

"These haven't been cut."

"I tied him."

"You sure?"

"I was here, Carl. You weren't."

"Maybe I should have been."

He stood. Put his hands in his pockets, took them out again.

I said, "I'm not arguing with you right now."

"Is there something you want to argue about?"

"I'm saying we should get out of here. Look for the coach. If we can find him, maybe we can—"

"How are we going to find him, Trev? Put up posters? 'LOST—Half-Starved English Teacher. Contents of Teenager's Piggy Bank Offered in Reward'?"

"At least I'm trying."

"You fucking should."

"What's that mean?"

"Just that the last time I was down here, the coach was tied to that post and my gun was in the workbench drawer."

Our brains were running at the same speed. They must have been, because it took both of us the same one second to turn to see the workbench drawer upside down on the earth floor.

We both went for it. Carl got there first. Kicked the drawer instead of turning it over with his hand, either to prevent leaving his fingerprints or because he needed to kick *something* if not me.

The revolver was gone.

"Shit," Carl said. "This is some seriously shitty shit."

"He wasn't even supposed to know it was there."

"Unless somebody showed him."

"You're blaming me for this too?"

"I said 'somebody.'"

"Who? Why would one of us do that?"

"Maybe it wasn't one of us."

Carl faced me. What I could read in the lips, suddenly gulping for his next mouthful of air, made it clear. He had seen something too.

Laughter. Coming from upstairs. The coach's, along with at least one other. Whinnying and cruel.

I can't remember if Carl started up the cellar stairs first or if I did. But we were both running, clutching handfuls of the house's cold air and throwing it behind us.

The laughter was now impossibly loud, a chorus of false joy shrieking out from the cracks in the walls. Sound so dense it thickened the space we moved through, slowing us to the floating leaps of astronauts.

Carl rounded through the kitchen and down the main hall. The nylon of his parka squeaking through my fingers as I followed a half-stride behind him. And then, in the next second, he was pulling away. Because I made the mistake of glancing into the living room on the way past.

There was the boy. Standing behind a naked Heather Langham, his pants a coil of denim around his ankles.

The two of them framed by the tall side window, the *fuckt* still there, Heather's fingers cutting lines around the letters. The boy slapping himself against her, oblivious to anything but his grip on her waist.

Then he spun his head around to face me. Except it wasn't the boy's face. It was mine.

"Trevor!"

Carl was waiting at the bottom of the stairs, looking at me quizzically, knowing I'd seen something.

I could have run past him, opened the front door (if it could be opened) and left Carl on his own to find out what the boy and the coach found so funny. There was no one left to save, after all. Whatever we'd done, and the reasons we'd first done it, didn't mean anything anymore.

Yet when Carl started up the stairs, I was right behind him. When I got to the landing, he was already halfway down the hall, led by the laughter that was coming from the one partly open door. The same doorway through which I'd seen the boy standing over a face-down female body on the bed.

Carl slowed. It wasn't cowardice that held me there, watching, but a command.

Carl's turn first.

He booted the door open.

Then a cowardly thought *did* enter my mind: I didn't need to know what Carl now knew. A second-hand report would be enough. And judging by the stricken look on Carl's face, what was to be seen belonged to a different level of awfulness altogether. It was the party the boy had invited us to.

But instead of doing what I meant to—turn around and start back down the stairs—I made my way along the hallway to where Carl stood outside the boy's childhood bedroom.

Because that's what it was, wasn't it? A room that, in its past, had been caught in the uncomfortable in-between of small-town sixteen, of the age and place I was myself.

"Carl?" My voice girlish in the empty hallway.

He didn't answer, didn't move.

We're going to have quite a time.

The coach stood across the room, in the same place where the boy had stood over the body on the bed. In the dim light, his degradation was fully visible: soiled pants, running nose, the beginnings of grey beard. And he was wearing lipstick. A smearing of rosy red extended beyond the lines of his thin lips, yet still carefully applied, a drawn mouth of female wantonness, all curves and pucker. It was the lipstick colour Heather wore—no, it *was* Heather's. Taken from her before she died, before the coach left her in the cellar.

He looked terribly afraid.

Isn't he pretty? Go on. Give him a kiss.

"You have to go," the coach said, his voice raw from laughter. Laughter, I could see now, he'd been forced to perform.

"Not without you," Carl said.

"You'll die if you stay."

"Nobody's dying here."

"Too late." The coach showed his teeth again in that not-smile of his.

"Come with us," I said.

"I can't leave *now*."

"Why?"

"If you're here long enough—if you *listen*—he won't let you."

"There's nobody here but us. It's just an empty house."

"No such thing as an empty house."

That's when the coach raised the gun. It had been in his hand the whole time, but it hung so loose, aimed at nothing but the dust bunnies at his feet, that we hadn't noticed it. He brought it level to his waist. Aimed it at us.

"He told me to hurt you," he said.

The coach stuck the index finger of his left hand in his ear, as though blocking out the sound of a passing siren. And with his right hand he raised the revolver. Screwed the end of its barrel into the other ear.

"But I'm not listening anymore."

Carl started toward him first. And though I couldn't see his regret, his wish to fix what he'd been a part in breaking, his already enveloping grief, I knew that it was in Carl as much as it was in me, and that the coach saw it in both of us. Because, right at the end, he was his real self again. Not the boy's talking dummy, but our guardian. Fighting off the voice so loud in his head we could hear it too—*Wait! Not yet! You don't want to be alone in here, do you? Don't you want to keep your boys close?*—to push the revolver's barrel a half-inch deeper into his skull and pull the trigger.

13

AT FIRST, what is even stranger than seeing that it is Carl descending the stairs of the Thurman house and passing between us is the way he simply turns the bolt lock on the front door, pulls it open and steps out onto the porch.

"I never knew you could open that thing," Randy says. "I never knew you could just walk out."

Tracey tried to, I think. *But the house wouldn't let her.*

From the threshold we peer out over a front lawn carpeted in leaves midway through their transformation from brittle yellows and oranges to black custard. And Carl squishing his boot prints into them as he walks to the sidewalk, where he faces us. Slips his hands into the pockets of his jeans and shudders at the night's chill.

"You faggots coming or not?" he says.

We follow him, equalling his brisk pace but not quite catching up. He stops at the railway tracks that cross Caledonia and starts left, crunching over the gravel that aprons the long, steel tongues. It is as it was before: Carl leading us into some night-time adventure, a bit of badness we trusted him to guide us through, even if we knew it was not *entirely* safe. Driving too fast in his dad's LTD II with the headlights off. Vandalism. Trespassing. Smoking homegrown possibly sprayed, he said, with angel dust or PCP or acid, evil-sounding supplements whose potential harms we had no clue of but did not ask about before inhaling.

In fact this was one of the places, hidden within the web of metal struts that buttress the tracks over our heads, the traffic of Erie Street passing in a tidal wash thirty feet below, where we would gather to smoke or pass one of Randy's father's *Hustler*s between ourselves. (I have just now the memory of a twelve-year-old Ben studying one of the centrefolds and, pointing at the complicated mechanics of the model's upturned hips, asking, "Does the pee come out *there*, or *there*, or *there*?" and none of us certain of the answer.) What's different is that, unlike then, it is now something of a struggle—and not only for me—to crabwalk up the cement slope of the trestle and into the weeds that have pushed through the cracks. By the time the three of us have found positions where there is limited risk of our sliding down onto the pavement below, we are panting like dogs.

"I hope your feelings won't be hurt," Carl says eventually, "if I say that you both look like hell."

"Funny thing to say. Coming from you," Randy says.

"But I'm the junkie, remember? I'm not even supposed to be *alive*."

"That's your excuse?"

"That and the fact I've gone three days without a shower."

"So we smelled."

If I didn't know better, I'd say Carl was the actor among us, not Randy. Of course Carl would be up for different parts: the mob hitman, the craggy roughneck, the retired boxer looking for one last bout to redeem himself. There is the aura of brutal experience about Carl that would be useful to the camera. He is lean too, his face pulled back over hard cheekbones and chin. The years, however harsh, have left him with a mournful handsomeness.

"That was you at the Old Grove, wasn't it?"

"Hello to you too, Trev."

"I *saw* you."

"You think I'd miss Ben's funeral?"

"That's what we were betting."

"Well, I was there."

"But you were *hiding*."

Carl doesn't flinch at this. As though he hadn't heard it at all. "I came as soon as I heard."

"How did you hear?"

"You left a message. It went down the line of some people I know. And when I got it, I called in some favours and got enough money to get a standby ticket."

"You took a flight?"

"From out west."

"Where out west?"

Carl grinds his teeth. "You sound like a cop."

"I just think it's strange, the way you've turned up."

"You mean me being in the house?"

"Yeah."

"You were there too, weren't you?"

I let this go for the moment. "Why did you run? When I saw you at the cemetery?"

"I didn't want you to see me."

"Why not?"

"I came for Ben. To say goodbye. That's all I had the strength for."

"And spending five minutes with me and Randy would have been too much for you? Saying hello might have tired you out?"

Carl scratches his ankles. He's not wearing socks, and the skin is blue from cold. "You sound angry, Trev."

Below us, another eighteen-wheeler hauling pigs to the slaughterhouse in Exeter wheels by, and I have to wait for the echoes of its shifting gears to dissipate before speaking again.

"Where's Tracey Flanagan?"

"I heard she's missing. That's it."

"Is she in the house?"

"What?"

"Did you see her?"

Did you hurt her? I want to ask. *Were those your hands that pulled her back into the dark?*

"I didn't see anybody."

"Because that's why we were in there. We were looking for her."

"Good for you."

"So you don't know anything about it?"

Carl places his hands on his knees. Shows us the dirty fingernails. The pale knuckles.

"If you want to accuse me of something, say it so I can walk over to where you're sitting and stick my fist down your throat," he says. "But if you're just a little worked up, if those shakes of yours have eaten away at your brain and twisted the wires in the part that tells you when it's time to calm the fuck down, then I'm ready to forgive you. Which is it?"

"It's Parkinson's. And if you talk about it again the way you just did, I'll be the one to take some of your teeth out the hard way. Understand?"

Carl starts over toward me. But when he gets within range of my trembling, cross-legged self, instead of throwing a punch as I—and a stiffened Randy—expect, he places his hand against the side of my neck.

"Look at us," he says. "A pair of grey-haired geezers."

"I tried to fight it, then I tried to ignore it. Nothing worked."

"Me, I tried to end it," he says. "That didn't work either." He spits a thick gob and watches the white foam snake down the concrete away from our feet. Then he elbows me in the ribs.

"I'm still waiting for you to tell us," Randy says directly to Carl.

"Tell you what?"

"Why you were in that house."

Carl climbs up onto one of the steel struts and sits on it, perched with his legs swinging beneath him.

"You own a nightclub or something, right, Trev?"

"Used to."

"Get a nice price?"

"My real estate agent is still sending me flowers."

"There you go. Even Randy here has been working. I saw you in that Rug Rubber ad a few months back."

"You *saw* that?" Randy says, clearly touched.

"You were dressed up in fur or something?"

"A dust bunny."

"Yeah! And then this giant worm—"

"The Rug Rubber."

"It ate you."

"More like it sucked me."

"That's right! You were *good*, man."

"What's your point here?" I ask.

"My point is I don't have any money. And not just 'I'm a little short this month,' but *nothing*." With the departure of his smile he grows instantly thinner. "My plan was to come into town, pay my respects to Ben and get out on the train that night. It was pretty much all I could afford to do anyway."

"But you didn't go."

"No."

"Why not?"

Carl is standing now. He'd like to pace, but the slope of the trestle makes it too difficult, and he is left bent over at the waist, shuffling under the girders.

"I haven't used in over six months," he says. "It's been hard. The hardest thing I've ever done. But I've been clean for longer than a week for the first time since I was thirteen years old, and it feels good. I'm actually *proud* of myself, know what I mean? Then I come here. And as soon as I get off the train I can hear his voice. The boy's voice. Telling me to do things."

"Like what?"

"Give in. To go out and cop a rock, fuck myself up. He wanted to see me fail. No, not even that." Carl wipes the back of his hand under his nose. "What he really wanted was to watch me die."

"It didn't work," Randy says.

"But it almost did. The first night I'm here and I'm calling up some guys I know, asking who's dealing in Grimshaw these days. Less than an hour after they put Ben down in the ground and I've got a loaded crack pipe in my hand, sitting on a bed out at the Swiss Cottage, where they've given me the off-season special, telling myself that if I smoke this shit, if I go back to that life, it'll kill me."

I don't want to ask this, but I do. "Did you light it?"

"I wanted to. The voice was *telling* me to. The boy was saying how my life was never worth much anyway, so why not enjoy myself a little before joining my old buddy Ben for a nice, long dirt nap. I came close about seven thousand times over the next day and a half. But no, I didn't."

"You could have come to us," Randy starts. "We would—"

"I *know* you would have helped, Randy. Or tried. I know you both would. That's why I came to look for you tonight."

"You looked for us in the Thurman house?" I ask.

"Over the nights I stayed at the Swiss Cottage, I'd go for walks around town. One way or another I'd always end up at the bottom of Caledonia Street, keeping away from the streetlights, looking at that fucking house. And then I saw Trev going into the McAuliffes'. Figured that's where you were staying. So that's where I headed first tonight, to see if you were there. But I didn't get as far as Mrs. A.'s door."

"What stopped you?"

"The house." Carl looks up through the slats at the slices of night sky overhead. "What I saw in the house."

Randy shoots me a look. One that says that he's not going to ask, so it's up to me.

"What did you see, Carl?"

"A girl in the window. One of the upstairs bedrooms. Remember, Trev?"

A picture of the boy returns to me: standing over the bed, over a girl's body, the pattern of blood on the walls. I have to squeeze my eyes shut and open them again to push it away. "I remember."

"She was looking down at me," Carl says. "Just a kid. A totally scared-shitless kid. Trying to claw her way through the glass but at the same time not wanting anyone to hear her, y'know? Because she wasn't alone in there."

"Was it Tracey Flanagan? Heather?"

"No. It was nobody I knew."

"Okay. So you went in."

"The truth? I wasn't looking to rescue anything other than my own ass tonight, but yeah. I ran in there and up the stairs and kicked that door open—all the very *last* things in the world I wanted to do—and nobody was there. Then, maybe a minute later, I heard sounds downstairs. Footsteps. I went to the top of the stairs and looked down and there was Randy. And then you too."

From far away there comes a low roar. At first I take it as the approach of a freight train that we can feel through the trestle's rails and ties—cattle cars and fuel tanks and Made in China whatnot that will soon be passing over our heads. But the sound rolls on a moment, growing in intensity, before abruptly receding. Thunder. Unseen clouds that have stolen the few stars from the sky.

"We were talking yesterday. Me and Randy," I find myself saying when the air is still again. "About what we saw in the house when we were kids."

"The real things? Or the other things?"

"You saw him too then, didn't you?"

Carl locks the fingers of his two hands together. A here's-the-church-and-here's-the-steeple fist. "Him?"

"The boy in the house."

"*We* were boys. And *we* were in the house."

"It wasn't us. You just said you heard him as soon as you got off the train."

"Heard. Not saw."

"C'mon, Carl. We all saw him."

"Then tell me. What did he look like?"

"Look like?"

"His *appearance*. If you both saw the same person—if I saw him too—we should be able to agree on the colour of his hair, his eyes, the length of his nose. All that."

It's the damnedest thing. But no matter how many times I have returned to the boy in my mind, no matter how vivid his presence in my dreams, I cannot conjure him in the details Carl has just asked for.

"Randy," I say, "why don't you start?"

"I'm not sure I can."

"Why not?"

"It's like being asked to describe, I don't know, air or something. Or loss, or anger. You can't say what shape it takes, only what it does to you."

Carl claps his hands together. "If *that's* what you saw, then I've seen him too."

"I could say more than that about him," I say. "He looked a lot like me."

"Or like me," Randy says.

"Or me," Carl says.

A second rumble of thunder reaches us from an even greater distance than the first. Yet this time, it continues to widen its sound. Bearing down on Grimshaw with sustained fury.

Carl says something, or tries to but the noise is too great for us to hear him. It's just his mouth opening into a circle and clenching shut, over and over.

Pain! Pain!

Then the terrible clatter of the wheels rolling over us. The trellis's steel crying under its weight.

"Train! Train!"

I wait for the black cars to pass, my arms around my knees. Close my eyes against the glint of Carl's teeth.

It's only the train, I know. But something sounds as though it has joined us down here. Something that is screaming and will never stop.

Over the time it takes to reach the Queen's and check Carl in with my credit card, I am wondering the same thing. I wonder it all the way to Caledonia Street, where I stop at the curb opposite the Thurman house.

Why don't we talk about it?

Why, after all these years, do we not even mention the elephant in the room—the elephant in our *lives*—that is what we did and saw in the winter of 1984? One reason is that we promised never to speak of it again. And none of us wished to be the first to break this promise.

But it's really more simple than that. We are men. Defined by the bearing of terrible truths more than a fondness for sports, for sex, for the wish to be left alone. It is as men that we remain silent to our horror.

I totter up the stairs to Ben's room. Roll onto the bed and sit up against the headboard, planning to record another entry for my Memory Diary. But when I reach for the Dictaphone on the bedside table, it's gone. At first, I assume I put it down somewhere else. Twenty minutes of upturning pillows and cheek-to-the-hardwood scans of the floor prove that it's not here.

I look out Ben's window. Wonder if the boy took it, and is now listening to it over and over for his own pleasure.

Then I wonder something worse. What if it is now in the

hands of someone who hears it for what it really is, not a diary at all but the confession of a crime? What if Betty McAuliffe is holding it to her ear under the sheets of her bed? What if someone who knew it was here—Randy, or Carl, who would have seen me in the window—came in and stole it? This last one being the worst possibility of all. Not because my friends might be thieves, but because from this point on I will be unable to prevent myself from wondering if they are.

What I need is a little bedtime reading. Something to slow my mind from its restless thinking. Trouble is, the only thing I'm interested in is Ben's journal. This time, as I curl up in his bed, I don't have the patience to move forward from where I left off last time, and skip ahead to the final pages.

September 14, 2008
Woke up this morning feeling strange. Not something strange in *me*, *but something that had touched me in the night. A stranger in my room.*

I sat up in bed and saw that I was right.
A message smudged onto the inside of the bedroom window:

i found him

After this, the diary returned to its record of soups Ben had for lunch for a few days. No sightings of the boy, no shooing visitors off the Thurman property. And then the final entry:

September 20, 2008
This just happened.
It is the end of things, I know. Forgive me. I have done my best but I am tired now, so tired it's almost impossible to write this, to

push the pen over this paper. I am tired and alone and I want only to be with him, to comfort him. It's funny. It's so stupid, but it's taken until now to realize how much I've missed my father.

Forgive me.

+ + + + +

Another message on my window tonight.

I had been keeping watch on the house, and turned away only long enough to get the glass of water I'd left by the bed. But when I sat down again it was there:

daddy's waiting

I slid the window open. The night smelled of lilacs and carnations. Not a good smell, though. Flowers left too long in dry vases.

He was sitting on the front steps. Stooped, elbows propped on his knees. He <u>had</u> been waiting. He looked even more tired than me. Like he'd been running and had just stopped and was trying to remember what he'd been running from.

My father stood when he saw me. I can't exactly say what expression he wore. It was defeat, among other things. And sadness. So lonely it made him look hollow.

He turned and walked into the house. Like he'd been called in for bed. Like it was the end of a long, long day.

Forgive me.

Later that same night, Randy called to tell me Ben was gone.

MEMORY DIARY

Entry No. 14

We watched them come.

A lone police cruiser at first. The officer's shirt straining against the bulge around his waist. When he came out he wasn't wearing his cap anymore.

We stood together. Unseen behind the curtains in the front room of Ben's house, his mother out on a grocery run. When the paramedics and bearded man in a suit who must have been the coroner finally emerged with the black bags laid out on gurneys—one, and then the smaller other—we held our breaths.

We remember all this, though still not everything.

And some of the things we remember may not have happened at all.

———

The letter, amazingly, was Randy's idea.

We were sitting in the Ford before school, no more than twenty minutes after Carl and I had witnessed the coach blow the side of his head off. I suppose the two of us must have been exhibiting some symptoms of shock, but I can't recall any tears or stony stares into space. Maybe this was because everything, as they say, was *happening so fast*. And we had each other. The most horrific events remained an inch within the bounds of the manageable so long as there was at least one Guardian to share them with.

We quickly agreed that hoping it would all go away was no longer an option. Neighbours might have heard the firing of Carl's revolver. Or perhaps someone passing by saw the coach in one of the windows. Or maybe someone other than us—a junkie kicked out of his room at the Y, young lovers looking for a wall to screw against—had smelled the morgueish taint in the house's air and knew it to be more than a poisoned rat. In any case, Heather Langham and the coach would soon be found, if they hadn't been already. And the likelihood of their trails leading to us, one way or another, was high, unless we could prevent an investigation from starting in the first place. A story that made sense out of what we knew to be senseless.

They were both teachers, seen to be friendly, sharing books in the staff lounge. One night, a shared flask, an empty house. But something had gone wrong—the blows to Heather's skull showed that, along with her hasty burial. A day or two passed, long enough for the coach to be pushed all the way over the edge, and he returned to the scene to do himself in. Some version of a narrative like this happened all the time, if not in Grimshaw then in some other hicksville they flashed the name of at the bottom of the screen on the suppertime news.

Two problems, though. One: the police had to see it this way. Two: if we were going to go in this direction, we had to start now.

That's when Randy mentioned the letter. He pointed out that, if we wanted it to look like a murder-and-then-a-later-suicide, a confession from the coach was the way to go. The trick was that it would have to appear as though it were composed when he was still alive.

Ben pulled out his wallet and unfolded a piece of paper from its slot.

"We'll use this," he said.

It was the paper the coach had signed but otherwise left blank. A confession he challenged us to fill in ourselves. Which is what we did.

We went to Carl's apartment. There was an electric typewriter under his sofa that we plugged in, and we typed what we hoped would be taken as the coach's admission of guilt:

321 Caledonia

We folded it into thirds, deciding against an envelope. As an afterthought, Carl typed URGENT on the outside.

Our first idea was to drop it off at police headquarters. But Carl, who'd been inside the cop shop more than the rest of us, remembered they had security cameras at the front and back doors. We were stumped for a minute after that, until I suggested leaving it at the *Beacon* offices. No cameras there, and there was the possibility of someone in its sleepy newsroom coming across a piece of paper marked URGENT and going to the trouble of reading it.

This was how Ben (who nominated himself, and who somehow seemed right for the task) came to run the three blocks from Carl's to slip the folded paper into the mail slot next to the front doors of *The Grimshaw Beacon*.

When Ben met up with us again, he said, "My mom's out shopping. Then she's getting her hair done."

"So?" Randy said.

"So we can watch from my place."

One of us probably should have pointed out that this was an unnecessary risk. Besides, spying on the authorities as they arrived at the Thurman house to push the soil off Heather Langham and elbow the bedroom door open to the coach's bloody spatters—it might make us feel even more guilty than we already did.

But we started over to Ben's house without discussion. The thing is, we wanted to see. To observe others go inside and come out changed.

We got away with it. The family-destroying trial, the humiliations of prison. There was none of that for any of us. We were free.

But getting away with the sort of thing we did can ruin a man. It can ruin four of them.

Here's another thing I know: there are people who have got away with things all around you. Mothers and fathers, the fellow who helps lift your stroller onto the bus, the ball of rags you walk by when it asks for change. You might work with them, play beer-league ball with them, sleep with them. Good guys. And you'd never know they were one of us.

Few in town knew Heather Langham when alive, but in death, she was treated like a favourite daughter. After her body was returned to the aunt and uncle who had raised her, Grimshaw organized a memorial service in the Municipal Hall auditorium that ended up drawing a standing-room-only crowd of earnest snifflers and speech-makers. By the end, the framed photo of Heather they'd set on a chair at the front had been encircled by bouquets, wreaths, dolls and teddy bears, as though the mourners were undecided whether to treat her as a fallen soldier or a stolen child.

A couple of rows near the front had been reserved for her students, who were asked to play at the end of the service a piece of music she'd taught us. This was how Carl, Randy, Ben and I, along with a dozen other honkers and tooters, came to grind our way through "The Maple Leaf Forever" before one of Grimshaw's largest-ever public audiences. Somehow, our ineptitude only magnified the moment's poignancy.

The coach's farewell couldn't have been more different. A patchy gathering at McCutcheon's Funeral Home that we all attended—the four of us, that is, not the whole team, though among the few other players who came I recall Todd Flanagan, apologizing for the baby-formula stains on his blazer. I don't remember who delivered the eulogy. Perhaps there wasn't one. There were no photos of the deceased, no open casket; the coach's ashes were collected in an urn that, as Randy whispered to me, looked a little like the Stanley Cup.

The only other attendee I specifically recall was the coach's wife, Laura. Maybe it was the circumstances of her husband's death, or maybe she was too broken to manage the weight of the moment, but even she was dry-eyed. Locking and unlocking her fingers and checking her watch as though nervous about missing her train out of town, which perhaps she was, as none of us ever saw her in Grimshaw again.

After Miss Langham and the coach were found, it was impossible for even the most rabid fans to conceive of the Guardians continuing any further in the playoffs. The league announced the team's withdrawal from what remained of the season, giving Seaforth a bye to the next round (where they were justly trounced by the elbowing, tobacco-farmer sons of the Woodstock Wolves).

Somewhere in there Sarah broke up with me. Or I broke up with her. I can't remember a definitive moment when we both walked away knowing it was over, perhaps because such a moment never happened.

Eventually, she started seeing other guys. Roy Kimble, Dougie Craft, Larry Musselman. Likable guys I would have been happy to hang out with had I not known they were taking Sarah Mulgrave out to the Vogue or a bush party, which forced me to loathe them instead, see them as slippery smooth talkers who Sarah, being a girl, couldn't see as the preppie liars they were.

We still talked from time to time. Painful exchanges in the school hallways or out by Nicotine Corner, where she would stop to ask how I was doing as I chain-smoked before heading in, late, for class. She asked about my mom and dad, and I asked about hers. She told me she missed me, and I said it was for the best. But all I remember thinking was *You were mine once*, over and over.

The next two and a half years of high school passed in a numbed procession of skipped classes and rec-room parties and daydreams of escape. We were perfecting our normal acts.

Every day we undertook another exercise in the impossible. We slouched, listened to the Clash and tried to pretend it never happened.

We did our best to fill the widening gaps within ourselves with distractions, building bridges that might find their way to the other side. For Carl, this meant drugs. More of the pot he'd been dulling himself with even before he first went into the Thurman house, but afterward supplemented with speed, acid, coke (even then finding its way into the hinterland). He soon assumed Randy's place as our dealer, serving half the student body as well, a job that introduced him to out-of-town distributors and mules, legitimately dangerous men we'd sometimes meet sitting at his kitchen table. To us, he looked so young compared to them as he confirmed the weight of baggies on his scales, handing over rolls of cash we knew to have been earned from other kids' driveway shovelling and part-time dishwashing. We worried about him. But I think the same things that worried us frightened us as well, and so we watched Carl's descent from an especially great distance.

It was Randy who seemed the least damaged among us. He went about cementing his reputation as the school's goofball, the floppy-eared puppy who enjoyed confounding success with the ladies. He even returned to playing hockey the following year, doodling around the net and getting rubbed into the boards as he had before. Randy was Randy. This is what you'd say when he fell onto somebody's glass coffee table at a party or accepted a dare to run bare-assed down Huron Street on a Friday night. Randy the jester, our fool.

As for me, I committed myself to perfecting the teen-age-boy cloaking device: sullenness, distance, a refusal to articulate any preferences or plans. I fell out of any clubs or hobbies, and just scuffed around. Daydreaming about all the shiny disguises money could buy.

Ben was the first of us to break, and we noticed it within days of Heather Langham's memorial service.

Whenever we'd call him or drive by in Carl's car to pick him up he'd say he had something he had to do, a chore or family engagement that required him to stay home. After a time, he abandoned these excuses altogether and simply said he didn't feel like going outside, though he welcomed us to hang out with him in his attic bedroom, which we increasingly had to do if we wanted to see him at all. Within weeks, it took all of Ben's strength to make it to school and home again three days out of five, the other two written off as sick days with signed letters from his mom.

"Somebody has to watch," he told me once. Ben was seated in what was now his spot, a wooden, colonial-style chair with curled armrests situated so that he could look directly out the window.

"Watch what, Ben?"

"The house."

"Have you seen something?"

"Once or twice. Something in there wants out, Trev. And we can't let it."

There was Ben's *we* again. The trouble was, this time, he was on his own.

More and more, Ben would spend his time sitting in his chair, staring out at the Thurman house. He told us it required his full concentration to keep its windows shut, the doors closed.

"It's like what the coach said," he told us. "There's some things you have to guard against."

"Fine," Carl said. "So why's it have to be you?"

Ben looked at the three of us. For a second, the strange intensity that had become fixed over his features was relaxed, and he managed half a smile. There was love in it. Love and madness.

"Because you're all going to leave, and I'm going to stay," he said.

For what remained of our high-school days, Ben faded from the sweetly dreamy boy we had known into a silhouette, a shadow in an attic window backlit by the forty-watt bulb in the Ken Dryden lamp by his bed. Sometimes, when I missed him but didn't want to ring the doorbell and have Mrs. McAuliffe, shivery and lost, let me in, I would stand a half block from his house and watch him up there. He rarely moved. And then, all of a sudden, he would launch forward and grip his hands to the window frame, his eyes squinting at some imagined movement within the Thurman house. How many times had he repeated this useless call to attention over the years between then and the day he looped a rope over the support beam in his ceiling, tied the other end around his neck and stepped off one of the folding chairs we'd used for epic coffee-fuelled poker games in his basement?

Even then, I wondered what particular corner of hell would turn out to be mine.

14

I WAKE UP BEFORE DAWN, so that it feels as though I haven't slept at all. Which perhaps I haven't. My dreams—if they *were* dreams—were a confusion of questions. Carl. Tracey Flanagan's whereabouts. The boy. The missing Dictaphone. Along with Sarah, who while a source of some comfort has been tainted in my mind by merely being so close to these other mysteries. It's like those nightmares where you, say, catch your brother in the middle of taking an axe to the neighbour's dog: you know it's not true, it's impossible, it never happened. And yet, the next time you look at your brother—or the neighbour's dog—he's been altered. A piece of him pulled into the world of night thoughts.

I work myself out of bed, fighting the collected hours of stiffness. Every muscle a hardened cord that must be warmed, then stretched, then retrained.

I'm finally standing when I see it.

A word I recognize through the hand it is written in even before I read its letters. The same tight, furious, misspelled scrawl we'd all seen drawn into the Thurman house's living-room window over two decades ago.

fuckt

A fingernailed threat cut through the dust. And written not on the outside of the glass, but on the *inside*.

Sleepwalking. Is this another Parkinson's symptom, one of the rarer ones to be found near the bottom of the list? How about sleepwriting?

I shuffle over to the window and wipe away the boy's graffiti with a balled-up T-shirt. When I'm done, it leaves the house across the street in greater clarity. I don't watch it for long for fear of seeing the awakened thing I can feel moving through its rooms.

To avoid any direct view of the house, I return to sit on the edge of the bed. It's still early. The house, the town outside, everything still. There is time to kill before Mrs. McAuliffe gets up and I can get into the shower without disturbing her, so I have another go at Ben's journal. More pages of his take on nothing.

I turn another crinkly page and come across something so unexpected I wonder if I am in fact awake at all.

A Post-it Note. On it a message dated two months before Ben died.

TREVOR—
If you have read this far, you deserve to know.

Look behind the vent under the bed. Read only if you feel the need to. Otherwise, burn it all and don't look back.

P.S. Don't go in. No matter what. Don't go in.

The grille easily pulls away on the first tug. I stick my hand in and feel around the duct, sliding under the bedframe far enough to slip my arm down all the way to the elbow. I pull out a soft bundle.

It's another diary. This one bound in pliant leather, slim and easily folded into a roll, bound tight by a strip of silver Christmas ribbon. I untie it and open the cover to find not more pages of Ben's handwriting, but clippings and smudgy photocopies. No notes, no accompanying explanation.

The first is a story cut from a tea-coloured page of *The Grimshaw Beacon*.

GRIMSHAW YOUTH VICTIM OF GRISLY ATTACK
ELIZABETH WORTH
Born January 27, 1933. Died November 12, 1949.

Tragedy visited the home of foster parents Paul Schantz and his wife, May, this past week when one of their charges, Elizabeth Worth, was found murdered in the home. Miss Worth was only sixteen years old.

"We loved her so much. She was a lovely child, so bright and kind. We have some difficult young people come through these doors from time to time, but Elizabeth wasn't one of them. It's heartbreaking to know she had the best of her life ahead of her," commented Mr. Schantz, who has been running the foster-care facility at 321 Caledonia for the past several years since purchasing the property from James Thurman in 1941. Prior to Miss Worth's passing, Mr. Schantz and his wife (who have no offspring of their own) had four children from four separate birth families under their care.

Mr. Schantz was not in Grimshaw at the time of the murder, and police have stressed that neither he nor his wife is a suspect in their investigations. As to alternative leads, authorities admit they are currently without clear directions.

Miss Worth's body was discovered by Mrs. Schantz in an upstairs bedroom early on the morning of November 12. While police are not publicly disclosing the details of the crime, the *Beacon* has learned that it was a brutal attack, the weapon being a wood plank bearing a nail or screw at its end. This weapon was used in fatally striking Miss Worth several times.

A memorial service for Elizabeth Worth is to be held at McCutcheon's Funeral Home on Thursday, November 17, 2 P.M. Any gifts of remembrance are asked to be made to the Perth County Family Services, which administers the guardianship of orphans such as Miss Worth.

Paul Schantz. The old man we'd visited in the Cedarfield Seniors Home. The one who'd warned me about the dead coming back.

Next, an inky carbon copy.

CORONER'S REPORT—SUMMARY STATEMENT
Perth County Coroner's Office

Dr. Philip Underhill, B.Sc., M.D.

Deceased: Elizabeth Worth
Age: 16

Report Release Date: Friday, November 18, 1949

Cause of Death: Brain hemorrhage from head trauma. Circumstances involved repeated strikes to the skull (numbering 8 to 12) by a wood board. A three-inch screw affixed to the board creating an open fracture in the cranium, likely in initial strike. Subsequent blows using same instrument cause of fatal cerebral injury.

Autopsy (Summary Remarks): Homicide (see above). Upon examination, deceased showed indications of recent sexual battery and physical struggle (likely the result of resistance to attack). Nature of injuries consistent with non-consensual intercourse.

A short piece in *The Globe and Mail*.

"Not Our Man," Police Say

Announcement Clears Foster Father of Suspicion in Case of Grimshaw Girl's Rape and Murder

By David Huggins

Grimshaw—At first, the murder of a young girl in this agricultural community was received by local residents with understandable shock. However, since parts

of a coroner's report were released to the public showing Elizabeth Worth, 16, was sexually assaulted a short
period prior to her death, this small, southwestern
Ontario town has been gripped by rampant speculation
as well as grief and fear.

Though community members have provided a "handful" of tips, police still have no substantive evidence or
suspects in the case.

For some, suspicion was primarily directed at the girl's
foster parents, and particularly her male guardian, Paul
Schantz, 47. Yesterday, however, police officially cleared
Mr. Schantz from any foul play when they announced that
he was out of province visiting an ill family member over
the time of the girl's rape and murder.

"We are aware that cases of this kind bring hardship
upon those living close to the events," Grimshaw Police
Superintendent Robert James stated at a news conference. "One form of such hardship is the way people can
muse about possible guilty parties. I am here today to
tell you that Mr. Paul Schantz is not under investigation
in this case."

Superintendent James's announcement was made in
apparent response to harassing phone calls and anonymous letters the Schantzes have received following the
release of the coroner's report.

The investigation has now turned to "other av-
enues," police said in response to questions from this
newspaper.

Another newspaper clipping, from the Province-Wide News
section of *The Toronto Telegram*.

SMALL TOWN REELING FROM TWO FOSTER
HOME LOSSES
First a Murder and Now Apparent Runaway
from 'Refuge for Lost Souls'

Grimshaw—A search is under way for Roy DeLisle, a 16-year-old foster child who went missing from his home in this sleepy community 150 miles west of Toronto. Mr. DeLisle's disappearance has left many residents of Grimshaw puzzled after the murder just last week of Elizabeth Worth, another child under the guardianship of Paul and May Schantz, the owners of the home where Worth and DeLisle lived.

While police are officially treating Mr. DeLisle's file as a missing persons case, two sources within the force told the *Telegram* that they are "exploring connections" between the young man's absence and the coroner's findings that Miss Worth was sexually assaulted shortly before her death.

"I would say that Roy DeLisle could rightly be considered a suspect at this point, yes," the police source said. "We'd certainly like to talk to him."

Though just a teenager, Mr. DeLisle has already compiled a disturbing criminal record and history of violence. The *Telegram* has obtained court documents showing that, during three of his previous foster home stints, Mr. DeLisle was twice charged with assault (both times the complainants being women), along with one charge of public indecency.

Local police as well as the O.P.P. are involved in the search, but their efforts have so far been frustrated by little information on the boy, whose parents died shortly after his birth, and who otherwise has no known family. Further, no photographs of Mr. DeLisle have yet been made available to investigators. "It's like he was never here," commented one provincial police detective.

Finally, another story in *The Grimshaw Beacon*, this one published on March 12, 1950, four months after Elizabeth Worth's death.

POLICE STILL FRUSTRATED IN SEARCH FOR GRIMSHAW TEEN

Roy DeLisle Missing Since November

"Sometimes runaways just don't come back," says frustrated Police Chief

By Louis Weir
Beacon Staff Reporter

Grimshaw Police and Ontario Provincial Police conducting a coordinated search for a missing Grimshaw boy who is considered the prime suspect in the murder of his former foster sister, Elizabeth Worth, have announced they are scaling back the resources being applied to their search. Roy DeLisle, who would have recently turned 17, has been missing since Friday, November 18, of last year, when he apparently left home for school in the morning but never arrived.

"We've done everything we can for now," said Donald Poole, Chief of Grimshaw Police and overseer of the search efforts. "Roy is out there somewhere, and we are hopeful that a member of the public will alert us to his whereabouts. We will find him, but it likely won't be in Grimshaw or the Perth County area or Ontario. Sometimes runaways just don't come back to where they ran from."

Paul Schantz, the foster parent who was acting as guardian of Mr. DeLisle for the four months prior to his disappearance, has previously alluded to the boy's "restless ways," and in an interview with the *Beacon*, speculated that Roy may have had a "wandering spirit."

When asked to comment on Mr. DeLisle's previously disclosed criminal history and attacks on young women, as well as his possible role in Miss Worth's death, Mr. Schantz would say only that such considerations are a matter for the police.

Mr. Schantz is still recovering from the tragic loss of Miss Worth late last year. Elizabeth Worth, 16 at the time of her death, was found murdered in the Schantzes' Caledonia Street home on November 12. Only two days after her memorial service, Mr. DeLisle was reported missing.

Though Chief Poole would not be drawn into open conjecture at his press conference, many have noted a connection between evidence that Miss Worth was raped before her death and Mr. DeLisle's missing status, not to mention the nature of his prior charges.

I finish reading lying on the floor. The first tendrils of dusty sunlight making their way toward me over the hardwood.

His name is Roy.

The boy was a real person once. A teenager the same age we were when we first entered the house to find Heather Langham in the cellar.

He killed that girl.

Of course it's possible that someone other than Roy DeLisle, her foster brother, assaulted and then murdered Elizabeth Worth. It could have been another kid at school, a teacher, a stranger. But it wasn't. It was Roy's "restless ways" that invited him to the party, the same way he invited each of us decades later. He had done bad things in the homes he was dropped into before the Schantzes', and he had done another, even worse thing to Elizabeth Worth. And then he was gone.

But wherever Roy ran to, he's back in the Thurman house now. That's why Ben watched. Made sure the doors stayed closed. Prevented others from going in. Ben had made a prison for himself in this room, but he'd done it to keep the Thurman house a prison for Roy DeLisle.

I'm folding the clippings to slip them back inside the journal when something else falls out from its pages. A plain envelope.

I know what's inside before I open it. Not from the feel of its shape through the paper, not its surprising weight. I just *know*.

And then it's there, a coil of delicate chain and gold heart in the palm of my hand. Heather's locket. The one she was wearing when we buried her.

As though at the sound of someone coming up the stairs, I hastily tie the clippings with the same ribbon and, not knowing where else to put it, tuck the package back into the air vent under the bed. But not the locket. I slip its chain into my wallet. Feel the gold heart press against my hip.

When I get to my feet again the dawn has finally arrived, though the streets remain quiet. I take a seat at Ben's window and try not to think. About the clippings, about the locket. Discoveries that explain everything. Or nothing.

It's this effort to sit and simply breathe that at first prevents me from noticing the man standing on the sidewalk, directly in front of the Thurman house.

He has been there for some time, or at least as long as it has taken me to focus on the view below. His back to me. Canvas sneakers and lumberjack shirt and a John Deere ball cap turned backwards on his head.

I recognize Gary Pullinger, Tracey Flanagan's boyfriend, a split second before he turns. His eyes searching the houses on the McAuliffes' side of the street, alerted to a sound, or perhaps by the sense that he was being watched. He appears lost. It's as though he had thought he was in another, safer town all his life and only now recognized the depths of his error.

And then he spots me. I can read the swift consideration of options passing through his mind. In the end he simply starts up the slope toward the hospital at an intentionally leisurely pace, an attempt to reinforce the illusion that he didn't stop outside the house at all, but merely paused to inhale a breath of the sun-sweetened air before continuing on his way.

But he *had* been watching the house. Looking into its windows. Searching for something he both wanted and did not want to see.

MEMORY DIARY

Entry No. 15

High school ended with a prom I didn't go to, a gradua-
tion ceremony I was asked to leave for shouting "Loser!"
during the valedictorian's address and a football game
Grimshaw lost, during which we gathered in Carl's Ford
at halftime. As soon as the next day, we were heading
in different directions. Randy to attend drama school at
a community college in Peterborough. Carl to hitchhike
out to Winnipeg to see an uncle of his we'd never heard
of. And Ben to stay in his attic bedroom, watching.

Though I'd applied to a handful of universities and had
even been accepted to a couple, I decided to move to
Toronto, find some work busing tables and try to become
someone else. It was a plan that my parents only half-
heartedly objected to. "Your room's always here," my father
assured me, his face rounded in a show of generosity, as if

he might have otherwise turned it into a massage parlour or dog kennel. He figured I'd be back. And while he wished me well, I believe there was some part of him that would have liked me to stitch together a life in Grimshaw as he did, be more contentedly defeated like him.

"Get ready to have your skulls explode," Carl said, lighting up.

The smoke blotted out the sun, the school, even the sound of fans cheering another of the visiting team's touchdowns.

"I guess we should talk about it," I said.

"I don't think we have to," Carl said.

"I'm talking about *not* talking about it. With anyone. Ever."

"I think we're pretty clear on that," Randy said.

"I hope so. Because there's no statute of limitations on kidnapping."

This took a minute to sink in.

"Let's make a pact," Ben said.

Randy turned to him. "You mean we should drink each other's blood or something?"

"Just a promise."

"Okay. We promise."

"No, we have to say it," Ben clarified. "And we have to *hear* each other say it."

We all nodded at this.

"What do we have to say?" Randy asked.

"We're the Guardians," I said.

Nobody seemed to have heard me. Except Ben.

"Okay. On three," he said. "One, two—"

We all said it. Three words that cleared the smoke from our faces, and we could see who we were.

15

I RIP THROUGH my wallet to find Barry Tate's card and call his number at the cop shop. Yet when his voice mail picks up, I'm frozen. Barry asks for "complete details" to be left in the message, but what are those? I saw a missing girl's boyfriend looking at a house. No more than that.

"If this is urgent," Officer Tate goes on, "press zero and your call will be transferred to 911."

Is this urgent? My heart certainly thinks so, taking runs at my ribs.

"Hi, Barry. It's Trev. *Trevor.* Sorry to bother you—gosh, I don't *think* this should bother you—but there's something I'd like to report. I left my cell number with you, right? Okay, so see you around."

I hang up.

Trev? Gosh? See you around? What could Barry possibly think when he hears that? I know what. *That poor guy with the shakes is losing his shit.*

I get dressed and head downstairs. The house is quiet. A good thing, because I don't want Betty McAuliffe to catch me running out of here with my shoes in my hands.

"Coffee only takes a minute."

She's standing in the kitchen doorway, arms crossed tightly over her chest.

"Gosh," I say for the second time in this new, going-downhill-fast morning, "I didn't know you were up."

"Heard you bumping around."

"Sorry to wake you."

"Didn't say you did."

The two of us wait. Or it's just me waiting, feeling for a way out the front door.

"I wanted to ask," I say. "Did you happen to see my Dictaphone around anywhere?"

"Dicta-who?"

"It's a little recording machine. Seem to have misplaced it."

"*That's* what you were doing up there. I thought you were on the phone for hours on end. But you were talking to yourself."

"I suppose it's a little strange, isn't it?"

"It sounded a lot like Ben to me."

"Well, if you happen to see it . . ."

"So you can keep up your observations," she says with an unreadable smile.

"I wasn't making observations."

"No? That's what Ben told me *he* was doing."

Mrs. McAuliffe starts back into the kitchen, but I stop her by speaking a name.

"Roy DeLisle."

"Is that a question?"

"I suppose he *is* a question."

"The boy who ran away. Is that who you mean? Years and

years ago. The way he disappeared after that terrible business with the orphan girl."

"Elizabeth Worth."

"My goodness. You know all the names."

"Ben passed along a little local history to me."

Betty rubs her hands together, as though lathering soap. "He went to the library sometimes. 'Research' is all he'd say when I asked what he was reading up on. I shouldn't be surprised it was that awful story."

"I guess that's why everyone calls the house across the street haunted."

"They do?" she asks, and though at first I take her disbelief as a joke, a lie so unbelievable it was never meant to be swallowed, her face tells me nothing either way.

"I grew up here," I go on eventually. "We all did. But I never heard anything about it."

"Why would you have? Those were things that happened half a lifetime before you were born."

"Still, you'd think someone would mention it. I mean, she was raped. She was murdered."

"That could only have come from your parents. And you were our *children*. It's our job to prevent you from hearing things like that for as long we're able."

"Until it just goes away."

"If you're lucky," she says, and shrugs. "Small towns are good at forgetting. They have to be."

I consider walking over to Sarah's place and asking if I can stay. Not just for the night or two she has already offered, but for as long as she'll let me. I'll do the cooking and cleaning. And as much of the nighttime fooling around as she and the Big P allow.

But having Sarah say no to such a proposal might push me over the edge into full-blown Benhood, and this worries me more than the idea of Roy DeLisle taking my hand as I walk.

"Trev! Over here!"

It's Randy, waving at me from the Queen's dining-room table he shares with Carl. Because they are who I've walked to, not Sarah. By the time I sink into the chair next to Carl, the waitress arrives to take their order.

"You hungry?" Carl asks me.

"I'll have what you're having."

"Steak and eggs?"

"Perfect."

"Hey, man, it's your credit card."

After my coffee cup is filled, I tell them about my discovery in Ben's room. The whole Roy DeLisle file. And how old Paul Schantz was the man looking after him when the bad things happened. I don't include any of my own thoughts about the commonalities between Elizabeth Worth and Heather Langham, Roy and the coach, how they all have been rooted to the Thurman house. They are thoughts I can read passing over their faces as I speak.

"He's got a name," Randy says when our food arrives. "*Roy*. I wish I didn't know that."

"It's like a lousy song that gets stuck in your head," I say.

"Worse," Carl says. "There's no music in it."

You've nailed it, Carl, the silence that follows seems to say. *Whatever he is, the boy is the opposite of music.*

"There was this too," I say, pulling out my wallet and letting Heather's locket spill onto the table.

Carl and Randy stare at it. Less shocked than stilled by the anticipation of some further action to follow, as if the chain might rise up and snake around one of our throats, squeezing out our next breath.

"That's Heather's," Randy says.

"Ben had it."

"How'd he get it?" Carl asks.

"No idea."

"Wait. Just *wait* a second," Carl says. "When we piled the dirt on her she was *wearing* that thing."

"I know it."

"So somebody had to have gone down there to get it before the cops found her. Gone down there to *dig her up*."

"I don't see any other way."

"Who would fucking *do* that?"

"I can answer that," Randy says. "One of us. We were the only ones who knew where she was."

"And the coach," I say.

"But he was tied up," Randy says. "And he didn't know where we put her."

"Unless one of us told him," I say. "Unless he talked one of us into letting him go long enough to do it."

"You mean unless the boy talked one of us into it," Randy says.

Carl lurches back in his chair and straightens his back, the gesture of a man fighting a sudden attack of heartburn. "What are we saying here?"

"More went on in that cellar than we thought," Randy says. "Which is saying something."

"Here's my question," I say. "Why didn't Ben ask which one of us did it?"

"Maybe he knew and kept it secret," Randy says. "Or maybe he didn't want to know."

"Or maybe he was the one who did the digging," Carl says.

Another silence. After a moment, I pick the locket up and return it to my wallet. We sip our coffee. Do a lousy job of pretending the last two minutes hadn't just happened.

Once the waitress has come and gone, filling our cups, I tell them about seeing Gary Pullinger standing outside the house this morning.

"Sounds like they have their man," Randy says.

"He's under arrest?"

"Not yet. But they've had him in and out of the cop shop, putting the screws to him."

"If he's still walking around, it shows they don't have enough," Carl says, draining his coffee.

"What would they need?"

"A body."

Once more, our thoughts steal our voices away.

"I called the police," I say after a while. "Left a message with Barry Tate. He's on the force here now."

"Hairy Barry?" Carl says.

"The very same."

"You sure that was a good idea?"

"It didn't feel like I had a choice."

"There's always a choice."

"I just want to pass along what I know."

"And what's that?"

"That Tracey's boyfriend stopped to look at the house where I thought I saw suspicious activity."

"Suspicious activity? C'mon, Trev," Randy says. "They already looked in there."

"Okay. So what should I do?"

"You should do what we're going to do," Carl says. "Get the fuck out of Dodge."

"There's a train at a quarter after five," Randy says. "You ought to come with us."

Carl places his hand on my arm. I can't tell if it's meant as reassurance or to stop it from shaking. "There's nothing here, Trev. There never really was."

"You think I *like* it here? Everything is telling me to go, just the same as it's telling you. But there's something else that knows we're meant to stay."

"Why? Why are we 'meant to stay'?" Randy asks.

"Ben was the guardian of this town, whether the town knew it or not. We owe it to him."

"Oh Christ."

"Think about it. He kept an eye on that house for twenty years. And then, after he can't handle it anymore, Todd's daughter goes missing."

"You need to see someone. Seriously."

"If we walk away, we're putting some other Tracey or Heather or Elizabeth at risk sometime down the line. We've already got a lot we're trying to live with. You want more?"

Randy rubs the freckles at his temples as though at the onset of sudden headache. "Okay, you crazy, shaky arsehole," he says. "I'll stay until tomorrow."

"You *believe* this?" Carl asks.

"I don't have to believe it. I'm staying because Trev asked us to."

I'm prevented from walking around the table and putting my arms around Randy by my cell phone, which comes alive in my jacket pocket, screaming its Beastie Boys ringtone. By the time my hand reaches in and grabs it, it's already switched over to my voice mail. I check the caller ID.

"It was Barry Tate."

"What are you going to do?" Carl asks.

"Call him back."

Then I'm up and wobbling for the doors.

Outside on Ontario Street I curse my hands. Fluttery as moths, the fingers swimming over the dial pad of my phone. Some hitting the right numbers, others forcing me to start all over again.

After I manage to record a message, I catch myself reflected in the glass of the Queen's picture window. With the spotted brick of the Edwardian storefronts behind me, I appear to be not holding a cell phone but nursing a small animal cupped in my hands.

And then it comes alive. The Beastie Boys hollering "Sabotage" into my palm.

"Hello?"

"Trevor? How you doing?"

"Thanks for calling back."

"My job."

It's immediately clear that Barry Tate is not prepared to be as patient with me as he was the first time around.

"I saw something this morning," I start.

"Oh?"

"Gary Pullinger."

"What about him?"

"He was outside the Thurman place."

"What time was this?"

"I'm not sure. Maybe six, six thirty."

"Was he attempting to enter the property?"

"He wasn't on the property, just the sidewalk."

"*Walking* on the sidewalk?"

"Standing."

"So you want me to arrest him for loitering?"

"I'm not telling you to do anything, Barry. I just thought it was worth reporting. Given he's a suspect in the Tracey Flanagan business."

"Who said that?"

"It's what I heard."

"Oh yeah? Well, you know what my supervisor heard yesterday? That me and my partner searched private property without a warrant. It wasn't a pleasant meeting, I can tell you."

"Sorry to hear that."

"And I'm sorry to hear you're calling me with more of this 'I saw something' news. What *did* you see? A kid walking along looking at houses?"

"He wasn't walking. And it wasn't any house, it was——"

"Your dad ever tell you about that kid who cried wolf?"

"Listen, Barry, you can be pissed off at me all you want. But I've got a feeling that Tracey Flanagan was in that place at some point, or maybe she——"

"You know something? You seem to have a lot of *feelings* about that girl. Now that could be an avenue I'd be willing to explore if you have something you want to get off your chest."

"This doesn't have anything to do with me."

"So let's not make it have something to do with you. Sound good?"

"Sure."

"Thanks for the call."

"And sorry about——" I start, but Hairy Barry is already gone.

By the time I'm back inside, the breakfast table is unoccupied and the waitress is clearing the plates. I call up to each of their rooms, but either they have agreed to ignore my call or they aren't up there. I leave a note for Randy at the front desk with my cell phone number and make my way outside once more.

It's my legs—kicking and side-swinging worse than at any other point since my arrival in Grimshaw—that seem to know I'm going to Sarah's before I do. I must now appear, as one of my doctors said I would eventually, as a "top-heavy drunk," leaving my shoe prints on dew-sodden lawns. You'd think, in my condition, presenting myself before a woman I like would be a bad idea. But the thing is, I don't have time to wait for good ideas anymore.

An hour after starting off from the Queen's I reach Sarah's place, thirsty and tingled with sweat. Pass my fingers through my hair. Rub a finger over my teeth.

"Trevor," she announces when she opens the door, as if looking out at the day and declaring "Rain" or "Snow."

"Gosh," I say, moronically, for the third time today, "I wasn't really expecting you to be here."

"Why wouldn't I be?"

"Figured you'd be at work."

"It's Saturday."

"Of course. Saturday."

She backs into the house, and I step inside and push the door closed behind me. Blink against the muted indoor light until Sarah's details return.

"You don't look well," she says.

"I'm not."

"Are you sick?"

"No more than usual."

"Then what's going on?"

"It's not something I could explain."

Sarah turns away and settles on the sofa in the living room. I follow her inside and sit next to her. I fight against leaning over and pulling her to me. Then I fight against laying my head in her lap.

"*Damn*," she says, suddenly shaking her head hard. "It's like old times, isn't it?"

"You mean you and me?"

"I mean you thinking you can't trust me."

"Sarah, it's got nothing to do with trust. I just don't want you to get damaged."

"*Damaged*? Like china? A box you'd write 'Fragile' on on moving day?"

"I don't see you like that."

"But you don't see me being able to handle anything either."

"It's just what men do."

"How's that?"

"We *protect*. Even if it means being alone."

"This conversation could have been one we had when we were sixteen."

"Maybe so."

"It makes me think that whatever was troubling you then is the same thing that's troubling you now. Am I right?"

"You're not wrong."

"So if it's been around that long, it's time you took care of it."

"Yes."

"Because you don't have a chance—and I'll tell you *this*, you don't have a chance with *me*—if you've got this secret thing floating around for the rest of your life."

She slides closer and kisses me. Then we kiss some more. When we finally pull apart, Kieran is standing in the doorway.

"I'm hungry," he announces. And then, with a grin my way, "Hey, Trevor."

"Hey."

"Want to come up to my room and check out my PlayStation?"

I look to Sarah, who shrugs. "You guys like grilled cheese?"

"And bacon, please," Kieran says.

"How about you, Trevor?"

"I think everything's better with bacon," I say, which happens to be the truth.

After lunch, and after declining Sarah's offer (seconded by Kieran) to stay for dinner, I ask if I can get a lift back to the McAuliffes'. But once the two of them have driven off and left me looking up at Ben's attic window, the paint of its frame scabby and puke-green in the midday light, I decide I can't go inside. So I start walking again. *Working out the kinks*, I tell myself, though the truth is, I'm nothing *but* kinks these days. If I didn't have my body's spasms and jerks, I wouldn't be able to move at all.

The Beastie Boys scream.

"Hello?"

"Hey."

"Randy? Still here?"

"Unfortunately, yes."

"What about Carl?"

"Gone."

"So it's just us."

"The gruesome twosome."

In the sky above, a passenger jet draws a line of smoke at thirty thousand feet. A border that marks Grimshaw apart from the rest of the world.

"What are we going to do, Randy?"

"I've got an idea."

"Yeah?"

"Let's just say I've done a little shopping."

16

RANDY AND I decide to meet for an early dinner at the Old London. He's already there when I lurch in. Sitting at the same circular table we'd occupied only two nights ago, a stretch of time that feels as distant now as the memory of summer camp.

"A cocktail, sir?" the maître d' asks as I take my seat.

"What're you having?" I ask Randy.

"Soda water. Got to keep the mind clear."

"Right. Orange juice, please. And coffee."

"And a couple of rare prime ribs."

The maître d' slips away, leaving the two of us facing each other across the ridiculous space of the table (I would have sat next to Randy, but that would have been even weirder).

"I know that keeping us here one more night was my idea," I admit after my drinks are delivered. "But maybe you could help me with something."

"Hit me."

"What the hell are we planning to do?"

Randy looks at me with dead seriousness. "We have to do something to put this place behind us."

"You think that's possible?"

"Who knows? We have to try. I think that's the key. If we do our best, maybe we won't have to think about Grimshaw every other second until we drop dead."

"Okay," I say, and sip my coffee. "So we try. Try what?"

"To face it. No more tiptoeing around."

"Ben watched for half his life and it didn't do any good."

"But Ben stayed *outside*."

The maître d' arrives with our meals, the bloody slices of beef set before us steaming and thick as novels.

"Are you saying we have to go in and stay there?" I ask.

"Not us. But we'll have eyes and ears on the inside all the same."

"How?"

"Baby monitors! Go on, say it. It's brilliant."

"It's brilliant. If we had a baby to monitor."

Randy sighs, savouring the rare moment of appearing smarter than someone else. "They've come a long way, let me tell you. Now they come with video cameras and motion detectors. You can pay me your half when you have a chance."

"And how exactly do these help us?"

"We do what Ben did—watch the house," Randy says, beaming now. "But tonight, we'll watch it from the *inside*."

"On the monitor."

"It's got a range of five hundred feet. And we'll be in Ben's room. But hidden. No faces in the window, in case someone looks."

"And where's the sensor?"

"Where would you least want to sit around all night in that place?"

"The cellar."

"Agreed."

"Agreed on what? Sorry, man, but I'm sure as hell not going down there to plant that thing."

"Already done. By me. Today. During *daylight* hours."

I watch Randy slice off a dripping chunk of meat and drive it into his mouth, his appetite the first giveaway that what we're going to do together this evening isn't a real stakeout, it's therapy. What's important, what gives the voodoo a chance of working, isn't the recitation of the right words or spraying of holy water, but that we believe the process might actually work. And so we are reinforcing our courage as we once did in the Guardians' dressing room before a game. Pretend warriors.

I can see as he chews and swallows and grins over the white linen that Randy doesn't really expect any confrontation to take place tonight. He's only acting as though it might for my sake.

"You're a good man, Randy."

"I'm glad you can see that. I just wish you had long hair and smelled a little better and looked great in a bikini."

"When was the last time you saw me in a bikini?"

"Please. I'm eating."

After dinner and several coffees, Randy and I start back toward Ben's house. It's night now, but a fog has darkened the air even further, rubbing out the details of Grimshaw's chimney stacks and the lights from its windows like a blindness. Cars nose through the slick streets. In the fog, Grimshaw feels at once familiar and altered, drained of some fundamental aspect that had previously marked it as a place for the living, so that I am left with the sensation of strolling into the afterlife.

At Caledonia, we don't immediately cross over to the McAuliffes' as we normally would. Instead, we stop at the spot where I'd seen Gary Pullinger standing, hands in our pockets, studying the islands of concrete that were once the front walk, before taking in the house itself. Given the finality of the evening—the last night in Grimshaw by the last of the Guardians who have come for the last time to brave the scrutiny of its windowed eyes—I am expecting to feel something different about the house. But it appears emptier and less consequential tonight than it ever has, unfairly scorned, even pitiable. The fog that passes between us and its door seems to erase its particulars, sweeping it away into a past that will soon claim what's left of it and leave an anonymous lot behind.

I can feel Randy wanting to say something along the lines of my own thoughts, a comment at how unbelievable it is that the four walls and buckling roof before us could be mistaken for a living thing. But I don't want the house to hear him.

"It's getting cold," I say, elbowing him in the side. As best I can, I start back across the street.

Randy passes me in the front hall and is already halfway up the stairs when Mrs. McAuliffe steps out from the living room's shadows.

"There's lamb stew in the pot if you boys are hungry," she says.

"Thanks, Mrs. A.," Randy shouts down the stairs. "Already ate."

It leaves me alone with the old woman. In the hall, she appears more frail than she did this morning and, at the same time, seems to be fighting this frailty by way of a bulky knit sweater (Ben's?) and corduroy gardening pants.

"What are you two planning on tonight?" she asks, stepping closer. "Painting the town red?"

"Nothing like that."

"You're welcome to use the TV in the basement."

"Thank you. But we're just, you know, hanging around."

"Playing records."

"Sorry?"

Betty giggles. "It's what Ben would say to me when you were all boys, spending hours up in his room, and I would ask what you were up to," she says. "'Playing records, Mom!' 'Nothing, Mom! We're just playing records!' But half the time I couldn't hear any music. Only you boys, talking and talking."

"Did you hear what we were saying?"

"No," she says, shaking her head. "But that didn't stop me from understanding things some of the time."

"A mother's intuition."

"Intuition, yes. But that's not all."

She knows. That is, she knows *something*, as we always suspected she did. How much she has guessed it's impossible to say, and I'm not about to ask. But what she is telling me now is that we were party to a crime of a most serious sort, and she has never shared this knowledge with another, not even her son.

Studying her now, I'm certain Betty McAuliffe was the only witness who watched us enter the Thurman house the evening we discovered Heather Langham in the cellar. What connections had she made once the coach went missing and then, soon after, was wheeled out of the house across the street along with the woman—only a girl really, rosy and unmarried and childless? It would have been impossible not to speculate. Not to conclude.

And yet, even with this knowledge, she had remained sweet Mrs. McAuliffe. Lonely Mrs. McAuliffe, baker of shortbread and pincher of cheeks and minder of her own business. This was love too.

"We'll be out of your way tomorrow," I say. "Randy's already checked out of the Queen's, so if it's all right by you, he'll be bunking on the pullout in Ben's room."

"No trouble. You'll find extra sheets and—"

"The linen closet. I remember."

She turns away, as if at the return of a TV program she had been engrossed in. "I'm off to bed myself," she says, beginning to turn off the lights one by one.

"See you in the morning, Betty."

"The morning," she repeats. Now in the dark, whispering it again, like a lover's remembered name. "The morning."

I find Randy stretched out on the bed, adjusting the dials on what looks at first to be an ancient cell phone, one of those banana-sized ones with the rubbery antennae that came out in the '80s.

"You gotta check out the picture on this thing," he says. "I rented a plasma screen to watch the finals last year and it wasn't any better than this."

I sit next him to see that he's right. A square screen that shows a wide view of the Thurman house's earth-floored cellar and, in the background, the bottom of the stairs leading up to the kitchen. An empty space except for a couple of crippled workbenches along the walls, random garbage balled up from where it was tossed down from the top of the stairs. The air greened by the night lens, so that the scene appears to be set on a cold lake bottom.

"They have these things for *babies*?" I say. "What for? To count the kid's eyelashes as it sleeps?"

Randy turns up the volume. A moment of microphoned vacancy washes out from the speakers.

"Something farts down there and we'll hear it," he says.

"With this thing? Probably smell it too."

For the first time, I notice it's dark in the room. The only illumination coming from the monitor's screen and what orange street light finds its way through the window. But as I reach to switch on Ben's Ken Dryden lamp, Randy grabs my wrist.

"We're not here. Remember?" he says.

"So we're just going to sit in the dark?"

"I'll hold your hand if you want."

"You *are* holding my hand."

"Oh."

I slide down to the floor and crawl over to the beanbag chair in the corner. From here, I can see the Thurman house's chimney, but little else. The fog has thinned somewhat over the last hour, and has turned to an indecisive drizzle, its droplets swaying and looping in their descent and, at times, even returning skyward.

"I saw Todd Flanagan today," Randy says.

"Yeah?"

"At the Wal-Mart."

"And you pushing a shopping cart with a baby monitor in it?"

"As a matter of fact, yes."

"How was he?"

"Not good. He was two minutes into our conversation in the vacuum cleaner aisle before he figured out who the hell I was."

"Poor bastard."

"He asked after you."

"What'd he say?"

"Can't remember exactly."

"Bullshit."

"Okay. He said it was really sad to see you all shaky and Parkinson's and whatnot, especially when you could have been the best winger the Guardians ever had."

"It's not half as sad as what he's going through."

Does fog make a sound? If it does, it whispers against Ben's window.

"Randy?"

"Yo."

"You think she could still be alive?"

"I dunno, boss."

"But what do you *think*?"

"Well, let me ask you this: Do the missing ever come back?"

"Sometimes. If they just ran away. Or if they wanted to be lost."

"Then those ones weren't really missing to begin with."

Over the next couple of hours the night grows still, both outside the McAuliffe house and within it. Betty must be asleep, as we haven't heard any creaks from the floorboards below since shortly after I came up. She has the right idea. It is only sporadic conversation between Randy and me—as well as changing shifts watching the monitor screen—that keeps the two of us awake.

"Coffee?" Randy asks at one point.

"Is that what you carried up here an hour ago?"

"I got a Thermos at Wal-Mart today too. State of the art."

"Am I going splits on that with you too?"

"If you wouldn't mind."

Randy pours us each coffee in the little plastic camping cups that came with the Thermos. The steam rising and reshaping itself like a phantom against his face.

"I have this theory," he says, sipping his coffee and grimacing at his instantly burnt tongue. "I may have told you about it already. I call it the Asshole Quotient. Remember?"

"Vaguely," I lie.

"It's kind of a natural law of human behaviour. A way of explaining why people just do shit things to other people for no reason. Unpredictable things."

"Assholes."

"Exactly. And I used to believe that no matter where you go, 20 per cent of the people you come in contact with are going to turn out to be assholes. You wouldn't know that's what they are, not at first, but they would always appear in a ratio of one to five."

"Sounds about right."

"No, it's *not* right. I was off."

"Twenty per cent is too high?"

"Too *low*. Over the last few years I've come to realize the number's closer to something like 30 or 40 per cent. Maybe it's an even fifty-fifty."

"You think things are getting that bad?"

"They were *always* that bad. It just takes until you're our age to see it."

"What evidence are you working from here?"

"Okay. Consider how most people have fewer friends the older they get. Why? You learn that the numbers are against you, that life isn't just going to be this hilarious succession of new and fascinating people to share whatever new and fascinating stage of your journey you find yourself at. It's why guys like us always end up *looking back* all the time. It's the only way you've got of beating the odds."

"Old friends."

"You got it."

"I have a question," I say, burning my tongue on my coffee just as Randy had a minute ago. "How do you know you haven't been wrong the whole time?"

"Wrong how?"

"About me, say. I'm as old a friend as you've got. But what if I'm not one of the good 50 per cent, but the bad 50 per cent?"

"I don't know, Trev," he says, saddened by the question itself. "I guess if I'm wrong about you, it's quittin' time."

Randy leans his elbows on his knees, sits forward in his chair to bring himself within whisper distance of me. "You think he would have done it? If it wasn't for us?"

"Who?"

"The coach. Do you think he would have killed himself if we hadn't—?"

"Yes," I interrupt. "It's what he deserved."

"What about us? What do we deserve?"

"This."

"A night in Ben's room?"

"Along with all the other nights of the past twenty-four years."

I'm wondering if this is remotely true, if we've even begun to understand the nature of the cruel and unusual punishments still to come our way, when the baby monitor bleats. An animal's cry of warning.

"The fuck was that?" Randy says.

"Your machine."

"Really? The motion sensor?"

"What other part of it would make a sound like that?"

"You think I actually read the owner's manual?" Randy stands and appears about to approach, but doesn't. "Anything?"

I stare at the screen. "Nothing."

"I'm not hearing anything on the mike either."

"Might be a glitch," I say. "Like when you put a new battery in a smoke detector and it beeps before you press the test button."

"That's never happened to me."

"Have you ever lived anywhere long enough that you had to replace a smoke detector battery?"

"Tell you the truth, I'm not sure I've ever lived somewhere that *had* a smoke detector."

Randy sits next to me on the edge of the bed. Between us, the monitor rests on top of the sheets, showing only the dark cellar, a hissing stillness coming out of the speaker. I turn the volume up full. A louder nothing.

After a time, Randy goes to the window. Peers down at the street. Places his forehead against the glass. "Ben thought he was looking for ghosts up here, didn't he?"

"I suppose he did."

"You ever wonder if he was the one who was dead all that time?"

"Ben only died last week, Randy."

"No. It was a long time before that. He died the first time he went in there."

Something in Randy's tone tells me he's referring not to the day we discovered Heather Langham but to the time when we were eight. When Ben learned of his father's accident that wasn't an accident and ran to the darkest place he knew.

"People can get over things," I say. "It just happens that Ben wasn't able to."

"You think he's the only one?"

It seems that Randy may be about to cry. Or maybe it's me. Either way, they are sounds I really don't want to hear. But just as I'm searching my memory for the distraction of a filthy joke, the one Randy likes about the midget pianist going into a bar, he slaps his hands against the window.

"The fuck?" he says.

"What is it?"

"Someone's there."

Randy starts down the attic stairs.

"Randy! Wait!"

"Stay here. Watch the monitor. Trust me, I'm not planning on going inside."

Then he's gone. I hobble to the window in time to see him cross the street and disappear into the shadows at the side of the house.

I have little choice but to do as I'm told and watch the screen. Five minutes—ten? twenty-five?—of studying the greenish empty cellar.

And then something's happening. Or it has been happening since the motion sensor was triggered, and I am only noticing it now.

Breathing.

Long intakes and exhalations, wet clicks in the throat. Something alive yet invisible. The screen reveals nothing. Nothing except the outline of shadow that slides over the floor. A human shape elongated by the angle of available light, so that it appears gaunt and long-fingered.

The house moves.

A tremor that turns into an earthquake, the walls and floor and staircase pitching. It makes me look around Ben's room to see if I'm being tossed the same way. But the earthquake hasn't reached the fifty yards to the other side of Caledonia Street.

"Somebody's picked it up," I say aloud, a statement I don't understand until I look at the screen again and see it bringing the ceiling beams into focus, the frayed wires veiled by cobweb lace.

A pause. Then the monitor is thrown to the floor.

The screen breaks into deafening static at impact. Just before it goes dead altogether, what could be the shattering fracture of the camera's casing, or feedback on the microphone—or a female scream.

Then I'm up. Fighting against my body's wish to find Ben's bed and lie face down, gripping the edges until morning. Past Betty McAuliffe's door and down the next flight, clinging to the handrail. Shouldering open the screen door to plow into the night.

I use my arms to keep balance, a breaststroke through air, until one hand freezes, a finger pointing at the house across the street. No, not the house. At the figure standing in the living-room window, indistinct but unmistakably there. Watching me just as I watch it.

[17]

I MAKE IT THROUGH the darkness of the mud room by feeling the air like a blind man. For the first several seconds there are no walls, no ceilings, no visible markings that might tell me where I am. Yet my memory of the space betrays me, and I slam headlong into the half-closed kitchen door, its hard edge cutting a fold of skin from my cheek.

"Fuck!"

The sound of my voice allows me to see, the widening aperture that turns the darkness into interior dusk.

I decide to check the living room first.

No, not "decide," not "check"—I simply drift past the door down to the cellar and find myself on the soiled rug, pretending I am being thorough when in fact I am merely afraid. I take the time to study the room, looking for signs of recent activity, but what I'm really doing is listening. For a footfall, a creaking door, a breath. For the boy to tell me it was him.

On my return to the kitchen, I notice the odours I hadn't the first time through. The slow rot of wood exposed to moisture finding its way through the walls, the cardboard stuffiness of uncirculated space. Along with something sugary. It makes me think of the dousings of perfume old ladies apply before collecting in coffee shops or church basements. It brings on the same gag reflex I have fought at every funeral I have ever attended: my mother's, my father's, the coach's, Heather's, Ben's.

I stand over the sink and turn the taps, though nothing but a hollow gurgle finds its way out. Through the window, the backyard looks limitless and wild in the dark, a habitat for prowling creatures. There is a sense that something is about to happen out there, the performance of violence. But when I turn away from the glass and lean my back against the counter, now looking into the house instead of out, I have the same sensation, only stronger.

On the kitchen walls, a similar scene to the one outside: the wallpaper mural of a pond, a background of forest, a drinking deer. A picture of terrible expectation. The hunter, when it comes, will walk out of *those* trees, not the real ones in the backyard. It will start with the frozen deer, then put its hands on the frozen me.

"Randy?"

My friend's name sounding like a plea in my ears.

I go to where I have to go. Nudge the cellar door wider with the toe of my shoe.

For a moment, the Parkinson's and I are united: both refuse to go down there. We are rigid, mind and body alike. Finding our full balance before attempting the turnaround, the first step of retreat, the shuffling getaway. Because there is a nightmare-in-progress awaiting me at the bottom, and I don't want to know how it ends.

I'm a boy again. A sixteen-year-old boy. Or even younger, for the whimper that escapes my lips is the sound an abandoned toddler makes in a supermarket aisle, a child just beginning to realize the potential depths of aloneness.

And then—before my eyes try to read something in the nothing, before fear takes full hold of what my body does next—I start down the stairs like the man of the house.

At the bottom, my feet sink a quarter-inch in the damp earth floor. It slows every step, cushioning the normal impact of *forward* and *stop*, so that moving through the cellar's space takes on the sludgy distortions of a dream. I wish it *were* a dream, though not nearly hard enough. Because now there's something you don't feel while lying in your bed: the sharp crunch of plastic underfoot that pierces the sole of your shoe.

It's a piece of the baby monitor's casing. Looking down, I can see more of its smashed anatomy over the floor. The lens splintered like ice chips.

I mean to say "Randy" but instead whisper "Please."

And with the sound of my voice I hear the scratching. So brief I do my best to interpret it as the creation of my own imagination. Then it comes again: the scrape of claws against wood. A mouse or a rat. This is what it must be. Just the kind of sound you would expect in an abandoned house.

Except unlike a rat's, the scratches are neither swift nor light. This is a single sound, deliberate and heavy. The slow slide of a clenched hand.

"Randy? That you?"

It's impossible to know how loud I say this, other than it is loud enough to not try again. In other houses, a spoken word can instantly humanize a space. Here it turns your own voice into a stranger's, a hostile impersonation.

I start for the stairs, as the sound seems to be coming from overhead. But when there is another scratch, I can tell its source isn't one of the rooms up there but is down here. It feels like it's emitting not from a walled enclosure at all, not from anything sharing this space with me, but from the space—from the house—itself. It's like hearing music and looking for the hidden speakers, only to realize it's a tune being played in your own head.

The scratching again. Weaker this time. But it allows me to follow it to the far corner of the cellar, no more than five feet from where we buried Heather Langham. *Scratch*, *s-c-r-a-t-c-h*. Coming from the spot directly over where I stand.

In the house I grew up in, there was a seldom-used storage area in our basement, a kind of loft tucked between the ceiling and the kitchen floor, designed to keep chosen items dry in case of flooding. The Thurman house is no different. Because there in the corner, visible by the outside light that comes in through a previously boarded window, is the trap door I can almost touch. Square, made of plywood, not much bigger than the drawer of a filing cabinet. And there against the wall is the folded wooden stepladder used to reach it.

I kick its legs open and start up. Try pushing the door open, but its wood has warped over time so its edges have cut into the frame, holding it in place. I step down and search the worktables. A hammer would be the best thing, but all I can find that might help is a rusted wrench.

Up again, and I'm knocking the wrench's round head against the door, whacking around its edges, working it up from its resting spot in a dozen hard-fought squeaks. And then, with a final, two-handed upswing, it pops open an inch and stays that way. A foul breath of air swirls down on me.

Why pocket the wrench, swing the door onto its back and step up the ladder to poke my head through and peer down the loft's dark length? Whatever lies in here is either storage for old

*Grimshaw Beacon*s or squirrels' nests or the place we have been looking for all along, the home to something worse than the boy. Why look inside when no good could possibly come of it? Because the time for looking away has come to an end.

So I pull myself up, my mid-air kicks doing as much work as the wobbly arms fighting to lift me over the edge. And before even the first full inhalation that might tell me if there's something living or otherwise within, I scramble inside.

A crawlspace. Where we kept the Monopoly and the slide projector in our house, but here appears to be empty. A two-foot-high gap that runs the full length of the kitchen, though it might be even bigger than this, as I can't see where it ends in the dark. It forces me to feel for whatever might be here. My hands stroking the cushions of insulation laid over the rib cage of two-by-fours that, each time I touch them, make me think of hair.

I'm not good in small spaces at the best of times. But this is worse than any discomfort I felt in the snow fort tunnels of my youth or the sweats that come upon entering crowded elevators. This is a coffin. It brings a new panic to every movement forward. Two wars are now raging inside me, both hopeless: one forcing my knees and hands to take the next prod farther into the dark, the other holding back the scream in my throat.

And now the arrival of a thought that instantly clouds over even these struggles. The growing certainty that, even if there's nothing to be found, I'm never getting out of here. This is a trap. Even as this occurs to me I think I can hear the crawlspace door being eased shut, a weight tugging it firmly into place.

The scratching again. In here. Close enough that I hear the slivers tear away from the wood.

Back. I've got to go back *now*. And I'm starting my wriggling retreat, rolling to the side, fighting to figure how to make my elbows do the opposite of what brought me this far, when I find the bones.

Up close, they are visible even in the near-darkness. I look over the remains and, before the spasm of revulsion, try to summon the names of the parts once learned for biology class. The flaring hips—that's the pelvis, right? The shoulder blades sound like a kitchen utensil. The scapula. But the shin?

Bones aren't white. This is my next thought. They're not the ivory of high-school skeletons but yellow-stained and black-creviced as smokers' teeth.

All at once, I'm throwing up the Old London's prime rib onto the boards.

Because the brief veil of shock has been pulled away. And because I realize the bones are Roy's.

I never really believed he ran away as it said in the news clippings. Some part of me couldn't swallow what old Paul Schantz told the reporter for the *Beacon*, that he didn't know where Roy was. Of *course* he knew. He took care of children. He was one of the good guys, watching over the lost, their guardian. If one of them had run away he would have looked for him, and kept looking until he was found.

But old Paul didn't look for Roy DeLisle because he knew the boy was already dead. Because he was the one who killed him.

I touch the hole in the boy's skull, where Paul Schantz delivered a blow that brought an end to Roy's bad imaginings. The back teeth of a hammer would be my guess. Something he could get his hands on in a hurry.

There's bad. Then there's worse.

After what Roy did to Elizabeth Worth, he could not be allowed to walk away. Roy DeLisle was, at sixteen, well on his way to building a career of ruining and murdering and running. The clippings mentioned his troubled history; Paul Schantz would have been aware of it too. But Paul would have extended the benefit of the doubt to the boy, offered a Christian second chance. It gave Roy the time to take Elizabeth Worth's life. And he would do it again to someone else, and someone else after that, something Paul Schantz knew as well as Roy did. People like the boy, the ones with the most terrible kind of "restless ways," had to be stopped, because there would always be those like Elizabeth— like Heather—who couldn't see them for what they were.

Paul Schantz was Grimshaw's original Guardian. A position later filled by Ben. And now me. Because old Paul had been right the afternoon we visited him. *There's always something worse than you think. Closer than you think.* Ben had known this from the day his mother told him his dad had driven into a hydro pole, and it's a knowledge that I've been doing my best to avoid. That we all do our best to avoid.

These thoughts prevent me from realizing how close I am to a dead thing. It sends me rolling back from the bones, suddenly frantic, my head slamming against wood below and above. The sharp end of a nail stabs the back of my hand. A metal bracket cracks against the brow over my eye, and it instantly swells into a throbbing egg.

Something is moaning in here with me. When it turns into a scream, I hear the voice as my own.

It strips away whatever control I still had over my movements and lets my Parkinson's have its way. I am moving, though neither forward nor back. A rolling, punching frenzy that has no intentions beyond the body's final expression of itself. Soon it will be stilled forever. But for now, like a beetle turned onto its back, there is only the writhing of limbs, a hysterical foreknowledge.

I stop when I collapse into the wall on the opposite side of the crawlspace from the boy's bones.

Except it's not a wall. A long mound of cloth and skin laid out over the insulation. At once yielding and hard. A concave belly. A shoulder knob.

A woman's body. Her skin glowing dull blue. Knees scraped raw on their fronts and backs. Hands flat against the wood, the fingertips watery as leaky ballpoints from trying to claw through. The palms resting on the lines of blood carved on either side of her.

"Tracey?"

I could touch her, but I don't want to. Because she's dead.

Maybe I was meant to come here to save her, to be the one to do what Ben only imagined doing, but I'm too late. Now I'm sharing a too-small space with the dead daughter of a friend, someone I could be said to know and to whom something terrible was done, and every part of me wants out, is shrieking its demand to scrabble back through this ratshit grave and *get out*.

She gasps. A single intake of air that comes with such effort she spasms, her limbs flailing before settling once more.

"*Tracey.*"

There is no reply other than her shallow breaths. Emaciated, filthy, cold. But alive.

She has fought against every indication that she would never be found, that all that remained for her was a prolonged, solitary death, and now I am here with her. The man with the disease that makes lifting anything heavier than a pint of beer an Olympic event.

But if she has managed to survive three days in here with only the boy's bones for company, I can try to pull her out.

It's done by counting inches. One for each pull on Tracey's ankles, my knees digging in and sliding the two of us back. There are moments I'm convinced that our movement is only me, attempting a directed retreat but merely shifting uselessly about. Clinging to Tracey as though she is my passed-out partner in a dance marathon.

But then, with another pull, I feel that we *are* moving. And as long as no part of us catches on another nail, as long as my heart keeps banging away, we'll keep moving.

I don't find the door so much as fall out of it. My legs slipping over the edge, kicking at the foundation's walls before my feet find the top of the stepladder. With this leverage, tugging Tracey all the way out is relatively easy.

Easier, that is, than holding her in my arms once we're both on the steps. And it is hot. A new heat I take to be a sudden spike of fever, or the blood rush that comes before blacking out.

After one step down, when it's clear I'm not going to make it, I use the relative softness of the cellar's floor as a landing pad. Turn my tumble forward into a controlled fall, so that when we make it to the earth floor it is as though I intended to lay Tracey there.

"Trevor the Brave."

Randy steps out of the dark. The words that come out of his mouth aren't his, but the boy's.

"Look at you, Mr. Shaky," he says. "But an old Guardian could never let down a damsel in distress, could he?"

My arms rise in front of me. A reflex. The limbs seeking counterbalance against falling backwards. It makes me feel like the Frankenstein monster from the after-school movies of my youth.

But Randy's attack doesn't come. He stands ten feet from where I stand over Tracey. Arms at his sides. His face falsely animated, as if he's trying to appear engaged by an anecdote he'd long stopped listening to.

A choking at the back of my throat, and I smell the smoke. Followed by the first tendrils of grey reaching down the stairs from the kitchen.

"We have to get out of here, Randy."

"I'd like you to stay."

"There's a *fire*."

"I know. I started it."

"Jesus Christ."

"Stay where you are," he says, though I'm not moving.

"You took her."

"You couldn't understand."

"Try me."

"It was a part."

"Part of what?"

"I told you you couldn't understand."

Through the veils of smoke, Randy's freckles appear enlarged. Spreading over his face like a hundred darkening bruises.

"How did she end up down here?"

"I wasn't fully committed."

"Committed to what?"

"The part."

"What the fuck are you talking about?"

"It was a *performance*. For once I had an audience that was really watching. And you know what I did? I messed it up. Mailed it in."

"Are you saying you were acting?"

"It's all I've ever wanted to do. And the boy knew that. The house knew it. And it asked me to show everything I had. To do one remarkable thing once in my life."

"To kill her."

"But I *didn't*. There was too much of me getting in the way of the character. Too much *interference*."

"Who did you think you were playing?"

"The lead."

"Roy."

"Who else?"

I've had rooms spin on me before. Boozy carousels or sickbed see-saws. But what's happening now is of a different order altogether. The cellar spinning, along with the house, the earth loosed from its axis and wobbling off into space.

"When did it start?" I manage.

"Sometime after Ben's funeral, I guess. That's when I heard his voice. First time in twenty-four years. Then it got so loud it was all I could hear."

"That night. You went back to Jake's after we left?"

"It was closed, so I waited. And when she came out I offered her a joint. I'm an old friend of her dad's. She said sure."

"She trusted you."

"I'm *fun*, remember?"

"So you decided to have a party."

"I asked her if kids still went to the old Thurman place. She couldn't believe I knew about it, that this freckly, balding guy used to get up to no good in here the same way she and her friends did. So she figured it couldn't hurt to smoke another joint for shits and giggles before heading home."

"Except you didn't smoke another joint."

"No. We didn't."

From upstairs, the fire is a voice that joins the two of ours. Wet and gulping, like a dog swallowing something it's found in the mud.

"What did you do instead?"

"Talked. I don't have a clue about what," Randy says, now grinning widely like his father, the loony salesman caricature they used in those Krazy Kevin! car lot ads. "Her boyfriend, maybe. How she couldn't wait to get out of this shithole. The future. I wasn't listening to her. I was listening to *him*. And when *I* was doing the talking, I was concentrating on selling my lines. And you know something? I was good."

"What did he tell you to do?"

"Make her stop."

"Stop what?"

"Laughing. Smiling. *Breathing.*"

I'm having trouble standing. The smoke has thickened, shrouding the large space so that, for moments at a time, Randy is the only thing I can see.

"I dragged her down here," he goes on, scratching an elbow. "Tied her to the same post where we tied the coach. Oh man, she wanted *out* of here—and part of me, the pussy Randy part, wanted to let her out. But there was his voice again. *Teach her a lesson. Leave her down in the dark until she shuts up.* So I left. Went for a walk, sobered up a little. It was cold. I was Randy again, give or take. And then I thought to myself, You've got a coat on, but that poor girl doesn't. So I ran back, came down here to find her quiet, eyes closed. Not dead, but pretty close. I saw that I couldn't let her go. I'd nearly killed her, and nearly killing someone is as bad as killing her, when you think of it. It's *worse*— because you can't bury a body that's strolling around, telling people what it knows."

"Randy, please. We have to—"

"I remembered how my house had a crawlspace under the kitchen floor. Yours did too, right?"

"You left her alone to die."

"*It's just another secret.* That's what he kept saying. *You're good with secrets. You all are.*"

Randy pulls something out of his pocket and tosses it at me. Somehow my hand grabs it out of the air. My Dictaphone.

"You broke the rule, Trev."

"I wasn't going to give this to anyone. I did it for myself."

"Which is the same reason I just told you the truth. To see if it changed anything."

"Has it?"

Randy appears about to work this through aloud, his finger partly raised in the manner of a courtroom clarification of fine points. Yet he says nothing. His mouth agape.

"Let us go."

My voice conveys none of the desperation I feel. It sounds as though I'm offering to take his place on the next shift in a Guardians game.

"I can't."

"Why not?"

"I've been alone a long time," he says, suddenly not himself at all. The boy's tone, lifeless and flat. "And I don't want to be alone anymore."

He grins again. Not Randy this time, not Krazy Kevin!, but the boy. And it's a glimpse of the afterlife. An eternity in here, waiting at the windows with Roy DeLisle. Watching the girls go by.

I make a move to get past him. Not a run, nothing so orchestrated as to be understood as an intention. A grasping of legs and arms and head in the direction of the stairs. But Randy pushes me back with one hand, his palm slapping my shoulder as if in greeting.

"Give me the locket," he says, and holds his hand out. Opens his fist to show a platinum band with a piece of emerald in it. I glance down at Tracey and spot the white circle below one of her knuckles.

"That was you? *You* dug Heather up?"

"Right there where you're standing," he points, and I take an involuntary step backwards. "But once I moved away I didn't want it anymore. I was just goofy Handy Randy again, and I couldn't bear it. Mailed it to Ben, no return address."

"Why Ben?"

"He *stayed*. And it belonged here." He takes a full stride closer. "It wanted to be here."

"You mean the boy wanted it to be here."

"And now he'd like it back."

So I give it to him. I step over Tracey Flanagan's unconscious body and pull Heather's gold heart from my wallet. Let its chain pour into Randy's hand.

As Randy unfastens the clasp and raises both arms to hook it up at the back of his neck, I slide the wrench out of my other pocket. He blinks down at it, amazed, as though it is a talking bird. I swing the wrench wide and strike it square against the side of his head.

He falls in two distinct motions: slow to his knees, then a formless slump onto his back. I fall to my knees too, bending at his side to feel his still-beating heart, his stale breath a whisper in my ear. I'd seen hockey players in this state before, unlucky puck chasers who'd gone headfirst into the boards. Unconscious, but not necessarily for long.

I scramble over to Tracey on all fours, slip my arms under her and forklift her up. Using the walls to keep her cradled in place, I get to my feet and swing around. Shuffle past Randy to the bottom

of the cellar stairs. There is only my own breath. And the fire
working its way through the house. Licking and swallowing.

You won't make it.

I hear this so clearly I assume at first it is the boy. But it
belongs instead to someone who wishes only to point out some
salient facts that might be escaping my attention.

*If you think you're carrying this girl up those stairs, you're crazier
than Ben ever was.*

So I'm crazy. Ben would have long known what I've come to
recently learn, and have confirmed as I take the first step up.
Sometimes, crazy *helps*.

It gets me all the way up to the kitchen, where I'm forced to
lay Tracey down again. There's the serious heat now, doubling
itself, cooking the air so that each breath is like swallowing oil.
Through the archway I can see that the fire has already claimed
most of the living room. A widening throat of orange and
black. The plaster walls collapsing. A carbon skin it is halfway
to shedding.

A cold finger touches the back of my neck.

I spin around expecting to see the boy. And for a second it *is*
the boy. Glaring at me, flushed and threatening tears.

"Stay with me," Randy says.

I charge at him.

My legs fluid, powerful. The fist that aims at Randy's head
and lands a solid blow feeling swift and Parkinson's-free, breaking the line of his jaw with a tidy, audible pop. I'm a Guardian
again. Young and fully armoured, meeting some Sugar King or
Winterhawk thug with unhesitating violence.

Stay with me.

I can't hear Randy anymore, but those are the words his
already swelling lips are working around. It's not the fire that

frightens him; it's not even death. It is the immensity of his loneliness opening wide inside of him.

I charge again. Driving my palms into Randy's throat. It pushes him over the linoleum edge and down the cellar stairs. For a moment he is a writhing outline against the dark. And then, without any sound of impact, he's gone.

I stand over Tracey, staring down at her as though trying to understand what she is.

Go!

I bend and lift Tracey over my shoulder. Hold her there, caught in an Atlas pose. Unable to step forward or back, disoriented by the smoke, the dizziness that came with lifting her.

NOW!

My knees start to fold, but I lean into it, turning their failure into a hopscotch march. The back door frame has already collapsed, forcing me through the kitchen, then into the hallway. The walls busy with fire. There is nowhere to turn where the heat doesn't take burning swipes at our skin. Tracey's hair swaying over my back.

Halfway down the hallway I stop. It's the cramping muscles, what feels like some kind of cardiac episode. It makes it impossible to carry her another foot, but in fact it is only the sort of thing that would be difficult for me even under the most uncomplicated circumstances.

But I got Tracey out of the crawlspace. Somehow I managed that. *I got her out.*

And if I did *that*, why can't I do *this*?

So I jerk ahead, waist first, a statue with one last, unhardened part. Lurch toward the front door.

This is me. I'm doing this. And with this thought comes a dangerous elation. *Not yet.* If I get out of here, I can sit on the curb and laugh my guts out. *Just not yet.*

I open the door with a single twist of the knob. A rectangle of smooth night appears. Then the cool air on my face, the porch steps groaning under my weight as I make my way down and tumble onto the lawn. Tracey Flanagan rolling off my back to lie on the grass, face up, eyes open and blinking. She looks as surprised by the stars as by the fact she is alive.

Then she turns my way. A shared recognition between us, as though we have known each other for uncountable years.

Randy.

I'm already working my way to my feet, crawling back up onto the porch.

The heat again. A line between the autumn night and the fire so defined it feels like passing into a different world altogether. Walking through something as solid as brick or stone.

The fire has encircled me now. I'm not sure if I'm in the hallway, the kitchen, or if I took a wrong turn into the living room. There is nowhere to go even if I had the capacity to move, which I don't. The brief reprieve from symptoms has already passed, leaving me rigid and faint.

He is only an outline in the smoke at first, unmoving and featureless. But with a single step forward he is more real than he has ever appeared to me. Oblivious to the fire, the lick of hair caught in his eyelashes and jumping with every blink. Coming to stand so close that even through the sulphurous air I can smell the rank, burnt-sugar sweetness of him.

Stay with us.

The boy holds my hand. On his face an expression of mock relief, a mimicry of Carl's features when we held hands in the Thurman kitchen the first night we left the coach alone in the cellar. But unlike Carl's, the boy's hand is cold, and his grip is meant not to comfort but to hold me in place. To keep me in the fire forever.

I fight him. Or I tell myself I must try to fight him, to wrench myself free. To *not listen*. But all my body allows is a brief spasm, just another of the symptoms that have no purpose or strength. So tired now the disease is all that's left. That, and the boy.

Stay.

And I will. Perhaps I never had a choice. If home is the place you spend most of your grown-up life working to forget, then this is mine.

Overhead, the sound of timber giving way. I look up in time to see a sheet of plaster breaking free of the ceiling before it crashes onto me, pinning me flat to the floor.

I had felt the heat before this—had been thickly swimming in it, drowning in it—yet only now do I lend it my full attention. It's because I'm burning. Trapped beneath what might be half a ton of century-old debris, the original nails and mouldings and support beams of the Thurman house. Still conscious, still within the reach of pain, but all of it to disappear soon.

The fire breaks a window. The high tinkle of glass atop the low growl of flames.

Then the boy is tugging at my arms. Apparently it's not enough for me to slowly burn to death. He wants to dislocate both of my shoulders too. When I don't move, he tugs again, and again.

Some part of me shifts. Yet other parts feel as though they are being left behind. Limbs torn from their sockets.

I open my eyes and work to turn my head to an angle where I might see who has put his hands on me, but the smoke has left me blind. If I am expecting to see any living thing it is Randy, horrifically burned. Randy, who seeks to pull me against him so that the two of us might be fused by fire.

The hands lift me up, throwing me onto narrow but strong

shoulders that carry me through the haze before tossing me into the air. There is a new pain to go along with the previous ones. Sharp teeth biting my skin in too many places to count, like being attacked by a swarm of yellowjackets.

And then the ground. Sudden and cool, and me rolling through the grass, clothes smoking and, if I'm not hearing things, some part of me sizzling. I keep tumbling in order to extinguish any live flames I've lost the ability to feel.

Now when I open my eyes there is the sky, the stars distinct, hovering close. Licks of flame reach out from the upper floor, as though the house is claiming the night for itself. It draws my sight to the shattered living-room window. The same window where *fuckt* had once been drawn in dust. The window I'd been thrown out of. What felt like stings in fact the cuts of glass teeth.

Then, through smoke so dense it is like another part of the wall, the boy leaps out. Landing on the ground with a thud, his body crumpling. His clothes, his hair, his skin blackened by smoke. His eyes the only colour—worn denim blue—that he lets me see.

"Trevor?" the boy says, but not in the boy's voice.

Carl grabs me by the ankles and, leaning back, drags me through the grass and away from the house. All of it ablaze now, the fire elbowing windows and bringing the ceilings down with oddly gentle crashes, as though the floors and walls have been cushioned by the heat.

When we make it to the sidewalk Carl lets go and sits next to me, the two of us able to do nothing more than watch the Thurman house flare and spit. I have a dim awareness of others around us—a clutch of bathrobed neighbours, a dog barking with the excitement of being outside, leashless, in the night.

No firetrucks or police yet, though their sirens join the undercurrents of sound. The murmuring witnesses, the yielding wood frame, the hissing voices rising up out of the smoke.

An ambulance arrives first. Stopping in front of the McAuliffe house, where we watch as the paramedics tend to someone lying under blankets on the front porch. Tracey Flanagan, who is able to sit up and tell them who she is.

Then Carl is pulling me close to him. His face appears freshly washed, streaks of white cut into the ash down to his jaw. But as he kneels with me I see that they are tears. Abundant, unstoppable.

There is nothing to do but what we have done all our lives, whether in our dreams or in our Grimshaw days. We watch the Thurman house and wait for it to show us how it is unlike other houses, how it is alive. The fire towering over its roof like a crown. The headless rooster still, as though, after decades of indecision, northeast was its final determination.

I suppose it's possible that someone else sees him other than us, though I hear no shriek from the onlookers behind us. So maybe it is only Carl and me who see Randy in the upstairs window. The bedroom where the coach died. Where Roy DeLisle stood over Elizabeth Worth's body, excited and proud, wanting to show someone the remarkable thing he'd done.

Randy is staring down at us with the false calm of someone trying to hide his fear. A soldier doing his best not to worry his family as the train pulls away, taking him off to war.

He takes a half step closer to the window frame and he isn't Randy anymore. He is the boy. Roy DeLisle as we have had to imagine him—a kid like us, looking like us. A kid expert at playing the same normal act we have played all our lives.

For a moment, Randy's face and the boy's face switch like

traded masks, so that, behind the curtain of smoke, their differences are slight, almost imperceptible.

Randy.

The boy.

Randy.

The boy.

They could be the same person, except one is terrified by whatever is to come, and the other is oblivious to the fire that swallows him. In fact, he may even be smiling.

WHERE DO HOSPITALS buy their paint? Is it wherever the leftover stock goes, the tints that the buying public have deemed too depressing or nauseating to use in homes where people actually live? Or is there thought to be therapeutic value to heartbreaking palettes, a motivation for patients to fake wellness enough to be discharged early if only to escape the pukey turquoises and hork-spit yellows?

These are among the deep considerations I ponder over my days in a semi-private suite in Grimshaw General. The bad news—aside from the walls, the institutional wafts of bleach and vegetable soup—is that the fire touched me in a number of spots, which has left me counting down the last minutes to my every-four-hours pain meds. The good news is that I know my roommate.

That it is Carl and not a stranger I have to hear stifling farts and watching *Friends* reruns and moaning as the nurses change his dressings on the other side of the curtain makes the time pass less awkwardly, if no less slowly. And of course, when we're alone, we pull the curtains back to talk.

Carl had taken a cab to the train station but not boarded the 5:14 when it pulled in. He couldn't say exactly why he decided to stay, other than "Something felt wrong, or was about to go that way." So he had gone to the place where wrong things were most likely to occur, keeping his eye on the back door of the Thurman house from his vantage point behind the see-saw. He had seen Randy enter in the late afternoon and then, some hours later, come running around from the side. He hadn't wanted to get any more involved than that, only to see who came out and when.

But then he had noticed the smoke. Soon afterward, going around to the front of the house, he had found Tracey Flanagan on the lawn and carried her to the McAuliffes' porch, banging on the door and telling Betty to call an ambulance. When he asked Tracey how she'd got out of there, she said my name.

"It's like each of us had a job to do," I tell Carl. "I went in to find Tracey, and you went in for me."

Carl fluffs his pillow, sits up straight, turns on *Jeopardy!* "Well, that's just the way it turned out. I see only what's right in front of me, you know what I'm saying?"

But of course he could see more than that. It's why he'd spent the cash I'd given him on cigarettes instead of a train ticket, why he'd smoked the lot of them while keeping his eye on an empty house. I didn't need to hear Carl admit to his belief in fate. It was more than enough to know that an absence of over twenty years and all the damage he had endured in that time had not slowed his run from the safe side of Caledonia Street to the other, to me.

We have no shortage of visitors.

On the less pleasant side, there are the police, who want to know everything and are frustrated by how little we offer them.

Carl and I stick to similarly vague stories. That is, the truth—minus the boy. We were just old pals who were concerned for Randy's emotional state following the suicide of a mutual friend, and figured he might try to harm himself.

"Why there?" each questioner asks. "Why *that* house?"

"Because it's haunted," we tell them.

In the end, their curiosity could take them only so far, as Tracey Flanagan's life had been saved, after all. The only crimes that were known to have been committed were done by Randy, and he was gone now. Other than the suspicion that we knew more than we were saying, the police had no charge they needed to lay, so they moved on, wishing us swift recoveries in ironic tones.

Betty McAuliffe brings us corn muffins and homemade raspberry jam, which save Carl and me from the frightening "scrambled eggs" and "oatmeal" that would have otherwise had to pass for breakfast. She tells us of her plans to sell the house. It's too big for her alone, and she doesn't relish the prospect of months of noisy bulldozers and nail guns across the street. There are some one-bedroom apartments she fancies over on Erie Street, overlooking the river. It is all she needs.

"So long as you boys drop in sometimes," she says, enticing us with ham sandwiches and a Thermos of good coffee, though she doesn't have to sweeten the deal to elicit promises from us.

Todd Flanagan comes by to say hello, but within seconds his rehearsed words abandon him, his gratitude and relief leaving him mute. So I do the talking for both of us. I tell him that it was an honour to be able to get Tracey out of there, that it was likely to turn out to be the most proud moment of my life. Then I tell Todd that his daughter struck me as smart enough and brave enough to recover from this, that my money is on her turning out fine.

He embraces me. Pins me against my pillow for a long hug I'm sure Todd has never given another man in his life, just as I am unused to receiving one.

It's not the only love I receive from the Flanagan family during my stay. Tracey opens her arms to me when the doctors deem her well enough to permit select visitors, and when I bend down to her, I am rewarded with cheek kisses.

"My dad was right," she says.

"About what?"

"He always said you were good."

She smiles at me, and I recall her telling me how Todd thought I was a pretty decent hockey player back in the day. I'm not sure I could stand on blades today, let alone skate around the rink. But I pulled this girl out. Me, the disease guy, Mr. Shakes. *I pulled her out.*

"I can see you're starting to like this hero stuff," Carl says when I return to our room. "Don't bother denying it."

Why would I deny it? A guy whose only boasts up until now were owning a disco for a while and having a decent wrist shot when he was sixteen?

So I'll take it. You're goddamn right I'll take it.

I look forward to Sarah and Kieran coming by more than just about anyone else. They're twice-a-dayers, bringers of chocolate and celebrity magazines ("It's all they've got down in that crappy store") and flowers.

The kid finds the whole bandages-and-IV business pretty interesting, and I can feel my stock rising in his estimation, my banged-up condition helping him to see me as an aging but furious warrior from one of his video games, rather than a middle-aged guy who used to date his mom in the unimaginable depths of history.

"I still owe you that car you lent me," I tell him when his mom has stepped out of the room. "The Ferrari."

"You remember that?"

"A promise is a promise."

Kieran nods his mother's nod. Tells me I can keep it.

Carl is here the whole time, of course. We don't talk in detail about the big questions, about Randy and how he'd fallen prey to the boy's invitations. I tell him about finding Roy DeLisle's bones in the crawlspace, how they were likely turned to ash in the fire, which would leave us the only holders of the last chapter of his regrettable biography. I also share my theory that it was Paul Schantz who put him there, and his quiet is answer enough.

Believe it or not, we spend most of the time laughing. Not gales of barroom hilarity, but the chuckles that come from old jokes retold, stories of childhood embarrassments and foolishness.

The doctors say Carl and I will be out of here soon. I offer Carl the use of my condo, tell him he can stay as long as he wants. Which is when he tells me that his boyfriend, Adam, is arriving in Toronto in a couple of days. That they're planning to get a place of their own in the city.

"Boyfriend?"

"It's been twenty-four years, Trev."

"I guess people change over that much time."

"No, they don't," Carl says, and rises onto an elbow to whip his pillow at my head. "They just become more of what they always were."

MEMORY DIARY

Entry No. 16

I have to believe that we weren't alone.

I have to believe that some of the things all of us did when we were young were strange. So strange that in recollection they strike us as the products of distorted dreams. Later, we may work to untangle these dreams, dismiss them, grapple with their meanings so that we might "move on." Or, more usually, we do our best to ignore them, to discount them as that-which-never-actually-happened. But they *did*. The bullying and being bullied, the greater or lesser perversities, the violence done to others and to us—all of it real.

And why did they happen at all? The imagination. The boundless possibility that goes with being a child, the brief period of ignorance before coming to understand that everything we do comes with a cost.

This will be my final entry. Not only because my memory of what happened to us over the winter of 1984 has found its end but because I will soon be unable to manage what I am doing now: sitting alone in a room, turning a recorder on and off, speaking aloud in a voice that anyone other than me might understand.

Right now, for instance, I'm in Sarah's room, sitting on the edge of her bed. It's where I slept last night, huddled against her warmth, my limbs calmed by the happy exertions of our keep-it-simple lovemaking. Why would I ever leave? Because there are only so many more days of my being capable of returning another's embrace, of being a man as most of us understand it. Soon I will be reduced to a human to-do list and little more. Sarah says that I'm welcome to stay, that Kieran would be thrilled if I did, that the three of us can face whatever's coming our way together if we're honest enough about it. She's a tough nut, as my mother used to say. Yet toughness might not be enough in my case. I'm losing myself, piece by piece, and there's no getting it back. It's likely to be the kind of process best left to me and professionals and Carl visiting now and again.

But you never know. You really don't.

I should stop now. Such considerations are getting close to overstepping the bounds of a memory diary, and I should colour within the lines I started out with.

So what's left to remember? Everything and nothing, if you know what I mean (and if you have piled on enough years to feel like your life is coming in for a landing rather than taking off, then I'm willing to bet you do). Anyway, I'm done with all that now. If the keeping of this diary has taught me anything, it's that the past is an anvil, or maybe a grand piano, the kind of thing that, in the cartoons of my youth, drops from the sky to flatten you into a pancake. And I'm too tired to try to stand up again after it does.

Except for this:

I seem to recall saying, sometime back near the beginning, that every town has a haunted house. But what do I know of every town? What I really meant, I think, is that there is a haunted house in every boy's life. A place where all the wants he is not yet old enough to act upon or even understand can be rehearsed or hidden away. A place he fears because he can sense its endlessness, how it reaches back into the pasts of other boys before him, as well as his own.

When I started this I thought I was recording a secret history, or maybe a kind of ghost story. I was wrong. It is a confession. I entered the Thurman house each time believing I was trying to do good, whether it was rescuing Heather Langham, or finding Tracey Flanagan, or saving Grimshaw from the darkest aspect of itself. But like the fireman who runs into the burning building upon hearing a baby's cry within, I really entered the red-brick shell on Caledonia Street not because of Heather or Tracey, or to protect future innocents from the likes of the boy, but because if it wasn't me, it would be one of the men next to me, my friends. I did it for love, in other words.

But if this remains a story of hauntings, has it ended, as such stories are supposed to end, with the restless spirits at peace? What lesson is to be drawn from a cautionary tale where the maimed survivor wouldn't alter any of the steps that led him into the one place he was forbidden to go? What kind of confession does this make when, even as I'm sorry for so much of what I've done, I still feel lucky to have been with my brothers in the doing of it?

ACKNOWLEDGEMENTS

Maya Mavjee, Kristin Cochrane, Susan Burns, Nita Pronovost, Nicola Makoway, Shaun Oakey, Anne McDermid, Monica Pacheco, Martha Magor, Sally Riley, Dan Levine, Peter Robinson, Kate Mills, Chris Herschdorfer—

Thank you.

ANDREW PYPER is the author of four novels and a collection of short stories, *Kiss Me*, which drew critical acclaim and heralded him as a writer to watch. His first novel, *Lost Girls*, was a national bestseller in Canada and a Notable Book selection in the *New York Times Book Review* and the *London Evening Standard*. The novel won the Arthur Ellis Award for Best First Novel. His chilling follow-up novel set in the Amazon, The Trade Mission, was called "remarkable and compelling" by *The London Times*. His third novel, *The Wildfire Season*, was a national bestseller and acclaimed in Canada, the U.S. and Britain. *The Killing Circle*, a national bestseller and *New York Times* Notable Book, was published in Fall 2008. *The Guardians*, as well as three of his previous novels, is being developed for feature film. Visit him at andrewpyper.com.